SLIPSTONE RILL

A GOTHIC MYSTERY

MICHAEL MATROS

ISBN: 978-0-692-19703-5

darlingroadpublishing@gmail.com

Cover design by Elena Foraker

**DARLING
ROAD
BOOKS**

For Maggy and Elena

ONLY LISTEN TO THE VOICE OF PINES AND CEDARS WHEN NO WIND STIRS.

— *RYONEN*

THEN

From on high, the wind plays the Chapel's loose wood and open stones like the taut strings of an instrument.

Down past the rill, deep in the trees, the dancing goes on as the light grows dim, with violins carrying the same song as the great structure on the hill.

The dancers' hands slip over those of their partners, palms so rough they catch and give with each pass and on to the next as they circle with wild smiles, faces moving in and out of the firelight. Violins and the guitar join the Chapel's harmonic as the wind brings it down the hill, over the rill, and far through the trees.

All of them together have created both, the instrument that is the high, fretted wood and stone of the building and the other instruments they all have learned to make and play when just old enough for their fingers to press the strings, calluses formed on their fingertips almost from infancy, both palms scarred, skin stiffened since taking up adzes and pull knives.

Together, sitting on a single flat stone, two small, serious girls and a brother hold their miniature instruments upright between knees, waiting their turn.

They know the song, they know all the tunes, but none of them smile with their older cousins, tight, nervous grips on the bows and necks of their instruments, ready for the dancing to stop, to be told to enter the firelight and play.

High up, through woods and over the rill, in the parlor of their cottage, Laura and her father sit on their paired rockers before the cold fireplace with its ash and bits of charcoal they never bothered to sweep away after the cool spring. With windows open they can just hear the sounds from across the rill. The man leans with his feet down to keep from rocking as he plucks at the strings of his own, ancient, violin, searching once again for the melody he's heard since a child, so he's told her a hundred times.

Watching from above the fireplace is her mother's portrait, painted, Laura knows, by some nearby artist, completed before the wave of disease took her away and all those others, took her away and brought her father home from the war, from his travels. Now her mother waits for them in the Chapel yard, close beside the stately crypt of her grandparents, but under a simple stone that says only Anne, with the numbers that tell of her short life.

On his chair, with violin and bow now placed upright on his leg, the Secretary sips from his small glass. There is very little of the whiskey left, now that selling it has become a crime.

Earlier she has written in her journal of the last few days' strange turns and then slid the small leather-bound book into the narrow space between her headboard and mattress. It is not a very secret kind of hiding place, but she knows her father would never go looking there or anywhere else, one's privacy at the heart of his personal ethos. It is a near-legendary quality that served him and his country so well as Secretary, before he left Slipstone and his wife and daughter for the European war.

Now he has placed his instrument into its case and exchanged it for one of the books he keeps on the table between them. The table is small and finely made, one of the many furniture pieces that her grandfather's craftsmen from across the rill built for the Chapel and their home. She has her own book on her lap and is turning the occasional page so he'll think she's reading, but anyway he is wearily nodding, chin toward his chest, up again a few times, and then down into his deep, steady breathing.

She waits just a little longer before lifting her lantern from the table. She kisses her father above his ear, and he seems to wake, but just for that moment, and then he's back asleep, a finger holding his place in the closed book. She knows that when he wakes later he'll grumble, his finger as always having curled itself back out of the pages, the book closed tight, place lost, and he'll slowly rise and take his own lantern back to his room.

These last few days Laura has carefully waxed the frame of her bedroom window with a candle stub so the sash will rise quietly, if not quite easily. Now, with her door closed behind, in her loose canvas trousers and the sleeves of her father's old wool shirt rolled to her wrists, she pushes up the window, takes up her lantern, pulls on the strap of the empty leather sack, and slips out into the darkening night.

SHE KNEW about the boy and his sister, not their names, but she has seen them on occasion in the settlement, in the shop, both in dungarees, just alike. She's heard them speak just the necessary words, haltingly, the shopkeeper Mr.

Suttle and his son both helping, as they follow the children's fingers pointing at harness fittings and other brass and leather she doesn't recognize, and as they sell them salt and buttons. Over time she has heard their language getting better. Once she saw them with a group of older men, all six of them with Mr. Suttle rolling a grindstone and then lifting it onto their wagon, all of them in the wagon then moving off with their horses pulling stolidly. That stone, Mr. Suttle told her, had been a month coming up from a quarry in another state.

"But there's a quarry just out past us," Laura insisted, "where the stones came from for the Chapel."

"Yes, where they *came* from," he said. "But the masons left long ago, after they finished the Chapel. No one's digging in that quarry now. And anyway, it's a different stone your Tinkers need for grinding. Harder, rougher than the sandstone your Chapel's built from."

"They're not *my* Tinkers."

"They would say they're not anyone's Tinkers. It's just a name they've come to be called because they can fix things, came with the masons, but these folks stayed on. Mostly they're carpenters; they work in wood. Of course, you know that. You've seen them with the doors and window frames and such they've built for your father while he restores his castle."

"His *Chapel*."

"Yes, the Founder's Chapel on the hill."

And so one day Laura, following the rill in and out of the sunlight, came upon them at the basin. It was *her* basin, partially dammed by rocks across the rill and eddied deeply over time, into a pool that no one should know but her. She was not quite surprised because their laughter had carried, but it suddenly stopped when the girl, then her brother, saw her there. Then they laughed again, or *he* did, and his sister dropped far enough into the basin for modesty, and he seemed even to rise a little, the surface of the water just where the ridge of dark hair began to spread under his lean waist.

Laura turned quickly away but as quickly back again. He stopped laughing, and he called, called her name.

"How do you know my name? You don't know me." Feet bare as always in the woods, canvas pants rolled above her ankles, she stood on the layers of short needles and leaves just away from the stony edge of the stream.

"Do you think we don't?" he called back.

"Maybe you do. I suppose you do. But how? Do you watch us? Do you *hear* us?"

"We hear when you call your father. And when he calls you." He was moving his hands slowly back and forth just under the surface, like swimming snakes.

"Are you Tinker kids? I've seen you in Mr. Suttle's shop, but you don't work at the Chapel."

Now the girl rose back up into the mottled sunlight but folded her arms in front. "We can't go up your hill, not with the men. It's *their* work up there. We stay with the children and the women." She turned to the boy and laughed, dropping her arms and splashing two palmfuls of water at his face.

He pulled just slightly away, hardly noticing the splash or his sister's lapse of shyness. "They won't *let* me go up," he said.

"Your *father* won't let him go up," the girl corrected. "Because of *you.*"

"Because of me? Why?"

"Why do you think?" She laughed again and pushed water again at the boy's face, and he laughed too. Then he moved behind the girl and folded his arms around her to keep her from splashing. The two of them swayed a little, him tight behind his sister.

"Are you coming in, or just watching?" the girl said.

TWO NIGHTS LATER, the way down from the Chapel was slick in the wet grass of the meadow, but of course she had her path around the little hillocks, and she had her lantern. In all her years here she had never gone so far from the house on such a dark, late night, but she knew the way well and all the level spots to reach the stones across the rill. As she started to cross, she heard the squeak of the bats in the air behind her, swooping and catching. Her toes knew where to grip the declivities of each stone, with the water high enough just to wash cold over her feet. When she was across, her toes picked up wet sand and tiny stones; then she pushed the soles of her feet through the leaves and needles to dry them as she continued into the trees. Before long the rill had twisted around, and she made her familiar way over the wide fallen tree that spanned the stream, but more slowly with just her lantern light. And over.

When she began to hear the music, it started her on a new direction, one she'd never followed because the trees were closer here and there was no natural path. And so she continued toward the sounds, the breeze at her back, as it always came down from the hilltop, and it seemed that the air carried its own sound, its own music, like a flute through the wood and stones of the Chapel and its high, heavy bells. When the string music stopped, there was laughter and clapping and a loud voice or two, and she heard the snap of a fire, and sparks were floating through the height of the trees.

It took a minute to find the cairn they showed her, not much of anything but an unruly stack of stones, not even her own height. Over time the two had built it, never quite knowing why, they told her, or maybe they just started throwing a few stones together and the thing grew, as they widened the base and started finding stones a little farther away, some just enough to close a fist around, some far enough toward the rill that Laura might have seen her two new friends if she had leaned out from one of the higher Chapel windows.

For a few days after their swim she had helped them build their cairn, a couple of hours in the afternoons while her father, the Secretary, toiled with his pen on the long story of his war that began on his travels and that he brought back home, where he found that the village Slipstone seemed to have gone away somewhere, gone away with his wife, Laura's mother. All that remained of his father's Chapel and cottages was empty and mostly roofless. And, so, it must be rebuilt.

Then with a silent and knowing nod to each other, the girl and boy had motioned her to follow another path, a different direction from the swimming basin and also from the musicians' circle. Soon they had stopped, and the boy had motioned proudly ahead. It had taken a moment before she recognized that sunlight was falling in the perfect, wide circle of a clearing. And around the circle had been another sort of tree, maybe twenty of them, all just the same, alike in their breadth and height, their branches with short blue needles and bark cracked into scales. They'd been planted there by their grandfathers, the girl and her brother had told her, and now, finally, they were almost the width for the first to be sacrificed for use.

"Sacrificed? You talk like they're some kind of *holy* trees, sacred," she had said.

"No, they're not," the girl had said. "But you can't find others anywhere here like *those* trees. You can call them Tinker trees if you want. We need those trees. Our people brought their own wood when they first came here, grand-mothers and grandfathers, but that has pretty much all been used, and not just for music and such. Tables too. Chairs and things. Some of them there on your hill. Those trees here are close now for use, and we'll be planting more."

Now this night, suddenly at the cairn, with the dark all around, she circled the lantern's light over the ground and somehow found a small, smooth stone that had not already been used. She pitched it toward the cairn, where it found a space and rested. She silently shut the slide of her lantern, and in the sudden darkness she could see figures moving against the firelight. She carefully walked a wide distance from the musicians, where they played on their circle of stones.

Then Laura heard her name whispered loudly, in two different voices, one right after the other, from behind at the cairn, and she turned away from the firelight back toward them.

"Was that you playing?" she asked, moving closer with her lantern. "I couldn't see in."

"It was us a little bit ago," the boy said. "It was probably our little cousins unless you've been hiding out here awhile."

"No, before. I know it was you, the two of you. There was this song you played, this tune, nothing like I'd heard before. Or not quite like."

There was silence for a few seconds. "You won't hear it

again," the boy finally said. "It's not something you needed to hear."

Another moment. Then, "Did you think I wouldn't come?"

"We knew you would," the girl said. And the boy said it too.

There were voices coming happily from the firelight in the pause of music, but they gradually quieted, and a slow thrum of guitar began to sound. It quickened gradually and fiddles came in, and voices too.

"What are they singing?"

"Just singing," the girl said. Then: "Dance."

Taking her hand, she pulled Laura gently into a slow circle, and then the boy joined with Laura's other hand, the music quickening. More quickly too, beginning a sideways run, hands tight between them, they circled the little mound they'd built of stones, and then the boy took his sister into his arms and they spun, and the two girls, then the three of them kicking up needles and leaves with bare feet and trading one to another, all three spinning together. The music quickened even more, with shouts and laughing loud from the firelight, while the three circled and spun, and it was only when the music suddenly stopped, and they stopped, that Laura knew her head was spinning too, wildly, and all three fell onto the hard surface of dry leaves. They laughed, and when she stopped laughing to catch her breath, the brother and sister laughed longer. Then, together, so much alike, they stopped too.

"Let's go over," one of them said, and Laura could never recall which one it was, but she raised herself to her elbows and then pushed to her feet. She followed them in a circle away from the firelight. It was only halfway to the rill and the basin, that she thought of her lantern. It would still be burning dimly, its wick screwed low, but it was easier than it should have been to follow the others without it, none of them quite running, but finding their way rapidly the way she'd learned those last few days. Then the clouds began to move aside, and the moon helped her find her footsteps. She could fetch her lantern on the way home.

The moon was also in the basin, rippling, when they finally reached the edge, with its pebbles and rough sand.

She was damp from the dance and the running. She watched her friends begin with their clothes, then looked down and worked at the buttons of her father's shirt and her canvas trousers. The three of them stood in the moonlight, at the edge of the basin, all of them white under the moon, but with the hair of the sister and brother dark, where hers, when she looked down at herself, shone light. Then the others stepped into the water. She followed them into the wide, cold reach of the stream, then deeper, and they stroked their way in separate directions through the water, circling one another, pushing out with their arms, and then, eventually, standing together, water at their ribs.

When the boy came over and was suddenly behind Laura, he felt warm at her back. She leaned into him, and he moved back just a step. But then she tried to come forward, and she knew she couldn't, because of his arms and his hands.

"No," she said. "Don't do that." She started to laugh, but then she stopped, because he was tightly behind her now, the length of him, legs against hers, pulling her. And now *he* was laughing.

And then his sister was close in front of Laura, and she was reaching too and laughing and pulling them all together, all slick with each other, skin sliding together with the sister's hands at her wrists and both of them pulling her to shallower water and then putting her down on the rough sand and weeds at the edge, holding her hard and not letting her up until they were through.

SHE PUSHES her window back down along the waxed edges, steps away from the side of the cottage, and goes to the shed with its bins and barrels of supplies. Inside, she needs to allow more light from her lantern, but then, before leaving, with the leather sack now heavy on her shoulder, she twists the wick back down low. Not far above her head, bats circle and dive. With the cold fury she has learned from her father, and with her lantern, she slips again down the wet grasses of the hill to the stream and steps onto the stones and across, hardly needing to watch her naked feet. She follows her way through the hard pack of the leaves, through the old oaks and alders.

The night sounds are starting to come on, but insects were louder at the rill than here in the trees. She knows the different owls that nest nearby and hears them, one at a time. She hurries along and doesn't pause even as she screws up the wick of her lantern. In the rhythm of her steps, the heavy sack over her shoulder hits and pushes her forward, chafing the bruises and cuts under her wool shirt.

She reaches the wide ring of identical trees, where they have been cultivated so carefully in their perfect circle. She eases the sack painfully off her shoulder and carries it into the center of the clearing. Here, so loud with voices and music two nights ago, she can now hear only some breeze, and she listens for it. And then she seems to hear the music again, the same kind of song as before, but it's not quite. It's the breeze, but it's music too, as it comes down from across the rill and through the woods, floating on the air from the Chapel.

Then she hurries. Pulling the sack to the first in the ring of trees, she opens the leather binding and reaches for the handle of her trowel. She has expected the ground to be tough at the roots, but she has sharpened the edge of the trowel, and she can lean into the tool and dig through the thick deposit of dry leaves and noodles into the earth more easily than she expected. When stones underneath stop her, she pushes the trowel between the next roots and digs as deeply as she can.

When she's done, she uses the tool to scoop out the thick pellets of salt from the sack and into each of the hollows she has dug. She layers dirt and leaves back over and goes to the next of the trees. She knows it will take her a few more nights to finish.

1

FRIDAY MORNING

In the dead of morning in Slipstone Village, birds ate all the crickets and took over the day's singing.

And I was up. I turned my music loud on the record player, bathed, breakfasted, read just a page or two, and was out on the stoop. I pulled the Rectory door shut but knew not to lock it. I might be seen, and you didn't lock your door in Slipstone Village.

In not too many steps, I was on Center Path, on the packed dirt and gravel, under moist, heavy leaves, my hands at my tie, then in my pockets, and my head went back as if I might start to whistle. No one else about. Every morning now the air was cool but almost warm like this, with low perfect clouds. Far down the path, the sun broke through the thin green leaves of spring onto my face, then off and on and off. I was getting used to this, and these mornings.

But soon there were others about.

I am a lover of dogs, and I always will befriend the mangiest stray. I have saved the most pitiful dogs from fatal injections at the animal pound and located homes for them to spend long lives with liver and lamb chops.

But I would murder my own dog, brutally, and with a smile, if my dog were a dog like Clancy.

And here was Clancy now. And with him, Elgin.

We all stopped.

"George."

"Elgin. Clancy."

"Ah. George." Elgin was a tall man, with shoulders. He leaned his big head back in the glory of the day. "It's another morning. Another morning. And a good one."

"With you and Clancy taking full advantage."

"It's a good one, this morning." He paused, just enough, and paused again. "Not quite as good, perhaps, for Jean." His head went even farther back, and he lined me up along his nose.

"Jean," I responded, "had quite a time of it. But bravely done. You could say, I suppose, that her Liszt carried on a little too long. Even after Galen turned the two pages that time instead of one. But then there was the other, Elgin, a new composition, the one she announced as a collaboration between the two of you. Kind of haunting, a little *familiar*."

"Are you suggesting that I...?"

"No, no, that's not it at all. Not familiar in that way. I have to congratulate you. It was beautiful in its...simplicity. Jean was playing the piece well, and I think her eyes may almost have been closed. Certainly, Galen's presence was unnecessary for any page-turning."

"Well, thank you, George. You may have appreciated her hard work, but your response wasn't quite what she expected, wasn't quite what any of us expected when the disturbance came like that, so suddenly. You must understand."

His choice of "disturbance" seemed, if not rehearsed, at least well considered, and I suddenly realized he'd expected to encounter me in just this spot on the path, expected to have a word.

"It was an awful thing, I know. And no one felt worse than I did. I hope Jean knows that."

"In fact, George, I'm not sure that she does know that."

"Of course she does, Elgin. She'd have to know something like that was an accident."

"Well, how *could* she know, George? How could know? The clamor is all she heard. How much was it, anyway?"

"I'm not sure. Sixteen cents, maybe. A dime, a nickel, a penny. Something like that, just fell from the top of my pocket when I shifted in the seat. Frankly, I didn't think to look for it afterward for a count."

"It sounded more like a dozen silver dollars," said Elgin, punctuating his comments with swoops of his meaty hands, "each one dropping to the hardwood floor of our little recital hall, rolling its way uninterrupted through seat legs to the edge of the piano bench, bouncing away and spinning for a minute or two, resonating through the room before losing energy and settling down to wait for the next." As Elgin described the dance of my coins, he assumed energy and almost began a dance of his own. Clancy grew excited with the performance and began to chase his cigar-stub tail, kicking up gravel on the path and twisting his leash around Elgin's wrist, finally bringing his master to heel.

"It was not," said Elgin, unstrapping himself and pulling up Clancy tight to his leg, "an evening that Jean – or any of the rest of us – will remember happily. As you may or may not know, George, I worked with Jean long and hard for her recital. And she did work hard, pure amateur that she is, who loves the keyboard but hardly knows how to touch it. It is a fact, to be sure, that everyone at the recital except Jean knew that Jean cannot play the piano. And that's what made your contribution so much worse, I'm afraid. At a performance of unquestioned musicianship, those distractions are cause only for anger, not the humiliation of the artist."

"Sounds resonate irregularly within our little recital cottage," I answered, "so I doubt if anyone noticed your sneezing fit."

"That damned Boz Dillings and his odious cologne. My allergies."

"Elgin, I'm sure almost no one recognized the source."

Seated fitfully by Elgin's foot, Clancy grinned up at me, whimpered, and panted. Suddenly he leapt to his paws, threw himself viciously in a torrent of growls and saliva after his own tail, stopped as quickly, gnawed his haunch, and looked back up. He whimpered, panted, and grinned.

THE DANGEROUS WAY the front door swung out so smoothly, the hinges dead silent, was a tribute to the meticulous guardianship of our sexton, Victor Blair. Friday was Victor's morning with his oil can, his wood and brass polish, with as many as twenty or thirty visitors expected to pull open the door to visit the Chapel on a sunny weekend.

No matter how many times I passed through the door, I always noticed the sweet odors of age. Victor's ministrations as caretaker could do nothing against the century of old wood, old wood polish, old books, old paintings, and old brass that filled the air. If he could, Victor would have bleached out all the smells. Instead, he had to satisfy himself with dissolving the newer grime.

On the table in the vestibule, Sara had laid out the leaflets as precisely as Victor would have done if that were his job, the top edge of each leaflet measured a half-inch down from the one underneath. Symmetrically placed on either side of the leaflets were framed photographs of the Secretary – in conference with the bishop, advising the governor, shooting with the President. Above them all, in its ornate oak frame, loomed the portrait of his father, village founder Jonas Hawkson.

"Sorry. I heard about last night. Sorry. Good morning."

"Sara. Good morning. Who told you about last night?"

"Sally was first, I guess. She's at all the recitals. I wish I could have attended. Well, I suppose I'm happy I wasn't able. Do you like what I did? What I did with the pictures?" Sara had slipped around the doorframe into the vestibule. Her hands were folded, head down, eyes up.

"It's very fine, Sara. This way the Secretary faces inward in all the photographs. Was that the idea?"

"Well, I guess he does do that. I just mean the way they're lined up better now. Sort of in a single plane."

"It looks very well organized, Sara," I admitted.

I followed her back between the right set of pews and the wall, under the green glass windows all leaning in at the same angle to let in the cool air of the April morning. We passed through the door to the sacristy, and Sara continued to her little office to tidy up for Friday morning. I climbed the old wooden steps to my office.

EVEN ON THIS bright morning the two small windows gave out only enough light to let me see dimly across the narrow room to my desk. I couldn't make out the pattern on the thin dark rug except for the rectangles where the shafts of morning light landed brightly on its surface. As I thought to do now these last few sunny mornings, I peered into the beams of light and saw, as I knew I would, that the dust was still high in the room, far from settled. Just this week, on another sunny morning, I had closed the door behind me and whirled through the office, opening and flipping through files, even taking the rug by a corner and shaking it a few times. I had then sat quietly, writing, admitting no visitors, as I timed the settling of the dust in the sunbeam. Based on those observations, I knew this morning that my visitor had left no more than a few hours ago, failing again, I supposed, to find what was so important no matter how much dust he stirred up.

Finally I walked the distance to the desk and turned on the green-shaded lamp. I slowly approached the old metal file cabinet and saw that the hidden bits of tape were still intact on the edges of the two drawers. If there was a search last night, what had been searched? It had been days since the files had been examined, and one day since I had sat at my desk to find a drawing left for me, a beautiful thing, actually, on some kind of thin parchment-like material, inked with a few greens and browns, the view from above of a wooded place, with a few tiny landmarks sketched and shaded in. A map.

It was now, behind me, across the room, that my office door squeaked open with another squeak right behind, the high pitch of Sara in extremis.

"Oh, golly, it's mice again. You have one, don't you?"

"No, Sara, no, it's just the door."

"The door? What's it *doing*?"

"The door you just opened. It squeaked."

"Oh."

"I'm sure the mice are gone," I assured her. "We'd have seen, well, seen that same evidence, especially in the drawer. Come look here."

"No, you open it." Another little squeak from Sara and she was halfway back through the door.

I unlocked the desk drawer with its little key and pulled it open. Two perfectly round tiny eyes, black in gray fur, looked up piteously. The creature didn't move except to breathe. "You see, Sara? I'm sure they're all gone, not to return." She remained huddled at the door.

"Well, all right, but tell Victor." She backed out the door and almost had it closed.

"Tell Victor? Why tell Victor?"

The door shot back open with my question.

"Victor says that 'mice don't visit, mice come to stay,'" she answered. It *did* sound like Victor, delivered with just the right sanctimony, and I realized that Sara's Victor was almost as clever as Victor's Sara, and just as poisonous.

"Victor's just teasing. Besides, he hates the little things more than you. More than *you* do, I mean. He'd be gone by now if rodents had taken up permanent residence."

"Sometimes I'd be willing for the trade." And the door closed fully this time, clicking shut.

I came out from behind the desk and walked quickly across the room to open the door.

"Sara," I called. "What did you want?"

Her voice came from around the corner. "What did I want?" Her head emerged shyly, her round black eyes hesitant. "Mice. I told you." And she disappeared.

2

FRIDAY NOON

At noon, or just earlier, I took my paper bag through the Chapel door and out to the churchyard. The shaded grass was still wet in the cool day, and the stones themselves seemed to have absorbed the morning dew and kept it in. I was cool in my shirtsleeves but didn't want to walk back in for my jacket. Sara always felt that the time, and the Chapel, were hers during that hour. I had decided soon after my arrival that she must have prayed, or hummed, or laid dust traps for Victor during lunch. She always seemed pleased in the early afternoon, though she would never have hummed in the presence of others. Instead, her small radio hummed with quiet voices.

As I walked in the thin damp grass of the churchyard, my paper bag in one hand, I reached down to rub the rough stones and push my fingers into the engravings, where bits of water still were collected. Recent markers stood among the older stones, but Chapel policies kept them modest and low, with carving required to be shallow into the surface. The newer stones were porous too, and markers only a few years old had begun to weather. The faithful here, who had returned with the return of the Secretary, measured family status by the remaining depth in the etching of their graveyard names after a hundred and more years of weathering.

The sun stood nearly above, but the Founder's sepulcher, set on the highest ground, seemed to give off shadows in every direction. The mass of the structure pulled me toward it, just as every visitor must veer in that direction, pulled at least for a moment by its gravity. Constructed like the Chapel of rough-hewn sandstone blocks, the mausoleum was roofed with the same slates, long weathered with mosses. In each side of the structure a cloverleaf opening allowed those tall enough, and willing to pull aside enough ivy, to peer in at the sarcophagus itself, a block of marble commissioned by the Secretary for his father and mother. Within, sealed over with interlocking leaves of slate, lay two maple coffins. At least they were maple according to my orientation, conducted by Sara upon my arrival in Slipstone. No one in living memory had attended the memorials for the Founder and his wife, and the crypt itself seemed to have grown impenetrable with the years of soil, rust, and moss.

The sun fell on my face again as I arced away from the sepulcher and walked farther among the stones, where some of the oldest markers stood slanted in the thin grass slope. On only a few of these pale surfaces was I able, tracing with a fingertip, to draw out the names of families disappeared long ago from Slipstone with the thinning of the populace in the years after Jonas's death and before the rehabilitation of the Chapel and village by the Secretary. Here were the Banters, the Crankshaws, somewhere the Stairnses, all the names inked into the parish records in a single volume shelved in the Chapel library. The few others of the founding family were here of course, but with the simplest of markers: the Secretary with his name and dates and two adjacent stones with only "Anne" and "Laura" and the years of those short lives.

The stone of Gammel Minken, the old Chapel archivist, was here too, its lack of weathering to signify his recent departure. Someday the ground would be broken for other villagers, there being area enough for those few I now lived among and for any others who might come along to take our place at the Chapel, in the shops, and at the market. I had expected not to be among them, but Slipstone had begun to draw me in, and I thought I might stay.

As the markers ended and the slope began to descend more steeply, Victor's tended grass gave way to native varieties, beginning now to push out their small, woolly blue and purple flowers. The grasses grew as high as my knees where the meadow began to take over the downward grade of the hill. If I walked farther, my pants legs would be quickly soaked in the dew that hadn't yet dried out of the long grass.

With my lunch bag gripped loosely, I crossed my arms, leaned back a little, and stared out over the downward slope of the meadow to where the stream glinted up as the noon sun managed to catch it. A slight wind had risen, and I heard a hint of the Chapel Song, as the phenomenon had come to be known, the breeze playing through the building's tuned apertures of wood and stone.

Back up the hill, I sat on a low weathered tomb that had become my lunch table and unfolded the top of my bag.

Barking now, the distant dogs called across the valley.

BEFORE RETURNING TO MY OFFICE, I walked up the Chapel aisle and proceeded behind the altar to the diminutive door that led to the bell tower. I twisted down the black iron handle, pushed my way in, and climbed into the cool, narrow space where the tight wooden stairs began to curve upward toward the dark. As I climbed, I leaned away from the center of the spiral and against the lathed wall that enclosed the stairway. The smells of old oil penetrated the air more and more sweetly the higher I rose, as the odor of the Chapel became concentrated here in this high wooden column. No dust had been allowed to gather in the grooves and notches of the old oak, although Victor never entered this part of the church.

In the darkness of the first landing, I located the electric bell switch and pushed it twice, quickly, listening for the thin sound of the buzzer in the high distance. As usual, in a minute or less, I heard the door squeak open above, and I began the next spiral up, climbing toward the dim light that spilled from the doorway.

Rachel Wren, small and just a little stooped with age, hugged the edge of the opening as I gained the threshold and moved gently past her into her room. She pushed the door shut and motioned me to my usual chair, where my small cup and saucer already sat on the console radio beside me. Rachel disappeared behind the curtain that closed off her tiny bedroom and lavatory and returned with her kettle. She twisted the dial of the hot plate, heated the water, and prepared our tea. Without speaking, she handed me a small piece of orange peel for my tea and placed a little dish of almonds on the cracked veneer surface of the radio. Then she stooped slowly into her chair, across the old rug from mine, and picked up her own matching cup. In the tiny space her harpsichord, a tiny virginal, just filled one of the small, angled walls in the oddly shaped room.

"Almost one," she said in her small voice, and she smiled thinly through the steam from her teacup.

"We'll both be at work in a few minutes, I guess."

"Me before you," she said, as she took another sip of the hot tea. "It's warm again up here. I can't decide why."

"But it has to be warmer here. All the heat funnels up from below. Why don't you keep the window cracked? You only open it to look out. Why not let it ventilate?"

"It's not that I'm *too* warm, George. I've told you. I said only that it's warm *again*. Maybe I like the warmth; maybe I need it." She coughed a little in the steam of her tea. "What I'm saying is that it's warm here in a way that it never is in April. The warmth up here tells me something about the way it is below, in the Chapel." She placed the cup firmly down on the small bookcase beside her and lifted herself out of the chair. She crossed the room, climbed onto the chime bench, and consulted the oversized face of the watch on her fragile wrist.

She paused with her right hand above the levers and then suddenly, with a nod, began to peal the hourly chimes. With her elbows cocked high to give force with each stroke, she leaned and pushed with a tiny fist onto one big wooden handle, then moved quickly to the next. The tumult of competing noises filled the little space of Rachel's chamber – the massive iron on bronze above us, the wooden handles as they clattered against the worn blue felt rests, and, some-how, impossibly, louder than the rest, Rachel's breath in her effort against the weight of the bells.

The chime of our small Chapel – not so grand as a carillon – and the image of the small woman in the attic pealing the bells constituted a significant draw for visitors up Slipstone Hill, although anyone in nearby Trellis could have heard the distant hourly chimes or Rachel's more elaborate performances. Expanded during the Secretary's renovations, the tower now carried the enormous weight of ten bells. Their cost, transportation, and installation had, it was said, exhausted almost all the Secretary's wealth.

As our brochure informed visitors, each numbered bell on the traditional scale had its name, embossed on its bronze from the Book of Revelation:

1. WORTHY IS THE LAMB THAT WAS SLAIN
2. TO RECEIVE POWER
3. AND RICHES
4. AND WISDOM
5. AND STRENGTH
6. AND HONOUR
7. AND GLORY
8. AND BLESSING.
9. AMEN.

The Secretary had also brought in a tenth bell, an E flat, which allowed the playing of songs in both major and minor keys, now by Rachel and, years earlier, by her predecessor and teacher.

Within and above the sounds of her pealing, at the center of the room was Rachel's small face, jaw set and lips out against the hard work of the bells, her nose up toward some point above me, and, as always when she tolled out the hour, her eyes jammed tight as her head jerked, front to side, side to back, in hard, jarring cadence with her bells. She played with a fury, as if those hourly chimes were the word of God, and of course they were. She pumped her arms and swayed in those short seconds with the fever of belief.

But as she stopped, and picked up the handkerchief from the brass arm of the instrument, she smiled with such pleasure, with so much delight at her performance, that I knew her belief in a spirit greater than music was abundantly stronger than my own. As the sounds finally dimmed and silence had just returned, she took back her seat and lifted her cup.

"Nicely done," I said.

"Thank you, George. But isn't it your custom to roll money toward the musician at a recital?"

"Rachel, my God, how could you have heard about that?"

"Who has the best view in the village?"

"Even *your* view doesn't penetrate stone walls. Who's been talking?

"Why, everybody, of course. It's the best thing in weeks."

"But who's been talking to *you*? You're never out in the morning."

"But I *am* out at *night*. As you know."

"As you tell me." I tried to stare her into some kind of admission, but, as usual, her own gaze was more determined than mine. Finally, I reached for some almonds.

"Shouldn't you be back at your desk?" she smiled. "Good example to the rest?"

"To Victor and Sara? They're too busy with their own battles to notice that I'm away."

"Do they know you visit me?"

"Of course. They know everything. It's a point of honor for each of them to know more than the other, to pass more windows, to peek into more cabinets."

I waited just a moment. "But *you* always know more than either one. And of course you've been here so much longer."

I hesitated, and then added, "You and Gammel Minken. Since...well, since the Secretary, I think."

When I looked up, Rachel was peering down into her tea, which was no longer steaming. She carefully dipped her fingertip into the cup and flipped away some piece of stem or leaf. I said, "Rachel?" and she kept her eyes at her cup. "Rachel? What is it you *do* know? What do you know about the nights here? Who comes in at night?"

"I'm like everybody else, George," she said. "I sleep at night."

3

FRIDAY AFTERNOON

There were phone calls to make Friday afternoon – the accountant, the glazier, the new trustee asking for the most knowledgeable docent to conduct his family's Sunday visit. Although Sara arranged most of the Chapel's weddings, I had learned in my few months that brides' mothers called less frantically, less often, if I contacted them early with assurance that no splinters would be waiting in the floor to catch their daughters' bridal trains.

I dialed the calls one after the other at my desk. As I talked, I peered up at the high windows in the room. The sun had moved its way from the morning side and now sent a kind of cool blue light through the southwest windows and onto the bookcase that stretched up the east wall of my office. The books there were old volumes on church history, studies of ecclesiastical architecture, various forms of hagiography – religious and otherwise – travel accounts, and other kinds of miscellany collected by my predecessors in this chamber, all priests until Gammel Minken the archivist and, just before me, John Patton.

Most pressing for the afternoon was the grant proposal

for the restoration, due to the Whitebeam Foundation in a month and requiring still more research into such historic matters as the quarrying of the Chapel stones in 1843 and their placement by Italian builders, conveyed to the American shore for that purpose by old Jonas Hawkson. Artists must be approached to bid on minor repairs to the altar fresco, which depicted a kneeling Virgin Mary at the Annunciation. I needed to locate the foundry that had fabricated the cross for the steeple so many years before, or at least to learn its name, and to measure the slates on the roof and decide how to replace those that had been cracked by storm or age. Victor, the sexton, had told me soon after my arrival that *his* place was on God's Earth, and that high ladders and scaffolding – and thus the Chapel roof – were best left to those with wings. I had looked up, expecting to find a gargoyle version of Victor, but instead I saw only the corruption at the corner of the old copper gutters, where moldy leaves had begun to push their way through the green corrosion.

THE SECRETARY'S books lined much of three walls in the Chapel library, where the occasional scholar studied, consulting pages under the ever-moving eye of Grant Sweeney, our part-time librarian and, soon, he hoped, Chapel priest. Grant was nearing his divinity degree at the university. Volumes were grouped on the shelves according to a classification devised many years ago by Gammel Minken, who had grown from boyhood in Slipstone Village to become the Chapel archivist, his education in a far-away college aimed solely toward that profession in this place.

Here were histories of various medieval cities of Western Europe. There were works on engineering, mining, flotation. Sealed cases held rare editions of Sannazzaro, Boiardo. The Secretary had found a good, early copy of Alessandri's *Genialium Dierum*, which, like the others, we protected within glass against the humid summers, a little gauge indicating just how moist the trapped air had become, though how to adjust the moisture was as yet a mystery to me. Most popular among the Italian books was a fine copy of Aldrovandi's ornithological studies.

High up, two windows of stained glass faced each other. To my left as I stood in its light, the Holy Virgin held up her hands as if checking for rain. The other window, with colors muted in a careful match with the Virgin's, depicted the Founder, robed as some ancient Athenian, one hand with a staff and the other reaching toward the branch of a broad tree.

The fourth wall of the reading room was given to a remnant of Renaissance tapestry depicting another sainted virgin, Cecilia, one arm raised protectively, whether in anticipation of marriage or the sword it was not clear from the fabric that remained. She was one of dozens of textile treasures boxed by the Secretary in heavy wooden cases in Italy and Germany and shipped back to the old village, to his old church.

Set between two bookcases was a handsome portrait of the Secretary, uniformed and with bold features, gazing far over the Piave River, where, after the retreat of the rest of his company, he would continue to face the advance of the Hun, alone, with his carbine.

The Secretary had been dead some sixty years when the pinewood case under the Founder's window, exhibiting the Secretary's Maggini violin, had its glass lid smashed with an unknown tool and its treasure taken away, the event simultaneous with the departure of my predecessor and leading to my own installation at Slipstone. The small wood-and-felt support upon which the instrument had been displayed now carried a small card with Sara's neat typing: "We at Slipstone Chapel regret that our Maggini violin has been taken from us. We hope that it returns soon to its rightful place."

With no visitors at the long table, Grant Sweeney was away from his desk, away from his rolling ladder, and away from the library. At the northwest corner of the room, the door to the cellar leaned open, and the glow of the bulb in the stairs beyond shone out dimly. I pushed the door wider and began to climb down, angling once with the stairs before reaching the hard dirt floor below. Down here the boards above my head were low, and they bowed slightly down, as if the weight of all those years of prayer would finally come crashing onto my head. Or onto Grant Sweeney's. I heard him shifting something around the next corner of the dim catacomb where we stored the Secretary's crates, many of whose contents had still not been catalogued, even after so many years.

As I came around the first of the crude wooden shelves, I saw Grant standing just under the low naked bulb, its light falling onto his shoulders and a book laid open in his hands. Reaching to his ankles was his thin black cassock, worn in solemn anticipation of his eventual ordination. At his feet was a heavy wooden crate with its top slats pulled up and away, a small pry bar laid across.

"Hello, Grant," I said, as quietly as I could.

His top half lurched back suddenly, rubbery, and I thought the book would fly out of his hands.

"George," he answered, shaken. "Hello. I just thought I'd begin to look through the next of these cases. Secretary's Alpine travels. Just look at this. It's a Galileo, late seventeenth. It's been here all this time." His white gloved fingers gently turned the pages to the front. "*Della scienza meccanica*. Pulleys and weights." His pale eyes were wide like a bird's, and a tuft of his thin hair stood up in a crest, just under the dim glow of the bulb.

"Good, good. I'm sorry to startle you. I thought maybe you'd heard me on the stairs." I knew, though, that Grant couldn't hear much of anything when he was busy following his finger down the page of an old book.

"But my goodness, the flocking," he continued, his thin fingertips picking ever so gingerly at the pages. "It's been here, this *treasure* has been sitting in this dampness for..."

"Yes, I know. We're lucky that you're..."

"Yes," he said impatiently, "it's criminal." He paused, and paused some more, as a finger traced the printed words, not quite touching the paper.

I realized the conversation had concluded. I moved behind him, past the edifice of the Secretary's crates and down the next row of shelves, where Chapel and village records were archived. Their boxes of thin pine sat tightly together, with the more recent series labeled in five-year sets. Earlier activity, though, was apparently less fully documented, with single boxes labeled for ten years, or twenty.

Most of the cartons had aged and grown dusty since their organization years ago by Gammel Minken. One box, though, was new, and of cardboard, unmarked by the fingerprints of historians and administrators, except, I assumed, those of Elgin Brattle, who had written the village history eight or nine years earlier and, with Sara's help, refiled some of the material. Copies of Elgin's thin volume, printed locally with badly reproduced black-and-white photographs, were available for examination in the vestibule, but sold only in Galen Jones's bookshop in the village proper.

I pulled the cardboard box out, set it gently on the floor, and opened the flaps. Inside was a series of crisp manila folders, each with a collection of correspondence, business documents, and other records. The papers had been stacked neatly before filing, and the typing on each label was perfectly centered, Sara's careful work when touching the sacred history. Only one thin folder seemed to offer what I needed: "Construction, 1842-44." I removed it and replaced the box. I carried the folder back past Grant, still rapt in his Galileo, up the cellar steps, through the library and sacristy, and up to my office, where I read through correspondence and other early documents about carpentry, roofing, and stonework. The foundry that had manufactured the simple, heavy cross on the steeple, now corroded after a century and a half, turned out to have been located in the state capital. With a few calls I learned that the foundry still stood, now well within the city boundaries. Its furnace was cold. The structure now housed a restaurant, a series of expensive shops, and a dance studio. In the neighboring state, though, the mine that sold the slate for the Chapel roof in 1843 was still producing. I could hear the noise of the operation in the background when I made the call.

Afterward I pushed myself back from the desk, left the Chapel, and walked the path through the woods to Slipstone Village and its downtown: the tea parlor, the bookstore and Elgin's gift shop, which also served as the village post office. Elgin sold stamps for his Slipstone postcards and was empowered to affix the Slipstone postmark. The small grocery sat at the corner of Treadle Street, and I walked there first.

No one stood by the counter as I came into the market

and approached the candy rack, but Thorny Webber heard me as I rustled through the bags of chocolate and mints, looking for an expiration date as recent as the last few months.

"None of those dates matter," he announced, invisible, down some aisle, as he must have seen me in his wide-angle shoplifting mirror examining the ends of the candy wrappers. "Those things stay fresh for years, all those preservatives."

"Just the same, the last chocolate almonds I bought here had all turned white. The years must bleach them out. I wonder, is Boz around?"

"Boz?" asked Thorny, as if he couldn't recall a Boz from among his army of cashiers. "Oh, Boz is on delivery. Gone to Rachel. In the bells. He'll take one little bag at a time up those stairs. Afraid of heights. He should try hauling a piano up there."

"You've carried a piano up the bell tower stairs?" It seemed unlikely that Thorny Webber could have wedged his own girth up those spirals, let alone a two-ton instrument.

"Well, a harpsichord, I guess it was, with a funny name, and I suppose Boz did help. Rachel hired us to tote it up, must have been seven, eight years ago."

"I thought you said Boz would never try hauling a piano up there."

"Well, he didn't, did he? I just said it was a harpsichord."

"I know her harpsichord and her harpsichord schedule. Concert daily at 4:15. I've been here two months now."

"That's right. Of course, you may be the only one who can hear her perform, right under her like you are. Of course, I know what a music lover you are, last night what with old Jean pounding it out and you throwing your money on the floor."

"I don't remember seeing you in the audience. Maybe you came in after the lights went down."

"In Slipstone you don't have to sit in the audience to hear the concert." He laughed with a single roll of his aproned belly, then paused and considered.

"Well, Boz should be back...he should be back *now*. I guess he and Rachel are sipping sherry up there. Any message?"

"I just need a little bicycle advice. His brakes are grabbing. *My* brakes, I mean."

I placed my small bag of candy on the checkout counter, its brown paper grown pale at the edge.

When I left the market, I climbed the short hill of Treadle Street and turned left to the shops, three nearly identical white cottages, each with shutters of Slipstone Green, each patterned with the shadows of dancing leaves in the afternoon sun. In his gift shop window, Elgin had arranged Slipstone notecards and T-shirts around the exact model he'd constructed years ago of the Chapel, its walls built of pebbles in mortar and its windows of isinglass. In the tea parlor window next door sat a small, round table with embroidered tablecloth, arranged with jonquils in glass vases, tiny white cakes, and two ladies at tea, their Chapel visit no doubt concluded. The two other tables sat neatly spaced behind, and I caught the flounce of one of the three Franz twins as she disappeared into the little kitchen.

Next door, the bookshop window was all business, exhibiting Galen Jones's new display of relics from her native island's celebrated women novelists. As I examined the arrangement – small volumes of brittle leather, a few scarves, and a woman's buttoned shoe – a hand came into the setting and adjusted a pair of fragile spectacles that had fallen forward onto their lenses. The hand tried to balance the glasses this way and that and finally leaned them against the old shoe. Galen moved into view, looked up from her design, frowned, and motioned me in.

"I shouldn't have those spectacles in the window anyway; they're too valuable."

"More than the books? My God, this is a find. How old?"

"It's 1880s and, no, it could never pass for a first. Thirty years too late. But, still, a nice leather binding and so shouldn't be lifted by someone without gloves. The oils, George. Please."

"And these spectacles?"

"Yes."

"Her glasses? You own them?"

"Yes. I told you. They have catalogs for these things."

"How do you even know she wore glasses?"

"The provenance is without doubt. I bought them from the same dealer who sold me her sister's shoe. And, no, please leave that in place; I've put it just right. You know how you are with things."

"How I am with things? How am I?"

"Well, George, think about it. It really was an awful moment last night. All that clattering. And poor Jean."

"Yes, poor Jean. A good thing she didn't look up at her page turner, where you didn't seem quite able to keep your face straight."

"Apparently you misinterpreted my expression. Besides, I was still upset over turning that extra page in the Liszt."

"Not enough moisture on your hands, obviously. A good lick of the thumb..."

Galen glanced around as the two ladies from the tea parlor pushed open the door, ringing the little entry bell.

They proceeded to crane their necks, looking to each corner of the bookshop and gauging where to begin. They both advanced toward the back room. Galen lowered her voice.

"Did you talk with Jean? Did you say anything? I mean *after*. It wasn't a good night."

"No, I couldn't. She left on Elgin's arm. And yours, as I recall."

"Well, she needed to talk with you."

"What did she say, Galen?"

Her voice grew even lower, and I leaned in to hear her.

"George, she didn't need to say anything. I've known about the two of you for a while."

She paused. I paused too.

"The two of us? Yes. Well, I'm not sure how much there is to know."

"Jean gets caught up in rehearsal, you know. And she talks. Sometimes she talks quite a lot."

"Galen, I think maybe Jean has more of an idea than I do about our friendship."

One of the ladies had returned from the back. She approached Galen.

"May I ask...," she began."

"Of course, you may ask. How may I help?"

"Oh, you're English."

"That's right," admitted Galen. "Dorset."

"Oh, my, Wessex."

"Yes, yes, all that. Now what may I help you find?"

"Well, my friend and I saw it in your window, well, this one," pointing, "and we thought perhaps you might know where we could locate..."

"I'm afraid the other shoe has long since disappeared," Galen quickly explained, and tried to turn away, back to me.

"No, no, the book, that beautiful edition, and..."

"Oh, I'm sorry, those items are from my small collection and only for display in my window."

"No, I'm sure I could never afford anything like...such an edition, but even the later ones are so hard to locate. She was so very young, wasn't she...? If you had any idea of where..."

"There's a reason, I'm afraid, that you may not find the one you want. It's quite a rarity. It is, after all, so awfully unreadable and never really sold very well, even years later, after all the commotion about the others. It's probably why mine is in such good condition; it was always put aside before anyone got very far into it, myself included."

As Galen and her visitor bantered over the juvenilia of English writers, I stepped into a back room and the few shelves set aside for books on music. In a moment I heard the front bell ring again, and Galen sought me out in the narrow shelves.

"I tell you, George, tomorrow I begin my lessons in American. I'm weary of little ladies finding me adorable because of my birthplace."

"Galen, forgive me, but in Slipstone your birthright is a gift others would murder for. Thank God Elgin finally abandoned his attempts at an accent."

"Oh, don't talk Elgin to me. He's sent yet someone else in here to ask for his book and admonish me for hiding it away from public view."

"Well, it isn't immediately evident the way it was, well...before."

"It certainly is. Here, right here, not only prominently shelved but its cover facing out."

"But surely a history of the village must sell more than any other..."

"That doesn't matter. I've told you, and I've told Elgin.

This is a bookstore, not a souvenir shop; that's Elgin's business."

"But with your agreement, Elgin can't sell books. And you can't sell T-shirts."

"Well, that's just an irony he'll have to live with. He shouldn't have sold me the shop if he didn't like my agreement."

"He sold you the shop because you were willing to buy it. And he couldn't keep it up with his wife dead and gone."

"He sold me the shop, as you must know, for my accent."

"He was charmed, I'm sure. Now help me, will you? I need a violin book. Something on Maggini, just some background."

"So you've decided to find the violin yourself, have you?"

"Just information for a report. Some comparisons with Guarneri and Stradivarius, maybe. Dimensions, materials, all part of a process in determining what the damn things cost."

"You must know what the Secretary's violin was worth. It has to be in the insurance documents."

"Completely undervalued. If the insurance company ever pays – and of course they may never pay because of the suspicious circumstance of the loss – the payment will never match the true value of the instrument."

"But now there's nothing left to insure. Why the need for information?" Galen tilted her head like a cat with a question.

"A trustee wants to find out about replacing the violin."

"But a substitute fiddle will never be the Secretary's fiddle, and that's what people pay to see."

"Well, actually, no one ever pays anything..."

"And why wouldn't it just be stolen again? Certainly you couldn't insure it now."

I lowered my voice. "We're thinking about a security system, you know, something..."

"Something even more sophisticated than Grant Sweeney squinting over the tops of his glasses?"

"Well, now that we're uncrating more of those other materials – books, old prints – there's too much of value just sitting there."

"I don't know that any book here is going to tell you today's market value of a rare instrument." She bent to a shelf, level with her knees. "Call a collector, a dealer."

"I am, I will. What I most need now is simple informa-tion about violins, about historic methods of instrument making, in order to carry on any kind of conversation. For all I know, a violin is carved from a single block of pine." I spoke to the top of Galen's head as she ran her finger over book spines and pulled a few out to check their contents.

"And the Secretary's wasn't just any Maggini," I contin-ued, "but an early instrument. More historically valuable than the later ones, but with an inferior tone."

"Is all that in the appraisal?"

"There was never any appraisal. All we know is what the Secretary told everyone. Early Maggini. From 1610 or so."

Galen looked back up, her finger keeping a place on a page. "And he'd pick it up and play some bit of Rossini, and the whole village would dance at his feet. Just how much is this trustee willing to pay for a violin to sit in a sealed glass case?"

"My god, Galen, it's no wonder you don't sell any books. Do all your customers have to pass a test? Did the old lady need to provide the girl writer's birthdate before you'd show her anything?"

"You know, that's really not a bad idea. And, George,

please don't eat those things in here; you'll get chocolate everywhere."

"Go ahead, have some."

"I didn't know these things came in white."

"They're a little past their date."

At the end of the afternoon I opened the old safe and laid the folder inside. Again I checked the small strips of tape on the file drawers and, sitting down at my desk, tore a page from my notepad. On it I wrote TELL ME WHY. TELL ME WHAT. I folded it, and printed HELLO, VISITOR on the front. I left the message centered on the desk blotter.

Before leaving, I stopped at Sara's office space to say goodbye. It was just a small area enclosed within a few short, thin walls and no door in the doorway, a situation I knew needed addressing for the historic preservation people. Sara was writing in her tight hand on her wall calendar. Chapel tours, student groups, weddings. Her desk radio emitted a low voice, words indiscernible, even from this close.

4

FRIDAY EVENING

Just at dark on any Friday evening, a Chapel docent, one of the three Franz twins, Melinda, Bea, or Gert, will have taken her guests by the elbow and indicated the dimly lit path through the Chapel Wood that must be followed to reach the village proper. As the visitors enter the dark embrace of the trees, they hear Miss Franz closing them out of the Chapel with a final turn of the big iron key. Only a minute or so later – but it can be a long minute in those woods – they emerge from the trees to find the tea parlor window pulling them to its light, and they flutter inside for what are left of the morning scones or the afternoon cakes, baked by the two Franzes not assisting that day in the Chapel. In Slipstone Village, at any time, any of the Franzes can be seen with flour whitening her gray hair.

But this Friday evening I had passed by an hour before.

My visit took me once more from my house, again down Center Path, and along the other side of Gunnell Street from the tea parlor's bright window, where I could walk invisibly under the dark maples, their foliage burgeoning toward full leaf. Tonight, my light wool jacket had become too heavy with the spring warmth and would go into mothballs for the season. I like my necktie up close but had loosened it by the time I reached the other side of the village, walked up the curved flagstone path of Alder Cottage, and rapped a few times on the green door.

I waited on the worn step, scalloped out over the last hundred years, where others like me had pushed their toes impatiently and waited for one member or another of the Clacton family to decide it was time to pull open the heavy old door. Now only one Clacton lived in Alder Cottage, and finally she appeared and asked me in, as quietly as she could, and as coolly.

"Hello," I said. "Thank you."

Jean returned to her little red rumpled armchair. She looked at her lap, at the back of her hand, at the window to her left. In the window boxes outside, some plantings were lit just barely from within by the reading lamp at the armchair. Finally she looked up at me.

"Would you like to sit down, George?"

"Should I make some tea first? Maybe some hot chocolate?"

"Don't you think the weather's turning too warm for chocolate, George?"

I let myself down into the other soft chair, across the thin patterned rug that covered a few of the wide pine floorboards. "You did it, Jean; it was beautiful. Especially the Liszt romance. It was worth all those mornings of practice, all that preparation with Elgin. That little room doesn't do much for sound, but your performance more than compensated."

"I think the hall treats sound quite fairly." She finally decided to look at me, and she paused magisterially. "It even magnifies certain ranges, the pitch of metal on polished wood, for instance, the sound of coins dropping and rolling and rolling even more and then taking their time to spin down to a final silence." Her voice had risen with each word of her detailed description.

"You know, Jean, your concentration last night seemed so complete it's astounding you were able to detect all the subtleties of my own contribution."

"I didn't need to, George. My friends described any subtleties I missed."

"Elgin, of course. I recognize some of his nuance in your narrative."

"No, not Elgin. Well, not only Elgin. I should wish it were only Elgin who told me more about your own performance than about mine."

"Jean, you played beautifully, movingly even, as you must know. I'm sorry. It's nothing I could help."

"You were slouching. I've thought about it; you were slouching so much the coins just fell right out of your pocket. You were *asleep*."

"Of course not. How could I sleep during the Liszt?

Then I paused and said, "I *am* sorry, Jean."

She looked back at her hands as they wrestled each other on her lap. In its turmoil, an elbow struck the small novel laid open on the arm of the chair, and it crashed to the pine boards. "This has happened to me all day," she wept, and she raised her hands to her face and spoke again.

"I'm sorry." I said. "I can't quite hear, with your..."

She turned up her face, all red and white. "It's you," she almost shouted. "Why does it have to be you?"

"Why does *what* have to be...?"

"You came to Slipstone. You were kind. You *are* kind, and then you just..."

I rose slowly to cross the wide pine boards and the thin

patterned rug to Jean, where she trembled silently, face in her hands. I am a large man, but there was no light behind me to cast a shadow as I leaned closely over the bowed woman.

I LEFT ALDER Cottage late and closed the front door as soundlessly as it allowed, tight against the jamb, painted so many times. I paused again on the front step and pushed my hands into my pockets, turning this way and that, catching the scents on the dark air of the cool spring night. From the village center came the smoke of a late-season woodstove fire.

Alder stands farthest south of the cottages on the village green. Center Path ends just beyond, its gravel thinning at the foot of an ancient and much-revered stone, the Hawkson Cenotaph. I stopped at the old marker and, with my fingertips, examined its lichened surface under the pale light of the stars. The weathered etching on Jonas Hawkson's memorial could barely be read, even under an afternoon sun, by anyone who didn't already know its message. Late this night I did know, of course, because Hawkson's words were printed on the Chapel letterhead, the motto in full circle, just as it had been carved into the Cenotaph one hundred years ago: *Give to the earth. Take from the trees.*

It was a phrase subject to any interpretation, and the interpreters had been many over the years, especially, most recently, those who would ascribe an environmental intent to the dictum. Old Jonas himself never explained the words, since they first appeared as the closing of his final letter to his only son Samuel, later to become Secretary Hawkson, a document found pinched under his dead hand, the old pioneer's heart stricken suddenly in vital old age. Now the phrase appeared not only on official Chapel correspondence, but also on incidental paraphernalia, such as the T-shirts Elgin sold in his village gift shop.

Give to the earth. Take from the trees. Slipstone Hill had germinated an abundance of hardwoods, the full range of maples and oaks, along with a variety of hickory known only here and submitted for official taxonomic recognition by its discoverer, our own Secretary, in his early days as boyhood botanizer. Unfortunately, biologists refused to accept *Carya hawksoni* as a valid new species, determining that the unusual orange of its fall leafage was due to the high iron content of Slipstone soil, not to the tree's cellular arrangement.

As I stood by the old stone, the wind came up the hill, as it does most late nights, and made its way through the greening leaves of the hardwoods that stand darkly on either side of the path. It came up from the valley, pulling with it the smell not just of wood smoke but of other, danker, odors I couldn't recognize.

As it will do, the wind played over the oddly aligned surfaces of the Chapel roof, along its gutters and downspouts, across deep-placed windows, and through the louvers in the bell tower above Rachel's loft, played the old sorrowful song on its instrument, the Chapel itself, crafted somehow by Jonas's imported builders, or created, more plausibly, as the unexpected trick of its placement on Slipstone Hill, where the night breeze could make it sing. Whether Old World magic or only meteorology, the music was another draw for Chapel visitors.

But tonight, as the wind receded, it carried something else too, a sound I could perceive just at its edge but could no longer hear after I listened for it. Then it came again a little louder and stayed within hearing, the keening song of violin strings, played high and sorrowfully, slow as an old woman, with long, sure strokes by the fraying horsehair of its bow. It was the Chapel Song, but now from a human source, the second time I had heard it performed by someone other than the wind. Last night on Jean's piano. And now.

I listened as the distant violin played, and then the wind renewed, and I turned and walked home, back along Center Path.

5

SATURDAY MORNING

From a distance they looked like small birds feeding, perched side by side on Center Path, watching each other and ready to fly. They seemed even to sway just slightly with the dying breeze of early morning. At least that was how Ginger Martin later described Jean's hands as he approached them through the foggy Saturday dawn, making his way toward the market's rubbish bin to check for bottles and cans. What he said, exactly, was, "I thought, birds."

When he finally saw Jean's hands for what they were, lifted elegantly on fingertips that were starting to curl in toward the palms, Ginger stood awhile and stared down at the small white things. I imagine him speaking to the hands a moment, asking a thing or two, pursing his lips and scratching with just a fingertip the exact point of his chin. Ginger had no one he could tell about what he'd found. It was much too early for Elgin to be walking Clancy, let alone starting the business day at the gift shop. Galen Jones must still have been in bed in her little house down the street from the market; her bookshop stayed shut until ten. Even the three Franz twins wouldn't open for tea until nine.

Ginger would have had the pocket of change he always carried and with which he counted out payment for his few purchases, but it would have surprised any of us to see him use the telephone outside the market. That would not have been one of his skills; he had no one on the end of any telephone to practice with. And so, on Saturday morning, Ginger did not call the sheriff. He finally did sit, though, cross-legged, guarded the two hands, and waited for help.

It was Boz Billings and Alice Felton who came up to him first as they headed to work at the market, Alice as always with her hands in her pockets and Boz walking his new bike, Alice on her way to the meat counter and Boz preparing himself mentally to stack cans and make deliveries. How would their faces have responded to the little white birds on the gravel, under Ginger's protection? Boz would have gone white when he stooped to examine the rough black sutures that closed each of Jean's wrists. Alice would have squatted in her jeans and flannel shirt, scientifically reaching over to touch the dead bleached skin or the stitching itself. She would have pulled Boz away, counseling him about spoiling evidence. Then both of them would gradually have turned toward the seated Ginger Martin, deciding together that it was Ginger who had delivered the hands there.

Boz, ever gentle, would have begun. "Ginger. Ginger, look at me. Where did you find these?"

And Alice: "Ginger Martin, what has happened? What terrible thing have you done?"

Boz: "Wait, Alice. Ginger, what is this?"

And Ginger, whose gaze persisted on an arrangement of gravel a foot south of the two hands, and who, if he understood nothing about how this set of hands could have parted from their wrists and come to alight before him, responded, Boz told me later, by turning his eyes slowly to the faces of his inquisitors, raising his eyebrows to match the rise of *their* eyebrows, and moving his great head almost imperceptibly from side to side. Boz asked Alice for the keys to the market, and he went to use the phone.

So now it was eight o'clock, when Slipstone opened its eyes, and the rest of us came to the village center.

I had arrived on Boz's old bicycle. After Boz Billings had bought his new bike to deliver groceries, I answered his ad in the post office and gave him twenty dollars for his ancient one-speed with coaster brakes. With its capacious saddle-bags, the heavy old bicycle was fine for errands in the village, and it made for good exercise to descend Slipstone Hill and work my way back up again, pushing hard on the big rubber pedals. Now, though, the sudden grabbing of the brakes down the hill was slightly worrisome, and it was beyond my mechanical knowledge even to examine, let alone manipulate, anything on this new purchase.

But braking was unnecessary here, and the fat tires never slid on the Center Path gravel, no matter how slowly I pedaled, and I pedaled slowly Saturday morning, away from my little house, the Rectory, and down the path again under the unfolding spring leaves of the hardwoods. Somewhere inside I still heard the record I'd been playing, the two-minute étude, and I tried to sing it on my bicycle with la and tra and other springtime notes I knew. Far off somewhere, hunters in the short early season punctuated my singing with hollow shots floating up. As I passed the other cottages, to the right was the white clapboard box that market owner Thorny Webber had bought years ago on the death of some native widow and where he first introduced the element vinyl to Slipstone, finding the wood siding of his new purchase subject to damp, insects, and the requirement of new paint. Thorny was immune to the disapproval of his neighbors, whose attempt to impose housing restrictions he blithely ignored.

In my sweater I was warming too quickly, and I stopped to fold the wool garment and slide it into a saddlebag. I could see no one on my side of the Center Path curve and heard no voice of trouble except that of a mockingbird who'd spotted Alice's fat tabby, prowling for morning game. An out-of-state car came by on Gunnell Street, a big sedan with two heads of gray hair doubtlessly intent on their Chapel tour.

As I came around the curve, I saw I was late for a gathering, and I pedaled closer. In circular randomness they stood, Thorny Webber, solid with arms crossed, strangely formal without his apron; one of the Franz twins, Melinda, I thought, with Gert scheduled for Chapel tours and Bea opening the tea parlor; Grant Sweeney, swaying in his cassock; and Elgin Brattle, struggling with Clancy, as the beast alternated between piteous whines at Elgin's ankles and headlong, salivating dashes to the end of his leash. Within this geometry moved Alice Felton, stork-like, stepping, turning, defiant.

"No, you'll leave footprints," I heard her scold, while she furiously wove a pattern with her pacing.

As I left my bicycle on its kickstand and approached, I saw Ginger Martin at the center of it all, sunk onto his haunches, hands gently on his thighs, refusing to look up. As usual, he was overdressed. On his legs he wore heavy tweed pants from someone's discarded suit. A thickly cabled fisherman's sweater, once white, sagged out from the open zipper of a what remained of a brown leather flight jacket.

The coat's rabbit-fur collar was drawn up over Ginger's ears, and Ginger stared ahead, finger back and forth at his chin, his eyes rapt at what could have been two rain-twisted leaves or two tea shop pastries or, more likely, a big pair of stiffened kidskin gloves.

"It's her hands."

I found myself coming closer, unaware of where I stepped or who had turned from her place in the ragged formation to meet me. "It's her hands, and they're cut off." The Franz had come up and was pinching the cuff of my shirt.

It was a statement I couldn't at first respond to, and I stepped closer to the group of my neighbors. The Franz moved with me and brought her hand farther up my arm to grip my elbow. "They've cut her hands off; we can't tell how. And they're all stitched up."

"What do you mean, her hands?" I was finally able to bring out.

"We think they're Jean's. Alice says they *are* Jean's. It's the ring."

Old Mrs. Clacton's pearl-and-ruby ring. Now daughter Jean's, loose now on her pale and birdlike hands. No one else seemed immediately to notice my arrival as I pulled loose from the Franz, passed between Grant and Thorny, and approached the fragile little figures on the gravel. The fingers had curled in close to the palms by now and my impression was of claws, the shriveled claws of the turkey vultures that flew the hills and streams around Slipstone, circling for muskrats, raccoon, sometimes deer, injured and dying. For an instant I let myself believe they *were* those birds' claws, and I closed my eyes at the vision of their severing.

"Don't, George," I heard Alice call from lengths away.

"The area needs to be clear." At the silence that followed her voice, I realized that a general muttering had stopped. I looked up at the faces within the small grouping, and the faces were all looking at me.

"It's Jean," Alice announced in the same voice she would use later in the day to list the market's specials in chops and chicken pieces. "It's the ring."

"Yes, I've seen the ring," I answered, as I squatted to look more closely at the sutures that tied shut the wrists, neat and evenly spaced, with tight, efficient knots. Around me, conversations started up again, Thorny in his string of bass monosyllables, Elgin calling opinions my way as he leaned back against the pull of Clancy, the Franz skittering to leave and then not. A slight movement just the other side of the hands drew my notice, and I tilted my head up to look at the huddled form of Ginger Martin, his eyes blinking slowly and his stiff forefinger tapping into his beard.

"He's not talking," Alice told me sternly. "He hasn't talked yet."

As I slowly rose and thought of questions for Alice, she glanced down the path, where Boz Billings, erect on his pedals, sped closer. He skidded quickly sideways in the gravel and leaned his new bike onto the nearest maple. "No one's there," he told us all. "I looked everywhere. I looked in every room."

At that, the group turned its collective gaze in the direction of Alder Cottage, far down Center Path from where we stood.

"Boz, you weren't to go inside," barked Alice. "Did you touch anything? What did you touch?"

"Well, the doorknob, I guess," Boz admitted. "But then I remembered."

"And you called first, didn't you?"

"Yes. And he'll be here very soon, he said. *Immediately*, he said."

And it was.

Just then our attention was pulled toward Gunnell Street thirty yards behind us, where Sheriff Aaron Crisp drew his brown cruiser to the curb, his roof light flashing in the morning sunlight. He climbed out, swung shut his door, and stepped quickly toward the path in his thin, precise way. Alice glared at each of us with a warning to stay clear, and she went to meet the lawman. The two of them huddled and pointed and nodded a minute, and she led him over, his hat brim level and his pistol perched hugely on his narrow hip. He leaned, then knelt, over the hands, Alice reluctantly allowing him closer than the rest of us. From his shirt pocket he drew an extendable pointer, extended the point, and touched each of the hands so gently that neither rocked even slightly, balanced as they were on wrist and one or two fingertips. After only a moment he rose.

"I've sent for the state lab," we heard him confide to Alice. Then he looked up and around at the rest of us and announced, "I've sent for the state lab. Does anyone know whose hands...whose hands these are?"

"Yes," Alice hissed at his ear, "I just told you, they're Jean Clacton's hands. The ring, that's her ring. I know the rings that people wear. I know their hands, the way they always reach..."

"And Jean Clacton resides...," he hesitated over the present tense, "...her residence is...?"

"Jean Clacton lives in Alder Cottage," Elgin spoke emphatically from the edge of the path, his dignity reduced by his struggles with the leaping and salivating Clancy. "And simply because Jean owns a ring something like the ring on those..., on that hand, is no reason to assume that those, that *that* is hers."

Immediately Alice stiffened, and was about to reply that, of course, and my god, Elgin, and so on, when behind us all, emerging from the Chapel Wood, closing the twenty yards over grass and early wildflowers, stumbled our sexton Victor Blair, his lean arms like sticks out of short sleeves, carrying, in grotesque inappropriateness, the Chapel's long-bladed hedge scissors. His mouth was a little open, even before he came close enough to use what he could gather together of his voice.

"There's something...," we heard him finally choke out, as he looked from face to face, unblinking. "There's some-one..." He stood there, swaying a little on legs far apart.

From far down the hill the sound of a hunter's shot came echoing up.

6

SATURDAY AFTERNOON

A s I leaned on a windowsill in my office later that Saturday, I watched twelve giant crows advance out of the trees and move warily across the Chapel lawn, picking up grass seed and beetles, watching each other to maintain an orderly distance. In the gray afternoon was a promise of rain, but no sound of thunder, no rising wind, only the thick sky. And, barking now, the distant dogs across the valley.

My note to the office visitor remained on the desk, apparently unfolded and unread.

The thick-paned window of green glass was pulled open, its fragile black chain reaching down for me to swing back and forth with my fingertip. Far beyond, and through the burgeoning spring greenery of a tall maple, I could see flashes of the state lab's yellow tape, strung in a perimeter around the crypt where the Founder and his wife lay interred. And where we – where Victor – had found Jean Clacton, delicately arrayed in her performing dress, inside upon the sarcophagus, thin leather gloves oddly flat and empty on her waist, where they extended from crossed wrists. Jean's repose might have seemed peaceful, but her eyes were pulled open in a look of sudden confusion, as if the surface where she woke felt like the cold and graven slate it was. Upon her dress was a dusting, thick in some places, of dry dirt.

We could see none of this as we first came to the sepulcher that morning, following the lead of, or rather bringing with us, a Victor not yet willing to say what had sent him to our little gathering on Center Path, but able only to gesture us down the path and around the Chapel to the churchyard. As we stood in the shadow of the heavy sandstone sepulcher, two of its sides bright in the morning sun and two still darkly cold, we could find nothing disturbed until Victor handed me his pocket flashlight and motioned me to aim it through the cloverleaf opening among the stones. Stepping to the side of the structure, I peered in and played the feeble beam over the length of the pale figure that lay there. Though shorter by far, Sheriff Crisp, standing on his toes and insisting on using his own pocket light, was able to look in as well.

He then stepped to the door of the crypt, and he tried to thumb the old latch while pulling on the handle. I glanced over to Alice, who winced at the new fingerprints but kept her distance.

"Who has the key?" The sheriff asked.

I looked at Victor, and he looked back. "I don't know that there is one," I answered, stepping to the door and examining the iron handle.

The sheriff paused just a moment until we all reached the same conclusion. "It seems like somebody has one somewhere. Don't you think?" Another pause. "Right now it's just as well. We need to back off until the lab gets here. Too many footprints already." He looked over toward Alice, who silently nodded her approval. Grant Sweeney, who had ventured to the cloverleaf opening, stiffened and looked down at his feet, hesitating to create more disturbance in the soil.

Thorny glanced over. "I think we can move away without disturbing too much more evidence," he reassured Grant. "We can't stand planted here all day. Boz, you want to come open up with me?"

"Just a minute," said Sheriff Crisp. "Is that Miss Clacton, or is it not?"

"Yes, of course," I told him.

"Of course," echoed Grant quietly.

"And you," the sheriff continued, "you, sir?" Finally Victor looked up under the small man's gaze. "What was it that brought you over here this morning? What cause did you have to look in that opening?"

Victor waited and thought. "I didn't have a cause," he finally replied. "I just looked."

Victor stood and fidgeted and wouldn't pull his eyes up off his feet. Finally he broke away from the little group and walked quickly toward the Chapel, still clutching his hedge scissors.

The sheriff wrote something tiny in his notebook.

BEFORE LONG, two investigators from the state crime lab pulled up at the roadside in their blue van, next to the wrought-iron fence of the churchyard. A stout woman of middle age stepped out, with a thin young man following her. They looked around at the tilting gravestones until they halted their gaze, as all visitors do, upon the sandstone structure of the sepulcher, central among the other, more modest, graves. I stood there alone, where the sheriff had stationed me. "Is that it?" the woman asked in a voice resonating from deep within her woolen suit.

"Yes," I said after they'd already walked past.

A few feet from the sepulcher's door the woman paused and reached back to impede her assistant's approach. They both stooped, and she indicated a flattened area in the grass, curving out from the entrance. She dispatched her assistant to the van, and he returned with plastic sheeting to place over the grass. He had also brought two pairs of some kind of broad-soled shoes, which, once on, seemed to allow them to approach the door more closely. I looked at Sheriff Crisp, who seemed about to mention that his own footprints might appear when the plastic was removed and the ground examined. But then he didn't.

The woman was in no hurry to gain entrance to the crypt, as she and her apprentice worked the entire door and stone frame with dust from small jars, using what appeared to be makeup brushes. The assistant paid special attention to the lock, latch, and handle, peering closely, his gaze moving side to side as he worked. He was then busy with a heavy camera, brought on a tripod from the blue van.

Occasionally the woman would jut her lips, push her glasses high on her nose, and nod to him. At one point she walked purposefully to the van's side door, stepped inside, and emerged after a minute with a small doctor's bag. She reached in and withdrew a ring hung with an assortment of heavy keys. I could hear them rattle as she moved them apart one by one with her fingers. Then she advanced again over the plastic sheet to the door of the crypt, chose a single key, twisted it a few times back and forth in the opening at the handle, twisted it harder, and was in the door.

. . .

As I CIRCLED the area outside the crime tape, I could see flashes of light coming from the cloverleaf opening of the sepulcher, as the young man photographed Jean where she lay on the cold slate lid of the Founder's sarcophagus. While the woman worked in the churchyard, examining the ground, measuring the distance between Center Path and the sepulcher, and quietly asking villagers to please go about their usual business, Sheriff Crisp set himself at Sara's desk to take statements. Alice Felton informed him that she would be assisting, but, after asking for the names and phone numbers of all the citizens on Center Path that morning, Sheriff Crisp sent her away to her responsibilities at the market, where she was to await her turn for an interview.

As the sheriff's official host in the Chapel, I helped gather up and escort the other guests to his side, first of them poor Ginger Martin. I had found Ginger at a tree by the edge of the Chapel Wood, in sight of the path, eating sandwiches and grapes that Boz had brought him from the market. I watched from a few trees away as he lifted the bunch of grapes to his face, the stem twisting as he went at the fruit with his teeth. He washed each bite down with milk.

"Ginger," I said as I approached, "are you getting enough to eat?"

By now he seemed able to talk, as well as he ever could. "Enough, yes." He smiled at me through grape juice and milk, with teeth that were astonishingly white and straight. "Boz gave me."

"He said he would." I hunkered down beside him. "Ginger, are you ready to talk to the sheriff?"

"Sure, yes," he said, as he continued to aim his mouth at the twirling bunch of grapes.

"I mean now. Are you ready to talk with him now? Can you do that?"

"I don't need to talk. I'm OK."

"It's good you're OK, but it's the sheriff who needs to talk. He needs to ask you about the hands. The hands you found."

Suddenly the grapes stopped twisting. Ginger brought them down to his lap and enclosed the diminishing bunch within his big hands, one hand streaked with dirt, the other with grease, and both with the clear juice of the fruit. "I thought, birds," he said slowly.

I stayed with him as he meticulously placed the remains of his lunch in his little paper bag from the market. He looked at me again and seemed to remember something.

"Let's go talk to the sheriff," I prompted.

"Yes," he said. We rose to our feet and strolled over to the Chapel.

I deposited Ginger at Sara's desk, and the Sheriff motioned me out. In the churchyard an ambulance stood heavy but quiet, its red and white roof lights flashing needlessly. A medic was just closing the rear door, and soon the vehicle drove off, no one but me to watch. The crime lab's van remained, its side door open to reveal big aluminum trunks, their lids hinged up.

I walked close to the sepulcher and heard the voices. "Over here. A few more of those drops, please. Let's dust up this surface one more time. I need one of those."

"Not one of these?"

"No, those. They hold a better edge."

I left the pair to the intricacies of their search and walked to the Gunnell Street shops. Elgin was alone with his Slipstone T-shirts, Slipstone stationery, glassware, writing instruments, and postcards.

He was working at the shop desk as I came in, and Clancy seemed blissfully at home on the floor beside him. He did not look up despite the noise of the door, even as I came close enough to see that his work was a series of figures drawn on graph paper, lined up precisely, a row of small adjacent circles, a row of perfect squares, a row of perfect squares with dots in the middle, a row of the letter *R* and the next of backward *R*s. He had begun uneven hexagons, coffin-like, when I spoke his name. The mechanical pencil stopped, but Elgin still gazed down.

"Elgin, are you going to be all right?"

"I'm all right, thank you, George." Still the bowed head.

"I came because the sheriff asked me to. He hopes you can come to the Chapel for a talk."

"The sheriff wants me? For a talk? I thought we *had* talked."

"An interview, I suppose you'd say. But it's not just you; it's all of us on the path this morning."

"Shouldn't he be here himself? Isn't that the way they do things? Maybe a deputy to the house? Besides, I thought the state police were here, or someone...official." Finally he lifted his great head and looked at me through shadowed, bleary eyes.

"It seems that the state helps out with forensics – fingerprints and all that – but something like this is first a local responsibility."

"Something like this? Something like *this*? George, what is *this* to you?" He gripped his metal pencil hard in his fist and pushed with his thumb as if to snap it. "How cold is your damn blood, George, you who..." Some act of will prevented his completing the thought.

"This is difficult, Elgin. It's going to be hard on you and me and everybody in this little place." He'd gone back to drawing his precise figures. "Don't talk to the sheriff now if you can't do it now. I can tell him."

His eyes were suddenly back up and wide and no longer shadowed. "You won't tell him anything for me, George. Not a thing. Now what time must I be there? And where? The confessional?"

As I left Elgin's shop I began to close the door quietly, when the two gray-haired visitors I'd spotted in their car this morning scurried up and began to enter the shop. "So it's open?" asked the woman. They were both in colorful sweaters, he with a notebook and she with a camera.

"It seems to be; the owner's just there." I pointed through the door to the desk.

"We sure picked the wrong day to see the Founder's grave," the little man said. "We can't get near it, with all the tape."

"I hope you didn't travel too far." I knew they hadn't; I'd checked the guest register after Gert Franz had turned them away from the Chapel.

"No, just from Loverton," answered the wife. "But I'll bet people start coming from all over once the story gets out."

"The story?" I tried to look quizzical. "The death today, you mean? I don't think someone's accident is going to bring much attention to Slipstone."

"Accident?" she snorted. "How can you say 'accident'? Aren't you the manager over there at the church? Don't you know about the hands?"

"I'm the administrator of the Chapel Foundation," I answered coolly.

"Then I'd be busy hiring extra staff if I were you."

"And maybe raising admission a little," added the husband.

"Our trustees, I think, would prefer to let the Chapel

itself, and the Secretary's artifacts, draw whatever visitors they may."

"Be sure and tell that to Greg Down," the wife smirked.

"I'm sorry?"

"Greg Down. From the *Citizen*. You know, on the Crime Page. He's over by the church now; we just finished our interview." She grinned and pushed past, and they closed the door clamorously behind them. I looked through the glass and saw Elgin rise to meet them.

As I set off toward the Chapel, I soon realized I was marching, as if I had some intention with Greg Down – something I could tell him, or something I could prevent his discovering. He was nowhere outside that I could see, but, as I approached the Chapel door, the two members of the state crime team came toward me. The woman's skirt was hanging a little askew, but her suit buttons were all done up tight. Her assistant's sleeves were rolled in careful folds, with his hands and forearms covered in grime.

"Is there a chance you have any distilled water?" the woman asked, somewhat insistently. "I seem to have arrived without any. And maybe a lavatory for my assistant." She herself had the appearance of never needing a lavatory.

"Distilled water? A few little bottles of drinking water in my office you could have, I suppose."

"No chlorine? Seals ever broken? I guess I could take a look at the mineral content."

"I'll bring them down," I offered.

"Oh, I'd be happy to come up. Your window doesn't look down on the little cemetery, does it?"

On our way to the stairs we passed Sara's office. Sheriff Crisp's thin voice came through her doorway, inflection rising, with Thorny Webber's profound bass following close, reverberating with "around about," "never understood," and other phrases I couldn't place in context, especially as the woman urged us on quickly with the rat-tats of her heels on the hard linoleum diamonds of the corridor floor.

"By the way," she finally announced as we began the stairs, "I'm Rella Derry, and my assistant's name is Bill." We had dropped off Bill in the restroom to wash his hands and arms.

I stopped to turn. "Yes, hello, I'm George…"

"Yes, I know, I know," said Rella Derry abruptly but with a smile as she motioned me upward with flips of her hands.

"You know?"

"Let's get that water now, shall we?"

"How did you manage to run out of distilled water? That van seems like it would…"

"Empty. Absolutely dry. Some of my colleagues – well, one of my colleagues – feels he can run through the entire inventory as long as there's plenty for him. Last time it was the hemostats. Try picking hairs out of sawdust with the tweezers from Bill's knife."

I thought I had closed my office door after a brief stop following the sheriff's arrival, but now it was fully open, and there, leaning onto the windowsill ledge, was Greg Down, propped on his elbow, jotting notes in his narrow pad, writing in a large hand, quickly flipping filled pages up and over, so unlike the small uniformed man downstairs at Sara's desk. He took time to scribble down a few more observations before looking up.

"Hi," he said. His big head, his little round glasses. "Hang on just a second." And he went back to his notes.

"Can I help you find something?" I asked.

"No, I just needed to put some thoughts together, thanks. Somehow the sanctity of the … downstairs…didn't seem appropriate. Besides, I thought I could look down from here. On the graveyard. Turns out I had my directions reversed."

I crossed the room to the old cabinet on the wall and took out two small bottles of mineral water.

"So, did you find your fingerprints, any fibers in the old tomb?" the reporter asked Rella Derry.

"As I told you, Mr. Down," she responded coolly. "I'd be happy to explain our techniques, but it's really not up to me to announce any results of our investigation."

"What about blood? Any blood other than hers."

"Wait, wait a minute, Mr. Down," I interposed. "Let me ask *you* a question first, if you don't mind. You don't mind, do you?"

"No, no secrets here."

"Please notice for a minute that you're standing uninvited in my office. Can you tell me why you felt entitled to wander in?"

"Well, the door was open," he said confidently, apparently surprised that I would think to question his presence. "Not open, exactly, but not locked. I did knock. And I remembered that after our interview – when you first took your job – you said I could come back any time."

"I suppose this isn't quite what I was thinking."

"I haven't touched a thing; just jotting down a few notes." He put his pen to his lip and hesitated. "How long's this been broken?"

"What? How long's what been broken?"

"The window lock. Here."

"I don't know. A hundred years probably. I never noticed." I refused to go look, but Rella Derry crossed the room, leaned toward the window, and adjusted her glasses.

"What do you think?" the reporter asked.

"Not for me to say," said Rella. "Not without a warrant."

"Mr. Down, are you suggesting that Jean Clacton's murderer climbed the stone walls of this building in order to visit my office? To sharpen a pencil, I suppose?"

"To look for a key, of course," he said. "How *did* he – or she – break into the tomb?"

"We refer to it as a sepulcher, Mr. Down."

"Tomb, crypt, same thing, isn't it? I just looked it up in your dictionary there. So where did the key come from? Do you keep it in your desk? The door wasn't forced, didn't you say, Dr. Derry?"

"There's no key to the vault, Mr. Down," I said. "At least I'd never seen one until she...," a nod toward Rella Derry, "managed to discover one of her own. Would you like to look in my desk? I do keep it locked, as you have probably discovered." With its tiny key from my pocket I unlocked the drawer and gently pulled it open. The reporter approached, leaned over, and jumped back with a little "oh."

Rella Derry started over. "What's there?"

"Only a friend," I answered, and we all three looked down. "A mouse, taking sanctuary. He's not very welcome in the rest of the building. And that's off the record, Mr. Down. I don't want our sexton and secretary reading about the rodent they've missed." I closed the drawer, and there came a fidget from the rear of the desk as the mouse ran down one of the back legs and across the rug to some hiding place or other.

Rella Derry opened one of the water bottles and began sipping at it.

SHERIFF CRISP DIDN'T TAKE much time with me that afternoon. As we talked in Sara's office, the phone rang two or three times, with calls from his dispatcher and a deputy. The sheriff had placed his hat on a third chair in the little office. His pistol lay in its black leather holster on Sara's perfect desk, its barrel toward one of Sara's family photographs.

I could tell he'd asked the same questions all day long: "When did you first know that something was wrong on the path?" "How long have you lived in Slipstone?" "How well did you know Jean Clacton?" "Did she have any enemies you're aware of?"

And then he asked me some others.

"Mr. Gilsum, why do you think Victor Blair happened to look in that opening in the vault?"

I waited a moment. "I've wanted to figure that out, and I can't. Did he ever try to explain?"

He wrote slowly and tidily with his ballpoint in a small spiral notebook, taking his time as he seemed to record every word of mine. He didn't answer my question, but he asked another: "When's the last time you entered the tomb?"

"I've never been in there. What reason could I have? So far as I know, there's been no one inside since they first installed the Founder and his wife. Well, not until now."

"What about the key?"

"There *is* no key. No key I've ever seen. Well, until Miss Derry found some kind of instrument that forced the lock."

Meticulously, he recorded every word. "I understand the deceased had some reason to be angry with you. Is that right?"

I expected the question. "I don't think Jean was ever angry with me. What are you talking about?" I paused just a second. "I don't think we knew each other well enough for either to be angry at the other."

He stopped writing and tilted his head up to see my eyes. Then he was back to the notebook, asking "Wasn't there a disturbance, something about disrupting her piano recital?" He turned back a few pages in his notes. "'Disorderly behavior in the audience,' someone called it."

"Elgin Brattle."

"Several individuals mentioned it."

"There was nothing. A few coins dropped out of my pocket and rolled along the floor. Jean probably heard them; I think she skipped over a few notes."

"Rolled along the floor," repeated Sheriff Crisp, writing slowly with his ballpoint.

"And, besides," I said, "what could that have to do with someone...with what happened? Did someone kill her because I made a noise in her recital?"

Sheriff Crisp stopped writing. He looked up and over into my face. "Did you talk with her afterwards? Explain what happened? Apologize?"

I decided and did not hesitate. "I wish I had. But, no, I never got the chance."

For once he resisted writing down my answer but still he repeated the words, almost absentmindedly, this time searching my face: "...never got the chance."

Then he looked back down at the hand with his ballpoint and said quietly, "It must have been another night then."

"Another night?"

"When you visited Jean Clacton at her home. When... someone mentioned seeing you approach her door."

"It must have been. Another night, that is. She's invited me there before. Coffee. Dessert. We're friends, not terribly close. We *were* friends, until..."

"Until someone carried her away and decided to cut her hands off." He looked up, his small gray eyes toward every part of my face.

We both paused, until I had to say something more.

"Maybe it's important. I don't think so. But someone's been in my office, at night. Looking."

"Looking at what, Mr. Gilsum?"

"Looking *for*. Looking for something in the file drawers, in my desk."

Sheriff Crisp had begun writing again, but then he stopped and tilted his head up one last time. "Looking for the key. Is that what you mean?"

THE CROWS HAD MARCHED across the lawn, from one edge of the woods to the other, picking up whatever they could find. One flew away, and then the rest. Behind them the yellow crime tape was stretched taut on its stakes.

"Tell me what you know, George. Tell me what you know."

I didn't look behind me at the interruption. I'd heard the boards on the stairway and wasn't surprised at the voice of my bookstore friend. "What is it you think I know, Galen?"

"I think you know how she got there. And I want you to tell me."

I turned around slowly and leaned back against the wall, my arms crossed. "And what else, Galen? What else do you want me to tell you?"

"That's all; that's enough. And I didn't say anything to Sheriff Crisp, George, if you want to know. He never asked a direct question about you and Jean."

"What kind of question were you expecting? Was there really anything worth mentioning?"

"Does the sheriff know about you – that you were... close?" She stayed at the door, but her voice came across the room firmly and distinct. Her cardigan was loose, and so was her hair.

"Your apparent version of *close* isn't exactly what I'd call us, Galen."

"And what would you call what you were?"

"Village neighbors, friends of a sort. No, I said almost nothing about Jean and me, but it's not something he pursued very rigorously, except that someone seems to have seen me at her cottage some night or other."

"Look, George, if you didn't have anything to do with what happened, if you don't know anything, you need to tell the sheriff about the two of you. Before someone else does.

"Someone else? And there really *was* no two of us."

"Do you think I'm the only one Jean talked to?"

"Yes." I walked halfway across my office, stood in the center of the rug, and slid my hands into my pockets. "That she said something to you about her imaginings astounds me. I suppose she took counsel where she could find it."

"She never asked for advice. She only talked."

"I'm sorry, Galen. I know. Jean was a friend, and I very much regretted, I hated, all the noise I made at the recital, the performance that you and Elgin and she had worked on so diligently together. But there's no need for you or anyone else to complicate her death. It's already complicated enough."

"The saddest thing, George, is that no one will ever account for Jean Clacton's *life*, let alone her death. There was too little there. The only complication is how it ended. Only her death will ever matter, and maybe someone can account for *it*. If not the sheriff, maybe that woman with her little bag and her tools and her quiet assistant."

I WALKED my bicycle to the market in the late, dim afternoon, with the sun still retreating early behind the high oaks and hickories of Slipstone Hill. Outside, two pickup trucks were slanted unevenly between the faded white lines, both with their tailgates down and each with a deer stretched dead in back. A doe and a buck, each with a dark red blister swelling low in the neck. Inside the hunters were loud in their shopping – beer, sausages, big sandwiches from Alice in back. "Whoo," said a scrawny young bearded man in old tan and canvas, as he found just the right change for his purchases, "her hands taken right off. Sawed, huh? Radio said just sawed off."

"The radio doesn't always know everything, now, does it, Jerry?" answered Alice, as she dropped everything into a brown paper bag and handed it over with a stern look.

I was looking through the shallow vegetable bins as I heard the front door close behind the exiting hunters. Boz was putting out carrots, and I took a bunch from his hand. "I just don't know how to act," he told me, smiling wide in a funny kind of question and rolling his head. "Nobody seems very sad; nobody seems scared. Mostly it's like nothing really happened. Thorny already took Miss Clacton's charge sheet out of the box and threw it away."

"What else could he do?" I asked.

"She's on her way; they're driving her...they're *taking* her to the state hospital for the autopsy. Everyone thinks there'll be nothing to find."

"Nothing to find?"

"She bled to death," called Alice, who had positioned herself up the aisle by the potatoes and onions. "Her body was bled white like an animal."

"But there were other marks," she continued in a quieter voice. "Some rubbing, an abrasion, I heard, a line around her neck. And her knees scuffed, with little pieces of leaf, and little tiny rocks."

"How do you know that?" I asked as she began to walk closer.

"I got a call."

"A call?"

"Her friends on the rescue squad," Boz explained.

"And they can't find any of the blood," Alice went on. "Her house is clean. There's no sign of trouble. Somewhere in the woods there's a big red pool, not even crusted over yet."

"And the dogs can't find it," said Boz.

"Those dogs will find it, don't you worry," Alice shot back. "If it's in this county, those dogs will find it."

She followed me back over to the butcher's case, where I asked her to wrap up some stew meat. "Boz can't understand how something like this can happen in Slipstone," she told me quietly. "But I had to tell him, Boz, there isn't any hill high enough to keep this kind of thing away. Everywhere, somebody hates somebody else. And sometimes this is how they show it." She tore off a length of tape to close up the white package of meat. "But Boz just won't believe it. All night tonight he'll be rolling around with those dreams of his."

"What sort of dreams does Boz have?"

"They're the longest, drawnoutest, most vicious things. Little boys with sharp teeth living in the woods. Animals you've never seen before with all kinds of knotty hair and razor claws. I try to talk him down when he wakes up afterwards, but there's no coming back from those dreams. They stay on his shoulder all day; it's like they talk in his ear." She handed me the package of meat and looked over the counter at Boz, where he had finished up the few bunches of carrots and begun making little pyramids of hard, pink tomatoes.

"What happens next?" I asked Thorny as he rang up my groceries. "What about Jean, her possessions, her cottage?"

"Somebody said her nephew's coming out. I don't know. I always thought she was the last Clacton left."

I knew he was right. There was nobody coming from anywhere to take Jean's things away.

7

SUNDAY MORNING

Every Sunday morning I woke to play my record of *The Thieving Magpie*, Rossini asking that I open the curtains, draw on my bathrobe, and make my way to the kitchen, clicking my tongue and nodding, a big man moving to the footsteps of a little bird. The day after Jean's death, or the day after we'd found her, I was half a step slow, and I saw myself staring out the kitchen window toward the woods behind, no idea how long I'd stood so still. My coffee was bitter and good, and I drank it with a plateful of rye toast and eggs.

On the kitchen counter lay an old leather bag that apparently had hung for many years, almost hidden, in the back of my bedroom closet. I had brought it into the light under the kitchen window and spent a number of hours reconditioning the leather, cleaning white residue from inside and oiling it day after day so the bag and its strap now yielded almost softly in my hands. I put some sandwiches inside, then pulled on my heavy boots and strong canvas pants.

The day was early and quiet, and I walked Center Path

as quickly as I ever had. At the churchyard I stood at the police tape and considered whether the footprints had all been lifted by the examiners, finally deciding they had. I stepped over the plastic yellow band and walked to the sepulcher. Rella Derry and her assistant had straightened everything behind them, even cleaning their fingerprint powder off the lock. As they had yesterday, I looked closely for fresh scars in the brass, but nothing had marked the years of tarnish, nothing to indicate a struggle at the latch. I walked around the little square structure in the short wet grass and tried to gauge the width of the cloverleaf openings, how big a set of shoulders or hips could make it through. My own body, I was sure, never could, and neither could the thin shoulders of someone like Ginger Martin.

I leaned against the sandstone and looked up toward the wooden shutters of the bell tower. Formed by the early sun, shadows of cottony clouds drifted along the dark surface and seemed to move the louvered boards. Rachel wouldn't ring the first hour of the day until seven.

The meadow grass was higher and even more lush than on Friday as I began to push through it behind the Chapel. I resisted the pull down the hill and walked steadily, leaning back, treading on the hard dry earth under the wet grass. After a few minutes, halfway down the hill, I lifted my arms as if for balance. I was alone, like the few trees in the meadow grass, with fragile blue flowers up past my knees. I reversed my body and moved backward downhill a moment, staring up at the dark, west side of the Chapel. It might have been Victor Blair who scuttled around the corner of the church, but the figure moved too quickly for me to see, if there had been a figure there at all against the dark of the stones. I turned back and made my way down the rest of the long slope to the edge of Slipstone Rill.

In my months here I'd never walked so far down this side of the hill. I was surprised at the width of the stream. The water ran quickly, although we'd had no rain for a week. I walked both directions a few hundred feet, onto sand and gravel, looking for an easy crossing, but then I came back to where I'd first descended. It was only here, I decided, that a person could cross and stay dry. And then I saw how. The rocks in the stream weren't laid straight across, but their order, after I started one to the next, was obvious and regular. The stones were flat, and high out of the water's flow, with the next easily reached from the last, especially if I didn't pause. They'd been arranged. And they were highly quartzed. They'd shine under the moon.

The stepping stones brought me onto a narrow shore of muddy gravel, and, when I stooped to look for tracks, I made out crescents in the wet sand that might have been sunk by boot heels. I fingered some of the pebbles at the edge of the cold water, and then I sank both hands until they stung. I stood and looked back up the hill, where the sun was lifting above the churchyard and warming my face. So far away, the Chapel hardly rose above the swaying of the grass. As I narrowed my eyes toward the sun, Rachel rang seven o'clock on the Chapel bells, the heavy sound rolling down the hill to the place where I stood. In an hour she'd ring again, and Grant Sweeney would offer a morning eucharist to the ten or fifteen parishioners who'd walk in from the village or drive from nearby. Grant's incense would drift up through the floorboards to linger for hours in my office.

I wiped my wet hands on my canvas pants, picked up my leather bag where I'd set it on a dry rock, and turned in toward the woods that began thirty feet back from the stream. There was a narrow opening, and at first I was forced to make my way slowly, through young pines so close their thick branches wove together. In a minute I broke through, and I found myself in a forest of old and new growth hardwoods, trees spaced wide enough for the sunlight to drop here and there on a flat floor of pine needles and last year's leaves. I moved my way farther into the forest along a direction that could have been a path, or just the way the rain beat down through the trees.

My way took me on a bearing just angled to the left, and I walked steadily, my boots on the hard level floor of leaves and dry yellow needles. At times I climbed under birches blown halfway down or over giant fallen oaks slick with decay, broken branches offering handholds. The forest was thick with smell, even without any recent rain. Fungus was everywhere growing wild, white molds in the cracks of rotting wood, dry green fungal lace along low branches, mushrooms sprouted out of the old needles but already withered. I kept walking what I thought was west, away from the sun, which had made its way higher now through the tallest branches. Whether or not it was an actual path I followed, I never had to hesitate to find the way the trees opened.

As the sun played in and out of the passing clouds, in and out of the treetops, I spotted in some near distance a kind of small deer or large gray fox or other frightened animal, weaving away from me farther into the woods. It was silent as it ran, and just a glint.

Eventually I reached a stream that flowed from my right and that I considered must be Slipstone Rill, circling from the south, farther into the forest. Back here the water had sliced its way some six or eight feet sharply into the earth, and I took a moment to find a place I could cross with dry boots – or to see if the path I seemed to follow would reveal the best way over this rushing brook and the steep sides it had carved. Looking toward a downstream bend, I saw where a fallen tree would take me across.

I walked along the stream bed, climbed onto the thick trunk, and tested my boot soles on the wood, where someone, it became clear, had long ago flattened the makeshift bridge with some kind of wide, sharp tool like a pull knife, creating notches that might once have provided more secure footing. I stood with bent knees and began my way along the tree, at first testing each footstep but soon finding the stability that momentum brings. Halfway across, confident with my balance, I stopped, bent my knees, and perched there, hunkered on the notched wood. I looked down at the water and gathered in the sounds of its flow.

The tree had fallen years ago, when the stream might have shifted its bank to eat away the ground underneath. At the far end of the tree, the roots spread wildly into the air to the left and right, but not the center, because someone had once chopped or sawn the way clear. There was something white there, hanging.

As I climbed my way through the narrow passage between the roots, one of them pulled a hole in my heavy sweater and grabbed at my leather bag. When I jumped through to the earth, my jaw was cut and bleeding and the strap on the bag was torn almost through. I leaned over and caught my breath, then looked up into the thick fingers of the roots, where the white thing I'd seen was hanging. It was held loosely by a scrap of fabric, and I took it into my hand.

The body of the doll was of something like sawdust beneath her thin flowered dress, with its tiny feet, shoeless and toeless, sewn tight with the stuff. The porcelain head was in one piece, with dark hair still secure on her scalp though matted with mud. Her wide brown eyes were newly painted, and they looked up serenely as I cradled her in my hand – or with serenity and something else – a look of loss, or fright. She was a pretty thing, although her features had weathered from little girls' caresses across what must have been many years. Her dress, I realized, was much newer than the doll who wore it, the stitching less artful than the features of her face should have deserved.

The sleeves of the rudimentary dress were overly long. I pulled the cuffs up over her wrists, and I saw that her hands were gone, severed cleanly away. Tight, meticulous sutures closed the wounds.

I SAT ON A SMALL, fallen log in dappled sun and ate my lunch; then I put the doll in my bag and began to walk again, angling to follow the flow of the stream. The sun was high enough now that I wouldn't be sure of my direction until it began to sink again toward the southwest. I wished I'd brought a compass, but I hadn't known the woods were so thick.

Once, as I walked along the edge of the rill, I saw ahead of me where the trees opened and the sun shone onto a wide place in the water. I came closer, and now I stood by the edge, on a level area of pebbles and thick sand. I could see that no stones broke the surface of the water here, or came high enough even to see through the dapple of the sunlight. The water might have been deep enough here to swim, or at least to cool off when the summer heat arrived.

I kept on, away now from the rill and farther into what openings I could find through the woods. I'd expected fields, a farmhouse, or a road by now, since I'd long ago topped the rise of forest I could see distantly from the churchyard. The trees here were older and let through less sun than before.

The ground rose and fell more frequently, and I crossed a half dozen damp or dry stream beds as I kept in my same direction.

Then, in a level area on the crest of one hill, there were stones arranged in a broad circle, stones weathered but flat across the top and a foot or so high, some twenty, the same sandstone as constituted the Chapel walls. They were not the stones of some ancient rite. Instead they suggested seats for a kind of meeting or performance. The ground within the circle was spread with packed leaves, but no seedlings, no other growth, had been allowed to develop there. I crouched within the circle and saw around me where small saplings had been sliced away close to the ground, their cuts still white and raw.

I rose and kept on.

As the trees grew more abundantly, with old growth keeping its place against the encroach of vines and saplings, I grew aware of sounds thinning away. I'd heard a few song-birds before, but now only a distant crow called out, high in the branches. The breeze was dead, even far above. My own noises grew louder – footfalls on the thick, flat leaves, the sound of my breath as I tired in my rapid walking. I stopped, stood still and listened for a long minute, then began to turn slowly in a tight circle as I watched the passing trees.

At one point then, a hundred feet away, I saw a break, a line where light fell quietly and the dust of old leaves seemed to hang. I slowly walked closer, touching trees with my fingertips as I cautiously moved along. All at once I came out into a band of sun, where trees had long since been cut away to right and left along a tenuous ridgetop to form an open field – open, but with an arrangement of short, rotted tree stumps, each a half-foot across, a circle of them, another circle in these woods.

I came and stopped beside the nearest stump. Its fragments of bark were grayed, dead of smell, peeled nearly away. I began a circuit around. Twenty dead trees in a circle fifty footsteps across, an area flat with the same thick mat of old leaves that spread all over the forest floor but with new growth sliced off clean near the ground.

And at the foot of each stump toward the center of the circle, a hands'-breadth of leaves was coated with irregular thickness, color of the darkest rust.

Give to the earth.

8

SUNDAY AFTERNOON

When I finally came out of the woods, late in the afternoon, the lower clouds were twisted like ropes, far up the hill over the Chapel spire. The sky was even darker behind. The rain began only after I'd picked my way back over the stepping stones of Slipstone Rill and started up the grassy incline. Big drops came down widely scattered, but the heavier rain held back until I had climbed the long hill and walked quickly through the churchyard. Grateful, but with some surprise, I found the Chapel door unlocked, and I entered the vestibule. I stood at the open door, breathing heavily, and felt the storm come up. The rain spattered from the front stoop onto the tile floor of the vestibule, and thunder came up close in the Chapel Wood. The torn strap of my bag was wound tightly around my fist.

I closed and locked the door, walked up the dark aisle, and continued back through the sacristy and library. The air felt heavy with the rain pounding outside and all the windows tight. In weeks before, I had already learned how powerfully thunderclaps could buffet this hill. There was iron, Sara had told me, not far below the soil in which Slipstone buried its dead, and lightning flew toward it heavy and hard when the weather began to warm. Lightning now flashed onto the library's south window, enough to show the diamond shapes on the old linoleum floor as I walked to the cellar door and opened it.

The switch at the head of the steps had been left on – by Grant, I assumed – and the series of bare ceiling bulbs was on to illuminate the main passage along the cellar, where aisles between shelves branched to the left and irregular spaces disappeared darkly to the right. No matter how often Victor swept the steps, dust settled again quickly, rising from the packed dirt floor of the cellar and the fifty trunks and boxes of the Secretary's travels. I walked carefully down the wood steps. If the shelves were ever taken down, the cellar might show itself to be shaped in the same broad cross as the church itself. The sound of the rain didn't carry down here, but I could feel the weight of the heavy air from the storm as I stood under the low boards of the ceiling.

I proceeded past the shelves at my left to the foundation wall below the library fireplace, where I had earlier cached the thing I had found on my office desk those days earlier. I pulled open the small square iron door to the ash cleanout and reached one hand far enough in to pluck out the fragile parchment I'd slid there earlier, rolled loosely and held gently by rubber bands within its plastic bag. The plastic was lightly dusted, despite my earlier care in preparing the cache with damp rags to remove the old ash and tiny cinders that had fallen since its last cleaning. I brought the document out under the light of the nearest bulb and carefully unrolled it. I laid it out on one of the simple, tall work platforms that Victor Blair or Gammel Minken had constructed at the ends of alternative shelves. I weighted the corners of the thick page with small but heavy books.

The map was sketched in ink, then painted with thin watercolor on something like parchment. With my fingertip I traced the walk I'd taken earlier. The village appeared, almost irrelevant, at the lower left of the old drawing, which must, I decided, be the southeast. The Chapel was nothing more than two rectangles intersected, and the churchyard was a dozen curved lines, suggesting stones. The woods took up most of the parchment, a series of short, angled hair-lines, spaced widely, drawn in an ink now turned from black to brown. Near the upper left corner was an absence of trees, almost an inch across its irregular circle, and drawn dark. A hollow, a hole. The stone quarry. When the unknown hand drew this map, trees had covered the long hill behind the church, but the wood had since been cut, I supposed, to build Slipstone cottages, with the hill planted for meadow.

Among the trees, eight inches up from the edge of the map, Slipstone Rill ran left to right, then turned upward, as drawn by an elegant hand, its flow suggested by delicate curves of the pen. Written within the stream, a word said simply *rill*. Nothing, no dotted pathway, marked the flat stones that had taken me across that morning and back just a half hour ago. As I considered my direction into the woods earlier, I began to see how the watercolor on the old map might be accurate in describing elevations, browns moving up in height to yellow, where the ridges topped off. The rectangles of the tiny Chapel sat on a field of the palest color, the hill descending into the darkest of the thin water-color browns at Slipstone Rill, the color then passing up and down through its narrow spectrum as the ground rose and fell through the forest.

My finger searched through the scratches of brown ink to find the way I'd taken through the woods. I came to the place where the rill curved around, but nothing indicated the tree where I had crossed the stream and found the doll. Then I pushed my finger a few inches farther and encountered two small cleared circles among the trees. I realized that one would have stones around it and the other would have stumps, although this map must have predated the cutting of those trees, which now were drawn with a circle of tiny cross-hatches for what must be their leaves. I began to move my finger up and to the left, imagining where I might have walked next, but then I stopped.

The sound might have been a little animal scratching along the stones of the foundation, hesitant, stopping, then quick again for a moment and finally silent. My mouse? Something larger? I re-rolled the map and laid it in the shadow of the closest shelf. I started up the main corridor to the other end of the cellar. The sound seemed to have stopped, but now I stood in the narrow space and listened again. The animal had started up again toward the steps, but now I heard some other sound.

Breathing. Regular and slow, but not secretive. Quietly I turned into the darkness toward my left.

I could see almost beyond the range of the meager light. There, where he had found the space to arrange his canvas bunk, lay the librarian Grant Sweeney, turned to the wall, fingertips stiff against the stone foundation, dead asleep. He lay in the cool cellar with his thin black cassock pulled up to his knees, legs white, down to a pair of worn socks. His shoes were set neatly on the floor.

I backed into the corridor and returned to the shelf where I'd laid the map. I examined it no further but quickly rolled it within its loose rubber bands for its place in the wall. Then I took the doll from my leather bag and wrapped it in the plastic I had earlier used for the map. I reached both back into the cleanout, a close fit, and swung back the iron door. It all took only a moment, but, as I lifted the door slightly to drop the catch into place, darkness interrupted me.

I waited a moment for my eyes to adjust, until I realized the dark was complete. With my arms out and circling for the shelves, I made my way to the corridor and back to where the stairs had to be; the faintest light appeared beneath the closed door at the top, where the dying sun still lighted the library just beyond. My hands now empty, I used them to help find my way up the steps, where I could reach the switch on the other side of the door.

But the door, as I somehow knew before I even tried the knob, had been locked from the library. In the uncertainty of the Chapel's electrical system John Patton had thought to cache small, cheap flashlights in selected corners of the building, especially at the edge of stairways, but there seemed not to be one here. I knocked with my knuckles, then my fist, but I could hear no footsteps coming back to me over the library linoleum. "Grant," I called through the door, once and a second time louder. Then I stopped. I said the name again, but this time more quietly, and in the direction of the cot below. "Grant, are you asleep, or are you gone?" I felt my way back down the wooden steps, along the corridor, and into the corner where Grant had arranged his cot. The canvas was empty – taut and still warm. I felt along the floor but couldn't find his shoes.

9

SUNDAY NIGHT

At times that night I thought my eyes had finally adjusted, and that I was just about able to discern the high corner of a shelf or the surface of Grant's worktable. But every phantom image would quickly vanish. Staring hard at my palm, I tried a dozen times to conjure up the outline of my hand, but every notion of whiteness evaporated when I moved my fingers. Three or four times I climbed the short stairway to hear how quietly I could move step to step, and to consider how quietly a smaller man like Grant Sweeney could move. One time at the top, after an hour or so when the sun must have gone down, I held my fingers just at the bottom of the door, but no light leaked under. So the library was dark too. Even if the rain had stopped, only the dimmest moonlight would have filtered through the stained glass of the library windows.

I was grateful for my heavy sweater while I maneuvered the cellar, moving aisle to aisle. As my hands explored the shelves, looking for matches, anything for light, I tried to identify the items there by touch. More than anything else, there were the cartons, gathered during the Secretary's lonely travels through southern and Alpine Europe. He had been a big man like me, but thinner those years, able to glide invisibly through a land during war, visiting homes and buying books, drawings, and icons, mailing them back, boxed for Slipstone Village. The Maggini didn't arrive until he brought it home himself.

Now and then I stood still and listened for whatever noises I could hear, a mouse scuttling over a piece of cardboard maybe, or rain and wind in the stones and wood above me. But nothing came through the blackness; instead, my ears created their own sounds from the insistent pressure of my pulse.

Finally I came to rest on Grant's cot. I took off my boots, pulled my feet underneath me, and leaned back on the foundation wall.

Later, when I opened my eyes, I knew I'd slept. I looked closely at the dial of my watch but still could see nothing. I held it to my ear, but its ticking had stopped.

It was very gradually that I sensed something new in the dark silence, and it took an instant to know how I perceived it. It was a smell, an odor that started faintly but, once I became aware of it, gained in thickness until it was most of what I knew around me. It may have been the smell that awakened me, because still there was no sound, even from whatever brought the odor so close. It was the smell of damp earth from under the leaves of the forest floor, or it was the redolence of some tincture or sour oil.

When he whispered, it was just at my ear.

"You can't follow it like you did today. That's not what you have to do."

He breathed out the smell of earth with his voice, as he continued.

"Did you think you'd find something, doing that, what you did out there? Did you think you'd fool me?"

I looked down toward my lap, where my invisible hands gripped each other firmly in the dark. They had quickly grown moist. My visitor didn't speak again for a while, though his smell stayed close beside me where he hunkered just at the edge of the cot.

"What is there to find?" I finally was able to say, "How can I know what *you* don't know? Are we playing a game?"

He waited a moment. In the complete darkness I looked in his direction as if he could see my face. I knew that somehow he *could* see it.

"Oh, it's no game," he told me.

I waited, but finally said, "I found the circle of trees from your map and the circle of stones. Is that what...?"

He sounded like he'd lost some voice from years of shouting, or that he hardly ever used his voice at all. Now his whisper became even lower in pitch, but more insistent. "You call it a map," he told me, "but it's not a map like you know."

We both waited for more.

"It's a story, is what it is," he finally said. "You have to read it, read it to the end."

"How do I know when it ends?"

"Mr. Gil-sam, you know *where* it ends. You know that, and John Patton knew that. And you both pretend you don't. It is in here somewhere, and you won't tell me. *Why* won't you tell me?"

"What is this...this *it* that is here?" I asked.

"You stole *everything* from us. You people up here. You always wanted us gone, and most of us went back, long before me. But some of us stayed. And now *I* stay, me and..." His voice trailed to silence.

With the dryness in my mouth I couldn't whisper, but I kept my voice as low as I was able. "Just tell me what it is. What can I have? Leaving the map, the chart, the *story* in my office means you could have gone anywhere in this place to find what you want."

"Mr. Gil-sam, I don't need to tell you something you already know."

I sat listening for the man's breath, but I wasn't sure I could hear it over my own. His smell left me for an instant but then was back. When I spoke, my voice had again lost its control.

"Jean's hands."

"Jean. Is that her name? It's no matter. She knew what she did."

"What she did? What could she have done?"

"There are things, Mr. Gil-sam, that are ours. That nobody takes. Not music that don't belong to you. That, and not what we need for our music. We will not abide that."

"The sheriff must know. Who else could have...?"

"That man will never think it's nobody else but you. He won't let himself think it's us. He don't want to know us at all. What he'll know is, it's you. It's you, Mr. Gil-sam. You been with that woman. He'll know that, oh, he will. You been with her over and again. And that night."

He paused. Then he added, "We seen you. You know that, don't you?"

"How would, how will...? You took her *hands*."

"No," he told me, still crouched beside the cot, "she gave us those hands when she took our music."

Those words hovered awhile in the darkness.

"And Gammel Minken...," I started.

"There is something that is ours, that we need, and that old man took and kept it. A young man then."

"But you, *you* could not have been alive..."

"We have been here long, and stories get told, and those stories are true. That picture, that map you call it, is only one of them."

"It's not a story I know."

"That story – that picture – shows what you did, you up here, the old-young man, all of you, then and now. We're almost all gone; the few of us will be given back what we need. You will do that."

Then he said, in slow and measured words, "Let this stay with you," and he took my arm in a grip so tight I couldn't think to resist. Then something started as a needle on the top of my wrist. A sting, then sharper, then pressure, and a driving kind of pain as the needle buried deeper to become a knifepoint between two tendons, hot as fire. He kept it there, and I couldn't tell in the dark how deep.

Somehow our corner of the cellar grew quieter than ever then, the two of us in the dark, my eyes forced tight with the pain, and his grip so hard neither of us had reason to struggle. And then, out of the quiet, came the song, up from his throat. He hummed it low toward my ear, pausing and humming. I could feel the song as it vibrated through his body and into his hand on my arm. Almost a lullaby. I closed my eyes.

And then no one was there.

10

MONDAY MORNING

I felt her finger touch my wrist, and I woke on the tight canvas cot. My legs were cold and my body stiff. With my face pressed against the green fabric, it took me a short moment to decide where I was. There was light now, but never bright down here.

"You never came out," she said. "Here."

I reached to take the plastic cup, the lid of Rachel's thermos, but my wrist buckled, and hot tea soaked the dirt floor near my boots. I looked to the back of my hand to see how bloody the damage was. The skin was only just narrowly slit, and blood had dried into a line between the tendons where the point of the man's tool had pressed in. I flexed my hand just to the edge of pain, and no more.

"What do you mean, I never came out?" I pulled myself upright and lifted the cup. Rachel poured out more tea.

"I saw you in the rain. You came inside when the storm began."

"And you waited; you stayed by your little window up there? Couldn't you have missed me when I left?"

"You never came out, George," she said calmly. "I would have seen."

I sat leaning over, my forearms hard on my knees. I drank the tea, a little at a time, trying to decide what time it must be.

"How did you find me?" I finally asked.

"How big do you think this Chapel really is?" she said, coming to sit beside me on the cot.

"And so you searched the building until you came down here, until you'd looked in all these little passageways? When did Grant leave the church?"

"George, I brought you some tea, that's all. It's late."

"It's early, you mean. It must be."

"Long after six; I have to climb upstairs."

"Rachel, drink some tea with me. Tell me what brought you down here."

"I have to ring seven. I have to go."

"Why did you wake me?"

"You were cold. Besides, you didn't want to be here."

"Why do you say that?"

"Well, you couldn't have locked yourself in here, of course. I'm sure if you had a choice, you'd rather be sleeping at home."

"*Grant* locked me in. He must have. Not deliberately, I suppose."

"If you say." She took the empty plastic cup from my hand, screwed it onto the thermos, and left. I left too.

The gravel on Center Path grew quiet under my boots when Rachel began to play her bells. Close to the tower, I thought I could hear the groan of the high oak beams as the ropes tightened, just at the strike of the clapper. I imagined hearing the levers hitting hard against the blue felt stops as Rachel closed her eyes and moved foot to foot. A few steps more took me from one pitch of the bells to a higher one, then another pitch yet, until Rachel ended her song with the seven long tolls of the hour.

FROM A DISTANCE, I saw a short line of visitors waiting at the tea shop door. On most weekdays, a few of them might drive to Slipstone for visits to the Secretary's archives, the items that Gammel Minken and Grant Sweeney had already rescued from their cartons and brought to the library. Today, though, the Franzes were entertaining a different clientele, all couples as usual, but more, and some of them younger. Their small gray European sedans were pulled in slantwise to the curb, with a black-and-green motorcycle among them. The motorcycle couple were holding open the door, the next to be admitted to a clean table in the tea shop. Neat, but in leather, they shared the morning's *Citizen*, he, bearded, holding the paper, she over his shoulder, running her finger down to read.

Galen's bookshop door was closed, and her sign said closed as well, but through the glass I could see her moving in and out of the shadows of her shelves. The stack of *Citizen*s still sat outside, the twine cut and a handful of quarters thrown on top. I set down a few coins and picked up a newspaper.

Reporter Greg Down liked modifiers, the expected ones: "gruesome," "remote," "historical" (he meant "historic"), "baffling," "brooding," "tree-lined," "looming," "unexplained." His account of Jean's murder spoke of irony: "hands severed savagely" but "wrists meticulously sutured." The story, dominating the front page, had "villagers huddling in hushed groups" and "a far-flung web of state and local law-enforcement officers following the slimmest leads." The reporter characterized my response to his questions as "unwilling" and the sheriff's as "reserved." Rella Derry he described as "professionally quiet." The coroner seemed to have refused Down's request to travel to the city and examine the body, but an unnamed source in that office had revealed to the reporter that Jean undoubtedly died from blood loss. The story suggested that a pair of police hounds were even now seeking the isolated bit of earth somewhere nearby, which must be pungent with Jean's blood.

Galen finally unlocked the door for the day's business. She noticed me through the glass panes in the door but quickly turned away. Folding the paper under my arm, I walked across Gunnell Street and up the path to the Chapel. I took long steps, and I was quickly through the Chapel Wood, up the narrow, sun-flecked path, and through the front door. As I entered the sacristy, I expected to hear Sara in her office, typing to the morning news, waiting to talk about the chaotic state in which Sheriff Crisp had left her desk.

She wasn't there, and it occurred to me that the door must have remained unlocked all night. I found and set the Closed sign out front.

Upstairs, no dust floated in the morning sunlight from my office windows. The invisible scraps of tape across my file cabinet were still in place. As quietly as I could, I unlocked and pulled open the desk drawer. My tiny friend stared back expectantly, waiting for his sunflower seeds, which I laid before him. As usual he refused to eat until I returned him to his privacy. I turned a page in my calendar and listed calls and letters to complete over the course of the day. Sara's answering machine downstairs would be alive with other calls I'd need to return from worried mothers of brides, a few canceling, a few seeking reassurances of various sorts. Having heard.

It wasn't too early to phone the Chair.

"My god, George, could you not have called?" she demanded. I could hear piano keys plinking behind her as a parent shopped for the right instrument.

"Actually, I did call. Your son said..."

"I suppose I *was* away from a phone, holed up at the lake; is that what he told you? I didn't even hear about it until last night. On the *radio*!"

"The village is full of cars this morning. The word's been out long enough, radio, now the *Citizen*. I've decided to close. I'd probably need an extra docent to open the Chapel, but the tea shop's full, and I'd be lucky if even Gert Franz makes it over."

"Which one's Gert again?" The piano notes behind her had promised for a moment to evolve into melody, but they only lapsed again into disorder.

"The pastries, she does the..."

"It's a good idea, George. Smacks a little of insensitivity, to open up so soon. The idea of community, the Slipstone community.... You say the shops are taking in business already? Making hay while the sun...not *Elgin*, I'm sure?"

"He wouldn't open until later anyway, but, no, I think Elgin won't be ready. He's handling the arrangements."

"The arrangements?"

"Jean. Jean's funeral. A ceremony tomorrow in the Chapel."

"Elgin and Jean? I didn't know."

"I didn't know either. I *don't* know. He was her teacher. Her piano mentor."

"Well, what about her family? Where are the Clactons?"

"The Clactons are all gone, most of them deep in the churchyard. There was only Jean."

"George." Her voice was quiet now and slow. Behind her, in the chamber of her shop, a piano arrangement was taking shape. It was nothing I'd heard before. It was left hand only, with the right just there for an instant, and there again, finding a melody. "George, who could it be? What kind of person does that? Who do they think it could be?"

"They don't think. They don't know what to think. They're looking for something. They have dogs."

The lightest of footsteps came up the stairs while I spoke with the Chair. When I replaced the receiver, Sara peered around the doorway and walked in. She wore a velvet jacket and matching beret. Though dark blue, they seemed especially colorful against her pale face and dark-rimmed eyes.

"Sara. It's terrible, isn't it. How are you?"

Instead of speaking, she stood in the doorway with her hands folded in front. She couldn't look up.

"Don't feel that you need to be here," I told her. "I've set the sign up that we're closed. I suppose you saw."

Her mutter was inaudible, directed as it was at the floor.

"I'm sorry?" I ventured.

"I said of course I saw the sign." A little louder now. And then louder yet: "What gives you the right?"

I could only stare.

"I'm sorry," she murmured. "I didn't mean...it's just that...how can you? Haven't you seen all the people? All the visitors? There've never been so many. All over the village, in the tea shop, mailing postcards. Look out your window at their cameras. They want to see us. The Chapel. The Secretary's effects."

"Well, don't you think it's a little, well, in questionable

taste to open our doors? Doesn't all this curiosity seem a bit...morbid?"

"But it's *curiosity*. It's what we've wanted." Accusingly, she looked straight across, a little like a wet bird in her velvet jacket. "Why do we take such care to polish and straighten, to set things just right?"

"Sara, shouldn't we observe a day of respect before we lay Jean to rest? Doesn't her memory require it?"

"Her memory? This is just what her memory needs." Her voice echoed off the diamond panes of window glass in the open room. "First her recital...," she paused, but only a moment as she darted a look toward me, "...is *disrupted*. After all those weeks of rehearsal. Didn't you ever walk near the recital cottage when she was practicing her new composition? Sometimes I think I can still hear it out there. And now this...*thing*...that happened. Isn't it the least we can do to let people...notice her for once?"

After Sara's appeal, her mouth remained slightly open in agitation. I walked a few steps closer and lifted my hands. "Well, Sara, can you help out with tours? I don't know if Gert can..."

"Of course," she interrupted, with an edge of disdain. "Who do you think used to welcome visitors before..."

"Yes, before," I raised my voice even higher than hers. "But you've been there to help in many other ways since I came. So now, today, will you arrange a schedule with the Franzes? If so, maybe we can open for an hour or two." I hesitated. "Or a little more. Talk to Grant. See if he can help with a tour."

"Grant? I really don't know that Grant can manage, do you?" Sara had become decidedly more animated. "He's scared of everyone who walks in the door."

"He conducts the Sunday service. How bashful can he be?"

"It's one thing to flounce around in a cassock with silver cups in your hand, showing off to those you grew up with. It's another to stand on the same level with people you don't know and answer their questions, explain the cornerstone, relate village lore, the Chapel history, tales of the Secretary's experiences, his solitary travels. Oh, Grant Sweeney knows the stories, all right, but I don't think you want him shuffling up the aisle with visitors in tow, mumbling a few words that only God can understand, or maybe not even God."

"You and Gert then, maybe Bea. And let Victor know."

Sara raised her eyebrows incredulously.

"Well, what about Victor?" I asked with growing impatience.

"You need to talk to him, that's all."

By following the chirp of what turned out to be an old push mower, its first use of the new season, I found Victor at the farthest corner of the churchyard, behind stones and trees, leaning hard into the mower against grass already high. As he saw me approach, he reached toward a pocket in his overalls, pulled out a small spouted can, and stooped to the two big wheels of the mower.

I stooped with him and rested on my heels. "How are you, Victor?"

I couldn't pick up his mumble as he aimed and clicked the oil can.

"How have you been since Saturday? You had the biggest shock of us all."

"It's no problem," I thought he said, as he examined the wheels and axle for a dry spot to oil. He found one and clicked at it, but the oil can seemed to have emptied. Still Victor applied five or six more clicks.

"Did the sheriff leave you alone?"

Victor finally lifted his long, thin head and stared hard. Under the brim of his old green baseball cap, his deep-set blue eyes were rimmed with shadow, and a darkness showed on the side of his face and left ear. The bruising was distinct and blue.

"What reason could he have to hit you, Victor? Why didn't you come tell me?"

"It wasn't the sheriff, Mr. Gilsum." His voice came up without his lips seeming to move. "It wasn't nobody."

"It was nobody who gave you that? Let me look."

Victor pulled his head away as quickly as I'd ever seen him move. "I hurt myself at home," he said defiantly, "and that's all there is."

We both still squatted by the mower, the mottled light playing around us. I could almost believe Victor's face wasn't beaten, but only shadowed darkly by sunlight and leaves.

I kept my voice low, avoiding any tone of challenge. "He asked you again, I'm sure, how you happened to look. How you happened to look in the sepulcher."

"He asked me that." He held the tiny oil can in both his large hands, and he examined the way it twisted in their grasp, its tip pointed toward his face.

"Were you able to tell him anything that might help?"

He began to push and release the sides of the oil can, setting up a slow rhythm of sharp clicks. "I told him. I told him. I just looked, is what I did. I just looked. Sometimes I do." He pushed the sides of the can faster now, steadily faster, and I suddenly reached over to cover his hands with one big hand of my own.

"Victor," I said sharply, "you have the key. You must have

it. Tell me where it is."

He shifted his gaze from the mower to my face and to the mower again. He balanced the oil can on one of the wheels and rocked it back and forth by a fingertip. "I told him," he barely said. "I already told him." He rocked the can on the wheel until I finally rose up straight and turned to walk away, when he said something else almost as quietly.

"What, Victor?" I towered over him as he hunkered by the machine.

"You asked about the wood, about someone to work on wood." His voice came just up to me but grew louder as we talked.

"I did? I don't remember that we've talked about it."

"A carpenter, you said. We need carpentry, isn't it so? The window frames, the door, getting done on the renovation."

"Well, we do need to hire someone, that's right; I just don't remember..."

"There's only one to do it. In the county there's only one. I've thought of his name, like you asked."

"Just when did I ask?"

"Zel Bander. Zel Bander. He stays with the Tinker People. He's one of the Tinker People."

"The Tinker People?"

"Way across out there." He poked his arm straight out and lifted his hand toward the rill, and the woods beyond.

"Is that out near you, Victor, out near where you live?"

"You can find him out there real easy, out off Big Run Road. That's where they do their carpentry. The Tinker People." His breath was coming out quickly. He wanted me to walk away. "There," he said, and he put the oil can back in his overalls. As I left, I heard the chirp of the mower start up as its blades tore into the damp grass.

11

MONDAY AFTERNOON

Thorny made me lunch at the market, turkey on wheat, and I ate at my office desk, John Patton's desk, the Secretary's desk, the desk of village founder Jonas Hawkson, a broad slab of dark-red wood, thick boards pieced together, with gilt-tooled leather stretched partway across its surface and a sleeping mouse in the only drawer. The desk was in the style of my cottage furniture and of much else in the village.

After eating, I went back downstairs, crossed in front of the altar, entered the little door to the bell tower, and climbed the curved steps to Rachel's loft. I sat with her a moment before she reached for her thermos. I drew a muslin pouch of tea leaves from my pocket. "Here," I said. "I have it mailed to me. Maybe you'll try it." She smiled as she lifted the pouch to smell the dry leaves.

"Good and black," she said, and she crossed the little room to put the pouch in the narrow cabinet over the table that served as her kitchen. As she came back toward her chair, she flicked her hand at a spot or piece of dust at the corner of her tiny harpsichord, the delicate virginal perched on its four tenuous legs.

"When will you play me something?"

"I play for you every hour, George. Haven't you been listening?"

"Something quieter than three tons of bronze struck by iron hammers." I stood and walked to the little harpsichord. I didn't dare sit on the bench, so much like a toy, and leaned to examine the intricate handiwork of its construction. "Tell me its story."

Rachel walked over slowly and sat at the keyboard. "That's right, you *should* know the provenance; I thought you did. It's the Secretary's, of course, so it's Italian, Venetian. It plays as well as any little one, any spinet. John had the quills replaced for me, and the tuning's stayed right these last two years, even up here with the damp."

"Did you play for John?"

"Well of course I did." She took a minute and said, "I'm sorry John's gone. It's good you're here, George, but I do miss John."

With my finger I traced the ivory inlay at the edge of one panel. "If the wood became damaged, how would you repair it, Rachel? Who could you find?"

"It won't be damaged up here. But if you came too close, I suppose, tripped it up and over, didn't like your tea one day and threw the harpsichord at my head, we'd have some trouble finding the right craftsman, I'd say."

"I've heard about some woodworkers – Victor told me – across the valley, maybe you've..."

"Oh yes, the Tinkers," she said wearily. "The Tinker People. Victor told you?"

"The only man in the county to hire for our repairs, he said."

"Zel Bander."

"Yes. That was his name."

She crossed from the harpsichord back to her chair, and she waited to continue, sipping at her tea and absentmindedly twisting her curl of lemon peel. "I wouldn't go looking for Zel Bander," she told me emphatically. "With any encouragement he'll bring his family and they'll camp on Center Path. Gypsies."

"Gypsies? Magyars with music boxes? There aren't many babies in Slipstone for them to steal."

"If Zel Bander is the only man in the county to do your work, you need to look in another county. Yes, his family – the Banderinos, actually – settled here to help as craftsmen during the construction of this Chapel. I say 'settled,' but apparently the Founder expected them to return to Italy afterward, with the stonemasons. Of course they didn't. How could they? *Why* would they?

"Then, with his return from Europe, the Secretary brought some of them up from their little...their little *compound* to help with the final woodworking details. For instance, the ornate frame around the fresco of the Chapel Virgin, which, you may not realize, was painted during the renovation by a young Tinker woman."

"I had thought – I'm sure Sara told me – that the artist was someone the Secretary had discovered in his travels, maybe in the Alps. Then, when the time came, he had someone locate her and arrange passage."

"Sara's version of Chapel lore is often slightly altered to correspond to her preferences."

"And the portrait of the Secretary's wife, Anne, in my cottage – in the Rectory living room. The same artist, I know from the style; Lisabetta is what Sara calls her, only Lisabetta."

"Yes, the same Tinker woman, Betta."

"If she was young then, could she still be alive, still live as one of the Tinkers?"

"I think not. No one has seen her, or mentioned her, in... well, many years. Actually, no one seems to know just how many Tinkers still live over there. I suppose most have died, or moved away."

"And Zel Bander?"

"I know there was a wife, maybe *is* a wife. There were children, but no one sees them anymore. For years a place in Trellis has sold the furniture they made. They still do some work, some carpentry, maybe even *fine* carpentry, but for customers from away somewhere. No one from here, no one ever from Trellis. Victor should know that."

Angrily she tossed her lemon peel into the cold tea and went to her tiny harpsichord.

"Tell me what you know about *this*," she said.

At first, the sounds from the instrument came hesitantly, unpracticed, and Rachel stopped. She folded her hands, pushed up the loose sleeves of her thin sweater, bent her head, and then began again. I don't know how long she played, but the melody repeated itself a half-dozen times in as many variations, a tune I'd heard in the last days from both a piano and a violin. As mournful as it sounded on violin strings in the night air, it now was quicker, plucked not bowed, but the melody was the same.

"It seems that tune isn't too welcome in public," I said when she had finished.

"We've all heard it, of course, for years, and I'll play it outside anyone's hearing – except yours today, or anyone else just beneath these floorboards. But *none* of us should play the piece, or even acknowledge it. It belongs to someone else."

"Someone else?"

"You know, George. Don't you know?"

"If that's the case, why did someone as fearful as Jean feel free to play it at her recital."

"Well, I suppose, you'll have to ask her teacher."

"Elgin, her piano mentor and her tutor in all things Slipstone. Ironic, I think. He's a latecomer, isn't he, not a true villager like Jean."

"But Elgin learned all there was. He learned it..."

"From *his* mentor, the archivist Gammel Minken. Is that right?"

"Yes, George, that's right."

"And Gammel Minken. Were you...were you children together?"

"Yes, children. There were not so many of us then. The Secretary away, and then back."

"And a daughter. Laura."

"Yes. Laura."

"Under her stone in the yard. She died very young. Was it influenza?"

"No. Not the kind of illness that took her mother, Anne. It was – worse than that, in its way."

"In what worse way was that, Rachel?"

She rose and walked the few steps to her other keyboard, for the Chapel chime.

"It's time for me to play this now," she said. "I'm sure you need to be helping out downstairs." She situated her fists over the batons of the keyboard and her feet over the short wooden levers.

The bells' vibrations descended with me through the narrow column of wood on my careful way down the spiral stairway. I began opening the little door behind the altar.

Only then did I hear much shuffling of shoes nearby, a

few coughs, and the low voice of a question. The answer rang out.

"The Hawkson whose name you saw on the Cenotaph," Sara announced, "we celebrate as our village founder, Jonas Hawkson, the father of Secretary Hawkson, who, after serving his nation as warrior and statesman, did so much to endow..." As she spoke her unending sentence, Sara lifted and lowered her arms, guiding the half-dozen visitors like schoolchildren or lambs toward the altar.

"Above the altar of course we have the Chapel Virgin," Sara continued, as I lurked nearby, "kneeling in a grotto during the Annunciation. A dove flies about her haloed head, with Gabriel depicted by the painter as a beam of light breaking through the leaves and falling on Mary's face. The artist has placed a flock of lambs at her feet. As we approach more closely, you will see that doves and lambs have also been embroidered into the altar cloth by those of us, I and others, with long standing in the village."

Abandoning Sara's performance, I reached my office to see the paper squares on my desk from Sara's message pad – the glazier about new leading in St. Cecilia's window, a worried mother whom Sara hadn't been able to appease, and, earliest of the three, Sheriff Crisp. "Needs to see you," read the sheriff's message in Sara's perfect schoolgirl script. And then she had underlined: "when you can."

I gently unlocked and pulled open the desk drawer. No one was inside.

TRELLIS, the county seat, begins gradually as the state road narrows. Outlying farmhouses stand among subdivisions, and lawns become smaller where wooden cottages and Queen Annes begin to line the street. Drivers soon find themselves funneled onto the circle of the town square. Past the musketed battle monument and greenspace, out the opposite spoke of the traffic circle, I drove up to the angled parking spaces of the courthouse, left my car, and walked inside the low cinderblock building. As if mere pointing wouldn't work, a woman in an unidentifiable uniform escorted me down half a hallway to the open door of the sheriff's department. No imposing partition blocked my way, no inch-thick glass and voice hole. And no officer of the day, only an empty desk with a logbook open on top and a swivel chair pushed away behind it.

I walked through one door and encountered a choice of three others. Two were open, their offices empty except for desks, paper, and, in one, a gun rack with rifles chained together. In the office with the guns, a radio had its volume set low. I could hear the music but not catch the words. I also could not decipher individual words from behind the closed office door, but only voices moving past each other in a kind of hum. Then they stopped.

Suddenly one of the voices came distinctly through the door. "Just a minute, Mr. Gilsum," said Sheriff Crisp. I didn't see the peephole through which he must have spotted me; I just backed into the reception area and sat on a stiff metal chair. Before long, the sheriff's doorknob rattled and the voices emerged, still low and unintelligible until the sheriff finally closed the conversation with "It's all right; it's all right" and guided Elgin Brattle into the waiting room. Elgin looked at his feet, and he couldn't manage even a "George" as he walked quickly past me and into the corridor.

"It's good you're here," the sheriff told me. "I need to ask a few things."

"That's why I *am* here. You called..."

"Yes, I certainly did."

I followed him into his office. We sat facing each other across the gray laminate of his desktop. He brought out his little notebook and ballpoint. He held the pen delicately within his fine fingers.

"Mr. Gilsum, why do you think Victor Blair happened to look into the tomb last Saturday morning?"

"As I told you the other day, I have no idea. He says he just does so sometimes as he works in the churchyard."

"Watching for grave robbers?"

"Squirrel or bird damage, more likely."

Sheriff Crisp wrote down all my words in his laborious, miniature handwriting. I wondered if he would ever look at this page again and, if he did, could he remember the questions, unwritten, that elicited my answers.

"When was the last time you entered the tomb?"

"As I said the other day, Sheriff, I've never set a foot inside that dank little structure. There's plenty to do in my office without my conducting archaeology."

"Where do you keep the key?"

"Sheriff, if you'd just go back a few pages in your notebook, you'll find the answers to all these questions."

"But where *do* you keep it?"

"I just can't account for keys to locks that haven't been opened in fifty years."

He didn't seem to mind my watching him write. He held the notebook tightly on the desk while he fastidiously drew each word.

"I understand you and the deceased – Miss Clacton..."

"I *know* her name, Sheriff."

"...that there was animosity between you and Miss Clacton at the time of her death. Is that correct?" He asked the question with his eyes fixed on my right ear.

"I believe I told you the other day, Sheriff, that Jean Clacton and I are, were, friends..."

"Were?"

"Well, yes, *were*; she's dead, isn't she?"

"You *were* friends at the time of her death, or you *had been* friends?"

"Jean Clacton and I became friends soon after my arrival in Slipstone just a few months ago. Like most friends, we were close some weeks, a little distant during others. We ate dinner together a few times at the hotel dining room in Trellis. Without booking a room, I should add, since you've no doubt heard more than you need of village gossip. I visited her cottage once or twice. Twice; she cooked something both times, roast pork and something with clams. She never visited me. I don't cook very often, or very well."

"How do you know it's dank?"

"Excuse me?"

He consulted his notes. "You've never set a foot inside the tomb. How do you know it's dank? It shouldn't be; plenty of air gets in through the openings." He looked at me wide-eyed, as if truly confused.

"I don't know if it's dank or soggy or humid. You're right; the air's probably just the same as the air outside. It's just that air in mausoleums is usually described as 'dank.' At least in the, the..."

"Collective unconscious?"

"Well, yes, I suppose that's what I mean."

"More often it's 'dry.'"

This time he looked up and continued looking. I kept my eyes on his. "Well, I guess that makes more sense," I offered. I waited while he took note of every inane word. "Is there anything else?"

"Let's see...no...well, yes, just this: In your opinion, just an opinion, that's all I'm asking for, is Ginger Martin capable of looping a line around someone's neck, killing her with a sharp instrument in the back of the head, carefully slicing off her hands, draining away every ounce of her blood, *removing* her blood, suturing her wrists, and arranging her body in a dank or dry tomb with all the accompanying unlocking and locking?"

He watched for a reaction and didn't write at all.

"Of course not," I said, feeling no change of expression cross my face. "The man's as gentle as a moth."

"I'm not asking about gentleness but ability. You've watched Ginger Martin make his way back and forth through Slipstone, asking for handouts, looking for cans and bottles, even though no one would ever leave a can or bottle or any other litter out in the open in Slipstone. You've paid him to help Victor Blair with tree pruning. What do you think? Could he do murder?"

"Is he strong enough? Is he coordinated enough? I'm sure he is. I've never seen him shake from any sort of palsy. I wouldn't let him up on a ladder, and neither would Victor. Especially with shears."

"How do you know?"

"How do I know what?"

"Whether Victor Blair would be aware enough of Ginger Martin's aptitude to decide if he should be allowed to climb a ladder with shears. Victor's a little dim, isn't he, not like Ginger maybe, but a little dim."

"Victor's just withdrawn," I tried to explain. "When he looks inside his head, I think he's a little scared of what he might find. And scared that someone else might see it too. When Ginger looks inside...well, I'm not sure there's much for him to find, frightening or otherwise. No demons ordering him to raise a knife to a...but what about, what did you say about looping a line, and the back of her head, a sharp instrument...?"

"Well, maybe it was a knife and maybe it wasn't, but..."

"Sheriff, was it a knife, was it a pickax, was it garden shears, what are you learning that no one else seems to know?"

"Nothing's been determined." Emphatic words from Sheriff Crisp, and a glance to his notepad. But then back up to my eyes. "Nothing, of course, has been determined."

"And, Sheriff, while I'm here, something else."

"Something else?"

"Our violin."

"Your violin."

"The insurance company's been calling."

"Yes, they have. Oh, yes."

"They called you too, yes? What can you tell them?"

"Oh, there's nothing about that I can discuss."

"Then there's something you know and *can't* tell me?"

"There's nothing at this time I can discuss. About the violin. I'm sure you told us everything you could at the time of the loss." He'd picked up his ballpoint again.

"Not the loss, the *theft*," I insisted.

"Well, *was* there something else you haven't mentioned?"

"No, there's nothing. Remember, I wasn't here. It was John Patton; John Patton was the administrator."

"And, of course, as we know only too well, Mr. Patton and the violin seem to have vanished simultaneously."

"Yes, and so the insurance company won't settle," I tried to explain. "They still refuse to settle until you tell them more, until you put some resolution to the case."

"Mr. Gilsum, how do you expect me to resolve the case, when you haven't found the violin?"

"I don't expect to find the violin. I do expect you to."

"We can find the violin, Mr. Gilsum, if it's there to find."

"Well, it's somewhere, isn't it?"

He had finally stopped writing. "Yes, Mr. Gilsum. It certainly is."

When I left the office, the woman in the unidentifiable uniform was sitting at the metal desk in the entrance room, turning pages unconsciously in the logbook as she waited with the phone to her ear. Her hair, dark and coarse, hung in thick waves past the collar of her uniform. A strong thin nose and a full lower lip. She waited for someone to speak on the other end of the phone.

IN MY SIX months at Slipstone, I'd walked past the windows of the *Citizen* any number of times and once, when Greg Down was preparing his story about my arrival at the Chapel, I found my way to the newsroom itself. The office took up half a short block on a shadowy side street, between a craft shop and a jeweler's. In front, the green-wire paper rack was empty; the metal coin tube must have been full of quarters, thanks to the story that made up the front page and most of the rest.

Security here was stricter than at the sheriff's department. The woman at the front desk challenged me as I tried to make sense of the wall directory, white plastic letters in black felt.

"Maybe I can help you? Classifieds is through this door and on back."

"No, the morgue please; I'd like to see someone about looking in..."

"We don't call it the morgue anymore," she smirked. "The library's upstairs. Wait a minute, please." I hadn't heard a ring, but she was answering, then "Just a moment, please." She pushed in a long black patch cord somewhere high on her console and removed another one from down low, releasing it to snap back into place. As she rearranged the connections, I began toward the door past her right shoulder. With some severity and an upraised finger she motioned me to stop. Through with her call, she swiveled the mouthpiece away from her mouth. "The library's upstairs," she told me again with finality.

"Upstairs?"

"Through this door and on back; stairs to the right."

I pushed through the swinging door, passed through the narrow channel between classifieds and circulation, and walked quickly past an arrangement of five desks – three vacant, two with young women talking on phones and scratching notes onto narrow pads. Neither raised an eyebrow to acknowledge someone passing by. On what was obviously Greg Down's desk, an array of notepads lay scattered on a curling, inky green blotter among news clippings, a glass jar of pennies, coffee mugs filled with pens, and, centered before the empty chair, a single paperback. Elgin Brattle's history of Slipstone Village. I continued to the back and climbed the stairs to the library.

The intermittent buzz of low fluorescents filled the little room and crackled among the metal file cabinets. The sound seemed to energize the wiry man at the desk. He rose quickly and came around to smile slantingly up at me. "Oh, yes," he said, quite confidently.

"Yes," I said too. "Can you help me find a few things?"

"I'm sure I can. Just what would you *like* to find?" He combed his fingers across his thin hair.

"I'm at Slipstone, the new Chapel administrator" – ah yes, his face said as he smiled knowingly – "and I'm looking for documentation of construction, repairs, that kind of thing." The wiry man folded his hands and nodded with absolute certainty. He was wiry like Grant Sweeney, men of libraries. I went on. "Our Chapel records are complete in some instances, but mostly in the details of transactions by letter and receipts. I'm looking for more, for more..." I hesitated.

"Of a context, Mr. Gilsum?" He announced my name knowingly, and with satisfaction.

"Ah. Yes. For a narrative."

"Oh, a narrative. Like Mr. Brattle's."

"No, not so...dramatic. I need more of a look from outside, a journalist's view, if you see what I mean. Something solid, something to appeal to, well, foundations."

"Yes, foundations. They *will* have something solid, won't they? And you don't want to overdramatize. Not after...the events."

"No."

"As you will see, Mr. Gilsum, our files for Slipstone Village occupy their own space here," – he gracefully unfolded an arm and hand to indicate two cabinets standing alone against a far wall – "but Slipstone also weaves its threads through many other drawers in this room as well, sometimes only tangentially related." Somehow his spidery arm grew longer as he swept it grandly back to take in all his domain.

"Unfortunately" – he lowered his tone, his chin, and his arm; he raised an eyebrow – "you will find some unevenness too." He peered at me over his lenses, as if only he and I could understand the decline of journalism through the decades. "And some of the most uneven material carries dates too sadly recent."

Managing not to grasp my elbow, he closely escorted me

to the first of the cabinets he had indicated across the room. He opened a drawer without looking inside and told me simply, "You'll find it all very maneuverable. Tell me if I can help. My name is Jeffrey." He returned to his desk and, with razor blade and ruler, began slicing lengths of newsprint from the papers before him.

The files were beautifully arranged, with labels in a careful hand. *Apiary. Apple grove.* Files both thick and meager with news from Slipstone Hill, on newsprint gone yellow, gone thin and brittle, the ink itself faded in some places to be almost illegible, halftones faded to ghosts, especially where creased.

Architecture, Chapel. Architecture – Secretary's Cottage. Armistice ceremony. Artisans.

Artisans. In the folder, and folded, lay a single article, a lengthy feature, with photographs, from fifteen years ago. The basis of the article was an interview with Gammel Minken, the long-time archivist, and the youthful bookseller and amateur historian Elgin Brattle, who was thick into preparation for his own history of Slipstone Village. Repairs to the Chapel foundation had uncovered carpentry tools, an Italian Bible, and a miniature chessboard, all wrapped in leather, left behind unaccountably by one of the Founder's imported carpenters. The discovery of the leather package had brought forth memories of the renovation during Minken's childhood. The European artisans were much admired for their talents, Minken explained, but local citizens feared for their daughters' hearts and virtue and were pleased when the project was completed and most of the craftsmen – though not all – returned to their home on the edge of some high Alp – exactly where in those mountains was not clear. A younger Rachel Wren was interviewed – this a few years before her isolation in the loft of the bell tower – to explain the process of inlay that created the elaborate patterns in the chessboard.

Bells and Bell Tower. Hawkson, Jonas. Hawkson, Samuel. Jonas, the village founder, was represented in only one folder, with a few hagiographic articles about the pioneer, who had left this world long before the arrival in Trellis of the *Citizen*. A half-dozen folders were dedicated to clippings about the Secretary, Samuel Hawkson, and his boyhood in Slipstone, his early political success, then the Cabinet years, his service in the war, and speculation on the two "missing" years in Europe. As I knew, his return to the village had been precipitated by the death of his wife, Anne, in the global pandemic, and therefore his need to attend to the upbringing of his daughter, Laura. His collections had preceded him by shipboard, carton by carton, to be sequestered in the Chapel cellar until his return.

Then, one yellowing article, in a folder by itself entitled *Hawkson, Laura*, explained the death of the girl, who had disappeared early one winter day and whose remains were discovered only during the next thaw after she seemed to have fallen from an outcrop high at the edge of the quarry – the same opening into the rocky earth that had produced the sandstone of her family's chapel.

"...whose remains were discovered." The identity of the discoverer was not revealed. An illness somehow worse than her mother's, Rachel Wren had told me during one of my visits to her loft in the bell tower.

The Secretary's obituary, also in its own folder, carried the date of a year after the death of his daughter. Most of the account had been retrieved from the earlier articles about his consequential life, a life dedicated to service but shadowed with sadness. The grand crypt that now housed the sarcophagus of his parents had been the Secretary's own design, but he had acceded to his young wife's wish for a more modest interment, as she had written to him when the sickness descended upon her. He now lay beside her, under another simple stone, his death the result, as the obituary implied but did not go so far as to verify, of a heart broken by his daughter's disappearance and death.

He seemed to have uncrated only a few of the boxes he had sent before him, and, to the knowledge of Gammel Minken, only rarely to have made his way into the Chapel cellar. As he had done for Anne and Laura before him, and then for himself toward the end, he commissioned simple caskets of native hardwoods to be crafted by the carpenters he had employed and befriended, a generation down from the family conveyed from Europe by his father so many years earlier for their woodworking. Banderino was their name.

I kept on through Jeffrey's folders.

Cenotaph. Center Path. Cross, lightning strike.

I pulled each file forward, fingertip by fingertip, closing one drawer and opening the next, pausing and reading only occasionally, glancing back surreptitiously at the wiry man with his razor blade.

I continued through the files so carefully tended by Jeffrey, or his predecessor, and decided to learn more about *Minken, Gammel.* The archivist's file extended in time to early days, when the Secretary still abided with his daughter in the Rectory, my small cottage. Gammel Minken had lived his childhood in Slipstone and returned there with his librarian's training to tend the abundance of treasures and fragments accumulated by Founder Jonas – so few as to easily organize and display – and his son the Secretary, with so much of his prodigious collection still stacked in those many wooden cartons in the Chapel cellar.

The clippings in which the old archivist appeared were sparse. The most recent, though, addressed his passing. Or, rather, his unexplained end, which occurred not so many years before my arrival in Slipstone. Gammel Minken's body had been found in the churchyard by the shopkeeper Thorny Webber, who had quickly reported his discovery to Sheriff Aaron Crisp. The sheriff, though, had been unwilling to disclose any details as to cause of death except to blame "an accident of unknown origin resulting in a sudden depletion of his life's blood." Thorny Webber and the mortuary staff in Trellis declined to explain further, and, with no later clippings, the *Citizen* seemed to have little need for more questions, except that a visit to the churchyard had revealed no sign of where Mr. Minken's lifeblood had been spilt.

Roof, Chapel. Roofs, cottages. Stonework, mortar. Stonework, replacement. Tapestries. Then, *Violin, Maggini.*

As I began to pull up the file I suddenly realized how quiet the room had become, and I looked toward the desk where Jeffrey had been razoring out his stories. Somehow he'd moved his chair back and got up and out without a sound. I turned back to the file and opened it in my folded hand.

The file was thin, like most of the others. The clippings inside ranged in shades of yellow from dark to just-now-turning to fresh. The earliest articles were stiff and brittle, and I lifted and unfolded them with careful thumb and fingertip, placing them on top of the cabinet. Soon after the Secretary's death: "Rare Instrument Now Rests in Chapel Case." A few years later: "University Visitor Bows Ancient Fiddle." Next: "Chapel Violin Reveals Master's Craft." Then: "Will Soggy Summer Soak Slipstone Fiddle?" And, finally, a series of stories from only months ago, the first under a front-page headline: "Priceless Violin Abducted from Slip-stone Chapel."

The byline, of course, was Greg Down's.

I felt a shadow cross my back. I turned my head.

The shadow was Greg Down's.

"Jeffrey's efficient." He smiled. "But he hasn't filed the murder yet, I'll bet." He reached for the file in my hand. He wore a white shirt, wrinkled all over, damp in places. His tie, striped blue and red, was loose. Not as large a man as I am, but broad all over, especially in the big white shirt. His hair was curly brown, eyes muddy blue.

"This violin story...," I began, "...the theft."

"The kidnapping." He grinned broadly in his broad face.

"The kidnapping?"

"Of course."

"And the ransom note?"

"Never delivered."

"Why not?"

"I haven't quite figured it out. He left the village quickly though, didn't he?" The smile broader still.

"Patton."

"Of course, John Patton. John Patton who engineered a break-in so contrived my mother could have seen through it. My mother *did* see through it. She was very pleased with herself. The glass of the case smashed to throw off the scent from someone who knew the combination to that little lock."

"It would have been a key, not a combination."

"I speak metaphorically, of course."

"What could he have gained? Who'd have bought a stolen Maggini? I can't imagine the market's so lucrative."

"Thus a kidnapping."

"With no ransom note."

"How well did you know Patton?" he asked.

"Not well."

"At all?"

"As well as you can know a man you've never met but who sat in your office for six years before you took his place. The spot on the desk where coffee rings soaked into the wood. His shelving system for books. But those could have been relics from the men he succeeded in that office. All clergymen except him and me, since the days of the Founder."

"So do you know that he left not only suddenly, but immediately?"

"How immediately was that?"

"He disappeared *with* the Maggini. Or the same time as. No one wants to talk about *that*."

"But there's nothing...no one has mentioned..."

"No one has mentioned," Greg Down said, "and no one will tell me on the record because, well, when John Patton left, when he *vanished*, nothing else vanished with him. Except, well, the fiddle."

"What do you mean? No other relics, collectibles, memorabilia?"

"What I mean is that he took nothing of his own. No clothes, no suitcase, no billfold, no toothbrush. Which, by the way, was found spread with a dollop of toothpaste, not quite dry. As if he suddenly decided brushing wasn't so important at that particular moment."

"But you learned this...off the record?"

"In Slipstone you can earn people's trust, but you have to keep it."

"People?"

"No one you don't know. By the way, Mr. Gilsum?"

"Yes?"

"About those keys."

I held up my empty palm. "There are no keys," I said in a quiet monotone. "Keys can't open anything shut so long, so rusted together. I don't know what kind of tool Rella Derry used to gain access. If there were keys, I'd know. And if I knew, I'd tell the sheriff. And probably even you."

He started to ask another, but I turned back, carefully replaced the folder, and closed the drawer. The reporter pushed his lips together, slid his hands into his pockets, and nodded goodbye on his way to the stairs. I walked past Jeffrey's desk and followed Greg Down at a distance, then out the building through its heavy glass front door.

As small as Trellis is, there is more than a main street, or Main Street, and I walked away from the direction of my car and around the town's few blocks, strolling at random past the bank and the hardware store, a café – closed – and a few other doors that led up various stairways to apartments, a dance studio, and a palm reader. Then, between a dress shop and a diner I had yet to visit, I found myself before a large, begrimed window with a few pieces of furniture on display – simple pieces, a chair, a table, a small bookcase in a light wood. Painted in faded gold, in half a circle on the window, was the name "Melton's."

There seemed to be no lights inside, but I tried the door and it opened noiselessly, no weight to it at all, a fragile thing, with no bell or other indication of entry. There *were* lights above, but unlit. The sun through the dirty window illuminated the interior, falling on more pieces of wood furniture, set around the shop without any sense of arrangement. Some of the items were large, ornate, and old. On the top of a hutch were displayed spherical glass paperweights with little candy-like flowers blown into them. Hinged down to reveal a series of thin pigeonholes was the writing surface of a darkly stained desk; on it lay writing paper, unused, printed at the top with "Trellis Bank."

No one seemed to be inside the shop, which was too spacious for the few items that may or may not have been for sale. There were no prices affixed anywhere.

I walked to the front window, where the furniture was situated on a raised display area. The wood was maple, but its color had darkened irregularly. The pieces were dusty, and so was the floor where they stood. They had been crafted with a careful hand. A child's desk was especially beautiful.

"Hello, hello," came a thin voice, and a thinner woman emerged from the shadowed area toward the rear of the shop. A plain muslin apron extended from her neck to her knees.

"Thank you," I said. "I was..."

"The wood is local. Our own maple." She was fifty, or sixty.

"And so made here in...?"

"Nearby, but awhile ago. There's a family out near, well, Slipstone, if you know where that is." She gave me a little questioning smile.

"A family?"

"I think it's one family; no one really seems to know. They fix things, but they were craftsmen before, as you can see." She approached and walked past me, head cocked a little, still with her questioning smile, and toward the window.

"Here, look at this," she said, as she stepped up onto the display area and pulled open the middle drawer of a small dresser. "See how smooth, and after years sitting here. See these..." She indicated the heads of dark pegs within the maple at the side of the drawer. "Always quite perfect."

She easily pushed the drawer back in, turned to a child's chair, and stroked the seatback slat.

"They made musical instruments too, but that was long ago."

"Was it? When would that have been?"

"When my father opened this little shop. He told me about them. Violins, other stringed instruments. Beautiful things, he said. A sound, he told me, that was already *old*, is how he put it, an old sound from newly made violins. Something to do with unusual woods, oils, varnish, these formulas they concocted. Of course they're all gone. The violins. I never got to hold one. Now, all we have are these few nice parlor pieces. We sell some to people driving through. Obviously there aren't many left. Those other pieces in the shop aren't really local. From nearby though. Not as fine of course."

Then: "Are you...driving through?" She looked past me, as if to spot my car at the curb.

"No, I'm in Slipstone now; I've moved to the village."

"Oh, of course. You're the new..."

"Yes, the new Chapel administrator. Just a couple of months now."

"Yes, of course," she said finally. She gazed into my face for a moment, then began to turn away, sliding her hands into apron pockets. "It's terrible. Poor Jean."

She left me there and headed back into the shadows at the far end of her shop.

12

MONDAY NIGHT

B ecause of the succession of the Chapel's priests who had inhabited the cottage in the years following the death of the Secretary, my house had become known as "the Rectory," with its English windows, its chestnut shelving, the simple wainscoting. In the many windows the small glass panes were the green of the Chapel glass, bubbled here and there except where replaced, one by me after the sash broke and the window fell too hard. The high, narrow, board-and-batten ceiling of the open den slanted up steeply. Off the kitchen, the pantry past its door was deep with uneven shelves holding cans and jars left by John Patton, his own brewed beer, abandoning the house so suddenly.

When I first arrived in the wintertime, and when no moon was out and I sat listening to records, the light changed from room to room by the different star groupings that shone through the windows. Some constellations I could almost read by.

As the trees leafed out, though, I found the starlight was gone entirely. The air in the den was so black I squinted at the glare from the little red light on my record player.

After these months I knew all the noises my house could make: the loose boards, the furnace on and off until a week earlier when the nights began to stay warm. Now at night some small animals scuttled around in the eaves. I sat deep in the old, soft leather of my chair, the Secretary's chair, as the needle scratched again and again at the label in the center of the record. In the darkness I finished my glass of John Patton's bitter beer and found my way to the kitchen for another, the smells changing from the dust of the chair to garlic and onions in the kitchen and back again as I returned quietly through the room's darkness to my chair. The needle continued to scratch. The only other sound was my breath.

But then there were two of us. And then, I thought, three, breathing there together, in the deep darkness. The others in front of me, near the center of the den. Standing on the thin rug. And then his smell.

"I've brought you the girl tonight, Mr. Gil-sam," he said.

"What do you mean, brought me the girl?"

"The girl Spinner. The playing girl. She's wanting her doll, and she'll play for it."

I could think of nothing to say. I said, "Spinner."

"She'll play for the doll. She wants to know where is it."

"Why does she think I have her doll?" I waited in the dark and listened to them breathing, the girl's breath shallow and fast. "All right," I finally said, "but there's nothing special about that doll. If it's hers though..."

"Oh, there's something special about that doll. She saw you take it out, reach into those roots and pull it out. Spinner was there and watched you. She left it in that tree when you scared her."

"I never scared this child. Or any child." There must have been light from some source because I thought I could distinguish the two forms, one so substantial beside the other.

"Oh, you did scare Spinner, you did. And that's her doll you've got. She'll play for you to get it back. That's why you've waited. That's why you've set in the dark so long. You knew we should be here tonight."

"You could have asked in the cellar last night," I told him. "The doll was right there. Why didn't you ask?"

"I didn't know you had it then," he said. "Spinner hadn't told me. And maybe she weren't going to, but I got her to. I got her to, and she told me. Told me in that way of hers."

As he spoke, there came the sound of something rigid tapping lightly onto the thin rug. *Bok. Bok.* For a few moments the tapping sounded together with the needle at the center of the record.

"I can get you the doll. But she left it..." I started to say, but didn't say, left it for *me*. For *me*.

The tapping continued at the same rhythm. *Bok.* Like that, lightly against the thin rug. *Bok. Bok.*

"You scared this child, and she let those tree roots pull that doll from her. That tree where you stood so long. That tree that's a bridge."

The tapping stopped.

Then, slowly, she bowed the first string, low and smooth, a single note, drawn out the length of the bow, the bow then gently lifting.

I waited. Then, "I've heard you play, haven't I? You play at night."

"Spinner, she plays day and night. She's not one for school."

"What do you call that song you play, Spinner?" I asked. "That melody at night, loud sometimes. I heard your father hum it once."

"No one's ever named that song." The man raised his voice angrily. "And if we ever talk about that song it won't be here, won't be now."

"Play me that tune, Spinner," I persisted. "That song you play at night, when it carries over the valley and up the hill. Here they call it the Chapel Song, the way the wind sings it past the bells and along the rooflines."

"She won't play it here; she can't." His voice started to break out of the low tones he'd used with me here and in the Chapel cellar. "That song is a dangerous thing, and you know it, Mr. Gil-sam. You know what happened when that woman played the song for those people. You think it happened for *you*, that we did it for *you*, knowing that you were done with her, and she wouldn't have being done with. You think we'll take a woman's hands off for you when you're done with her. We don't need to do such things for you. If you don't help us, we'll find another, the next one along, the one after you. The last one, Mr. Patton, he said he wanted to help us, but he was no help."

"Where did Jean learn how to play that song? Did she just pick it up by ear? Did you teach it to her, Spinner?"

"No, no, no," Zel Bander insisted. "I know pretty well who she got it from. And I'll see to him, oh I will."

"Like you saw to Jean Clacton? Like you saw to her?"

"Someone needed to show what happens."

"What *happens*? What happens when? And so Spinner's doll, and *her* tiny hands, gone like that. Was that a lesson too?"

"Spinner needs reminding sometimes of who she is."

"Well, who *is* she that needs such a lesson as that?"

He paused and almost answered but then didn't. Instead he said, "Spinner'll play you a different song, a different song from that one." His voice grew quick, even drier than before. "Go on, girl."

Now, still in my chair, I could just see their movements, just in outline, just the white edges of clothing and of the little girl's face, and something of the bow as it oscillated over the instrument. What she played carried lilts and dives in a minor key, in a melody slow and soft, softer somehow than any other violin could produce. I know that her music could carry its way from somewhere deep in the woods, over the rill, and up to the village, but now it hardly filled my small room. Her song wasn't the same but was much like the melody I'd heard her play late Friday night from across the rill, the song Zel Bander had hummed to me in the dark of the Chapel cellar, a song that never quite began and never quite stopped.

It wasn't Jean's piano piece, but it was *much* the same, out of the same hand and ear, out of the same earth.

I don't know how long it continued. It must have been over for a minute or more when I woke to the silence the instrument had left in the room.

In the dark I looked toward the place where they stood. "You see everything at night, don't you," I asked Zel Bander, "but what do you see in the daytime? Do you sleep at night or day?"

"We see in daytime, all right, as good as night. Today we saw you in the town, at the sheriff's, telling some of what you know, but only some. And someone else we saw there too."

"Who do you mean?"

"We saw him, your friend Mr. Brattle. We saw him, and he weren't supposed to be there."

"What do you mean? Why not?"

"And he weren't supposed to teach that song, neither,"

He paused to let me understand what that might mean. "We'll leave now. Just set there." I shifted in the chair.

"Just set there," Zel Bander commanded. "We'll go another way. What way that is, I guess you'll know too. Soon."

I heard them move from the rug to the wooden floor, one of them shuffling and the other stepping lightly. Their footsteps receded toward the kitchen, and I heard what could have been the soft closing of a door. Then the sounds they made were gone.

I realized the scratch of the phonograph needle had never stopped. I switched on my reading lamp, then stood and walked as silently as I could into the kitchen. I opened the door to the pantry and entered the darkened space. I passed the shelves, the bags of flour and sugar, John Patton's cans of vegetables and soup. I stood as still as I could, and I faced the back of the tiny room, where the shelves were almost empty. At the end of the floor, in the space between two boards near my feet, there showed a flutter of dim light. It shifted, flickered, and disappeared. A square of the boards squeaked and shifted as I put some of my weight there.

I came back to sit in the Secretary's armchair, and soon afterward there was another flickering, this time from my front window, and then a distant thunder. Seconds later, too rapidly, it seemed, for wind to have brought a storm so close, the next bright flash showed me the trees and the path outside my door, and not a second later a crash seemed to shake the cottage.

I thought of Zel Bander and Spinner and of Spinner's violin somewhere out in the pelting rain.

13

TUESDAY MORNING

I thought it was part of my dream – the mad animal running from my front door to Center Path and back, and again, faster every time. But then I knew better. And I knew I should leave my bed and open the door.

The running continued, even while I stood there in my bathrobe. Clancy whipped his empty leash behind him as he turned on his heel at the gravel path, racing to my flag-stone stoop and back to the path that Tuesday morning, his tongue lashing the sides of his brown-and-white cannonball head. Every time he turned at the path, his feet sprayed gravel, tiny stones still wet from the night's heavy rain.

Finally he stopped. He stood shivering near my feet in their worn leather slippers. Then he moved onto the slippers, his wet heat pressing against my legs through the thin pajamas. In his fright he would have pushed over a smaller man. The morning wasn't yet warm. There were clouds out, but the storm had blown northward during the night.

I bent for Clancy's leash, and he allowed me to lead him to Center Path, where we could see a hundred yards to our right toward the Chapel. In the distance a scarecrow figure slouched and weaved, slowly gathered speed and quickly lost it again – Ginger Martin on his trek to the village from whatever warm barn he had slept in last night. But in neither direction was there Elgin Brattle, whose firm and patient hand had never before lost the leash of his dog. I slowly looked down to my own hand, bound by the broad leather strap, and I stooped and laid the leash on the damp gravel of Center Path. Elgin would appear there in moments to capture his dog. I turned and walked to the house.

Clancy followed. And as I cracked open the door and tried to slip through alone, to open it enough just for me was to open it for Clancy too, and he came in and sat down and fidgeted, noisily splaying out his tongue to drip on the thin rug, just where my two visitors had stood last night. With the damp and nervous dog in my den, I retreated to the bedroom to dress. Then I took up Clancy's leash and led him outside again.

He walked me in the direction of the village, pulling as hard as I'd allow, his feet spitting back gravel with each determined step. No cars passed on the road beyond the line of trees to our left – too early yet for any visitors, even with the new curiosity of Jean's death. A few cottages down from my own, Clancy stopped at the walk to Elgin's house, unsure what direction to go next; I gathered he had tried them all in a search for his master. I led him down the narrow walk between geranium boxes to the stoop outside Elgin's door. I knocked, then knocked again, and waited, moving foot to foot, Clancy moving foot to foot too, claws scratching on the flagstones. From inside there never came even the false sounds that sometimes fool us into thinking someone's coming.

Then we began our way around the house through the damp grass. None of the curtains were drawn shut, but I could see no lights on inside or hear music or dishes or detect any other signs of Elgin Brattle. The windows gave me angles into the living room with its dark Persian rugs, the bedroom and the untouched bed, the kitchen. There were no stray dishes; the telephone sat prominently on its shelf with the cookbooks, a favorite spot in the house for Elgin the entertainer. All the rooms were clean, silent, and dim. Once around the house at every window, the dog and I climbed again onto the stoop, and I considered opening the front door to deposit him, but decided not to intrude on an empty house.

"Clancy," I said, as matter-of-factly as I could, "you'll need to stay home. Elgin won't know where to find you." I leaned to touch the sweating dog as lightly as possible with a single fingertip. He looked up to my eyes, desperation in his own. "He's just gone for a paper," I explained. Clancy opened his mouth, needing to speak, but I interrupted: "You must stay here like a good dog. You must stay here." I noticed that my hand had opened and that I was stroking the hideous dog fully on the head now, even rubbing behind his ears in a gesture of comfort and reassurance. Slowly I pulled away, slid both hands calmly into my pockets, and backed off the porch. Clancy followed me up the walk. At Center Path I picked up his leash, and we started toward the village.

Galen's cottage sat on a little hill down Treadle Street, after Treadle Street curved past Thorny's market. The houses at this edge of the village weren't all white with green shutters, as an unofficial Slipstone ordinance required of cottages along Center Path. Galen's house was a pale blue

– or green or tan, as the light was filtered differently from one season to the next, or from morning to afternoon. Today it was blue – a spring morning with the sun just out above the smell of the night's rain.

Galen came to the door in a dark-blue bathrobe, the pallor of sleep long gone from her face, with her green eyes full and bright, her short hair combed straight. She looked down toward Clancy even before acknowledging me, and her face was quizzical, perturbed, knowing – all in turn before I even spoke, contrite as I was for the early visit and for the slavering dog.

"So are you here to apologize for being here?" she asked when I'd finished my few words, her tone flat. She no longer looked down at Clancy but just at my face. "Something else?"

"I'm not completely sure. I think I needed to ask someone about the dog. I knew you had to be up. For the shop."

"Not a friend of yours, I ever thought, that dog. Not mine either. Tie him somewhere and come on in. Just for a minute. You're right; the shop needs to open."

"He won't let me leave him here. Or anywhere." Clancy nodded at this and dropped his rump onto my right foot, anchoring it in place.

Galen almost smiled, but not toward me. "Come in, Clancy," she said. "Have a muffin."

She invited me to the bright kitchen table, where I sat while the dog spread himself underneath, his panting loud and wet. "I don't believe you've been inside here before," she ventured, more challenging than polite.

I looked through the kitchen window by the table. There were no curtains to shroud the view into the woods in back.

"I wasn't sure I would be let in," I said as I tried to look past the tree line.

"And why not?" She stood above me. "Why not, George?"

"After Saturday. Your accusation."

She brought over two fragile cups and poured coffee. "Advice, not accusation. That you need to say what you know, to tell the sheriff, or those state investigators." She sat down across from me at the table, the dog between our feet on the floor.

"I've told them all I need to say, Galen. But there's something else more immediate."

"And it's on my feet. Heavy and wet."

"He was running furiously back and forth from Center Path to my door."

"He sounds like he was out there all night. He feels like it too. Can't we try taking him out awhile? These wood floors; he's so wet..."

"But he won't go. He's too afraid." I didn't know how to say it. "He wants me to know something."

She started to speak but poured coffee instead. She lowered and raised her head. "Is it too obvious to ask where Elgin might be?" she finally asked. "Is that why you're here?"

As I stared down toward the quickly cooling black coffee in Galen's fragile china cup, all I could see on its surface were forest and stones – the woods past the rill and the step-ping stones across the stream, the woods and the two circles there, stones and the cleared space between tree stumps. The breathing of the dog grew so loud I could hardly under-stand Galen when she spoke.

"Don't worry, George. I don't know if I *want* you to tell me. Can we decide that you should not?"

"I don't know if I have anything to tell you, anything that I could work into words. There's nothing that quite comes together, nothing I could explain without hesitating and then losing what comes next. But I do have something to ask."

"Is it something I can understand?"

"Can we talk about dolls? May I show you one?"

As we walked down Center Path, the dog leading frantically and then holding us up by tugging behind, we saw Alice Felton and Boz Billings far ahead, crossing the narrow gravel way, quickly moving toward the market to open up. Two of the Franz twins passed us slowly in their car on the road running parallel, one twin tight-lipped at the large white steering wheel and the other with bowed head, tired or praying. Melinda and Sally. Sally and Gert. Gert and Melinda. As we came even with the village shops across the road, Clancy pulled us in the other direction, up the narrower path toward the Chapel, leading us emphatically through the woods, where the sun had not yet filtered through. Galen and I followed silently, she in her gray dress and denim jacket and I with loosened tie, overly warm with the rapid walking. Clancy would have brought us up the ancient step to the heavy front door, but, against his will, I wrapped his leash around an iron spike in the old fence that outlined the churchyard and separated us from its leaning headstones. He leapt against the restraint just once, then settled on his haunches, panting vigorously and watching Galen and me walk up the two ancient granite steps. I unlocked the door, and we were through.

The Chapel was lit only by the dull light through the

pale green windows. Up the side wall, yards apart, were the alabaster reliefs that told the story of Jonas Hawkson, the stations of his cross, his early years as a young Eastern preacher, his wanderings by foot, ship, and wagon to spread the story of his God, his time in the wooded wilderness as he fought his way toward a hill he would clear for his Chapel. Duplicated in terracotta, a miniature set of Jonas Hawkson reliefs sold well in Elgin's shop.

I opened the library door, and we passed by the display cases and tapestries. Galen walked on the far side of the broken violin display, running her hand along the oak and stopping at the small brass plate. The case, all its broken glass long since carefully picked and vacuumed away, was lined in green felt, much like a billiard table, with two small joints of felt-covered wood contrived, after the Secretary's death, to hold his violin. Useless in the corner of the case was the tiny humidity gauge. Galen paused to read the inscription on the brass plate, but the light was too dim.

"'Maggini violin circa 1612,'" I intoned. "'Located by Secretary Hawkson near Florence, 1918.' You've seen the case empty. Did you ever see the instrument?"

"Of course, on my arrival, the first thing for all newcomers, before, well, yes, before...the *event*...before it was no longer here to see. Of course I learned about it as I negotiated with Elgin for the empty storefront."

"You'd never visited Slipstone before leasing the bookshop?"

"I'd never visited the States. Slipstone wasn't even a rumor for me before I learned about the shop."

I faced her across the empty case and took hold of the oak frame. "And how *did* you learn about it?"

"From the ad Elgin had placed in my local paper, in all the

papers nearby. He was trolling for just the right accent for this little ivied village of his. The right person to lease a shop. Rather a tedious interview process he took me through. The phone line kept breaking up; it sounded like wartime. Elgin explained it was the Slipstone exchange. Nothing ever quite up to date."

She looked into the case and ran her finger over the two wooden joints for the violin. "The instrument was just here, just waiting under this glass. No alarms necessary."

"No alarms. This being Slipstone."

I led her to the corner of the room, where I flipped up the switch to the cellar lights and turned the lock on the small door. She followed me down the narrow unfinished steps under the first of the bare bulbs, bright after the dimness of the reading room. The other bulbs lit us down the aisle by the rows of shelving.

Walking just behind me, Galen paused at each set of shelves. "There's so much here," she said, and stooped at one of the Secretary's wooden cases, set on a low shelf, inches off the dirt floor. "I've never quite understood its arrangement. Or *if* there's an arrangement."

"In the first of those rows back there, those are Chapel records – correspondence, drawings, receipts going all the way back. Some of the original sketches for the building and a few of the cottages."

"And this precious cargo still sits from his years of wandering. Have all these things been opened?" she asked.

"Oh, opened over the years, and sifted through for the best of the weavings, drawings, manuscripts, old editions. The items in those shelves and cases upstairs. Grant Sweeney is always sneaking down here, hoping to make new discoveries. John Patton was hired in part to bring order to all this, but when Gammel Minken died..."

"Yes, the archivist," Galen said, still fiddling with the lid of the trunk where she stooped.

"Right, the old archivist. Gammel Minken knew much of everything down here, kept Chapel records neat and orderly in those cardboard boxes. He had many of the Secretary's items precisely catalogued too, but only in his head. But there were still many to go. *Most* to go, it must be said. A dusty little man, Gammel Minken. Elgin was his protégé."

"Gert Franz told me Elgin's Slipstone history was dictated word for word by the old guy," Galen said.

"And then published after Minken's death," I said, "with only one line of acknowledgment in Elgin's book, a vague thanks for assistance. But while it was Elgin he should have been wary of, the old archivist would never have abided any of the rest of us had he lived past his...accident. Any of us from outside. John Patton. Me. You. Anyone who came from anywhere else. Better that Slipstone Village wither to no one here than fall to infestation by outsiders. Let the wind and rain take ownership as it did in the years before its revival by the Secretary. That's why I'm surprised Elgin went so far afield to find someone for his shop. I guess in Slipstone it compensates to be English."

"I've never seen why Slipstone villagers want to be English," Galen said. "Or why they think they are."

"Our little tea shop," she added, in a caricature of her own voice. "Yes, let's go for a crumpet, shall we?" She pushed herself away from the trunk and stood back up, dusting her hands against each other. "Well, show me what I'm here to see. This cellar was part of Elgin's tour, but I know there are secrets yet to discover. Maybe for you too."

She followed me along the final five shelves and to the stone wall of the foundation, under the last of the bare bulbs. Before I stooped to open the little iron cleanout door, I turned back to Galen and saw that she had remained several arm-lengths back. I couldn't read her expression.

"You're safe, Galen," I said. "I *am* a gentle soul."

"Just show me," she said.

With Galen standing above me, I reached into the opening. I made certain of the map rolled loosely within its rubber bands beside the doll. I closed my hand over the little porcelain-and-sawdust figure, brought it out, and carried it to the nearest of Grant's work platforms. Galen followed me over and watched as I removed the wrapping.

The doll was just the same, her face chipped and stained but still capable under the hard light of staring back, her mouth in a smile I couldn't quite read, something of surprise, but joy, too, under the fear.

"What do you want me to tell you?" Galen asked, as she took the doll from my hands. She went first to the empty wrists, shifted her look back up to me in some kind of accusation, then returned to the doll, pulling the sleeves up and turning the wrists to the light, then pulling a fingertip across the tiny sutures.

"Quick and clean," she said. "Scissors. A knife. Which was it?"

"The doll itself, what can you tell about it?"

She began gently to squeeze at the sawdust shoulders and body.

"What do you want to know? Just because I was once a little girl, you can't expect..."

"Galen, you know about these things. Was it mass-produced?"

"The term 'mass production' didn't have much meaning when this doll was made. Or the head anyway." She lifted the skirt and tested the give of the knees and the waist.

"What about origin and date? Or is the head the only original piece?"

"You tell me first. About the hands. And is it necessary to hide it in this little...cavity down here?"

"I found it near a tree, in the roots of a tree, in the woods, a fallen tree over a stream, over the rill, a kind of bridge. And it was just like that; *she* was just like that, hands missing."

"And if it's hidden so well, don't you care that I know?"

"Take the doll to your shop, Galen. See what you can learn in those collectors' catalogs of yours..."

"I do have one book with some dolls."

"...and I'll come by soon."

"I may have to keep her awhile. I have some paperwork that needs..."

"I'll have to come by for her this morning," I said. She creased her brow at me, more curious now than when she first saw the mutilated figure.

"I need to give her back," I said.

"To some little girl?"

"That's right."

"A little girl with a knife?"

"A little girl who seems to need her doll."

When we climbed back up to the library, Galen was clutching the doll, which I had carefully wrapped again. The time was just past eight. We were silent now, and we could hear a light wind against the windows, some of them loose in their frames. Galen led me by the empty Maggini display case, hesitating, about to break the silence. A voice from Sara's radio came in from her office by the sacristy, but only the low tones were able to carry toward us in the library. I couldn't tell if the voice was of a man or woman, talking or song, vibrating through the dark wood of the old building, luh-luh-luh, breaking a rhythm and back into it, l'-l'-luh-luh-luh.

WITH GALEN GONE through the front door, I walked back toward Sara's office. If it was a song on her radio, it had ended, and the weather report was on. The announcer said overcast, showers. I coughed, tapped on a rail outside the door to keep from startling Sara, and walked in. She was waiting, impatient with my noises, ready to tell me something.

"Isn't Elgin here? I thought he might be with you. I heard someone, and Clancy's outside."

"Is the fence still standing where he's tied?"

"Clancy's a perfect gentleman," Sara insisted.

"I'm glad to hear you say so."

"And why is that?"

"I was hoping you'd want to find him something to eat."

"We don't have anything here for that poor dog. And isn't that Elgin's job?"

"Sara, there are all sorts of cheeses and cold cuts and spreads and things in the refrigerator."

"You know that's for Jean's service. Gert Franz is coming at noon," she paused and grimaced, "to help me prepare everything. Besides, Clancy can't eat those things. He needs something for dogs. But Elgin, where's Elgin?"

"Clancy's with *me* this morning."

"With you? You hate the dog. And where's Elgin?"

"Well, he's not here."

"Then I'll find Victor. If anyone's got time to feed a hungry dog, it's Victor."

I left her to her mission and climbed the stairs. Without sunlight through the windows, the air in my office couldn't show any dust that might be settling. But I didn't think anyone had come in; the searching had gone to other places.

I chose Elgin's phone number from the single-page village directory, typed by Sara, updated regularly and laminated for me. In the new edition she had already excised Jean's number. I dialed Elgin's house, imagining the empty kitchen, with the phone on its ledge under three shelves of cookbooks. It rang a dozen times before I finally stopped it. Then I slipped my finger down the laminate of the directory to "Village Gifts," kept my finger on the number, and dialed it. I let Elgin's store phone ring, imagining Galen in her shop next door – listening to the faint ring through the wall to see if he'd answer. I hung up so she might continue searching through her doll book.

It was quiet in my desk, and I tapped a few times with the point of my pen. Still nothing, so I unlocked and gently pulled open the drawer. At first I didn't see the mouse, but then I noticed something different, a small pile of gray, shredded cardboard had been gnawed from what had been a box of paper clips. The bed looked fluffy and comfortable. The little mouse now sprang up to his begging position, nose high and waving, and I dropped a few sunflower seeds by his new bed. As usual, there was nothing in the drawer that needed cleaning, except a few scrapes of pine cone seeds or something similar. Through his crevice in the wood at the back of the drawer, he slipped out for everything but sleep and eating. He always came back home.

I reached for my telephone at the edge of the leather writing surface. I needed to call the glazier about the broken leading on the Chapel's west windows. And the tile man for the roof, who hadn't yet called back to set up a time to bring his ladders. But it was too early to conduct business, and my business for the day wasn't in the office anyway. Now, though, my phone did ring.

"When were you going to tell me about Elgin Brattle?" said the sheriff.

"Is there something to tell? I have his dog."

"Mr. Gilsum, I've asked you twice to let me know these things."

"There wasn't enough to call with. An empty house, Elgin's shop not open yet. His dog running loose. It's not enough. I thought a person couldn't be declared missing until after two days."

There was silence on the sheriff's end. I knew he had pulled out the little ballpoint pen from his shirt pocket and was carefully writing.

"What else should you be telling me?" he finally asked.

"There's nothing else to tell."

"Tell me this then, Mr. Gilsum. What are you doing with Elgin Brattle's dog?"

"Which do you mean: What are he and I doing at this moment, how do I intend to dispose of him, or how does he happen to be in my possession?"

"Sometimes a dog knows a great deal about these things," he told me in his most serious tone. "The trick is to have him reveal it."

"Sheriff," I said, "Clancy has already made it clear he hasn't a clue about Elgin's whereabouts. But I'll ask him again. And I'll tell you what he says."

"Mr. Gilsum, there's no need..."

"Right now, though, Sheriff, I have work to do."

I left my desk before the phone could ring again. Downstairs, I started past Sara's office and heard her on the phone. I could make out none of the conversation except the last three words: "...and only then." There was acid in her voice, and her hang-up was slow and deliberate. I looked in as she folded her hands, stared straight through me, unfolded her hands, and picked up a long yellow pencil, returning to her bookkeeping. As an afterthought, she reached angrily to the radio and turned the sound back up. The weather was already back on. There was now no decision about whether more rain was on the way. Walking past her, I didn't see any light from the library, and so Grant Sweeney wasn't yet in. I continued down that side of the church and into the vestibule. I slowly opened the front door, hoping to see the dog before *he* saw *me*, just to check.

Clancy was with Victor, and with an old couple I recognized. The husband and wife were both in starched whites and grays on their way to visit the library on one of its open days, to don some of Grant's thin cotton gloves and continue their examination of the Secretary's Italian bird books, the most-prized volumes of the natural history shelves. Clancy's face was buried in an old piece of crockery, pumping up and down at whatever Victor had found for him to eat. The old couple was early for their visit. I expected the crowd would come later. They would come every day until the next nearby sensation drew them away, or until Jean's death slowly dissolved within local consciousness.

I turned back inside and started toward Sara's office to have her reassure me again about details of the service. As I approached her doorway, though, I noticed the light from the library. I put my head inside to see Grant at his desk with a stack of volumes beside him. He was gradually moving his finger in a book that was carefully propped open only partway, to keep stress off the leather spine.

I came and stood above him, looking down at the wisps of thin hair that floated over his head. He was thin in every way, his nose, his fingers, the fabric of his cassock.

Someone my size could lift him in a hand. As close as I was, I knew he still hadn't seen me, so I moved back carefully toward the door and spoke his name as quietly as I could. "Grant."

He was thin as a bird, and like a bird he moved his head so quickly from point to point that the movement itself was invisible. "George." His voice was thin too, with his usual surprise at having someone come in, even the person most likely to.

"A few of your usual customers are outside, I notice. Are you open for business?"

"Oh, of course. For a few visitors, anyway. I'm hoping to close for a while before the service. To read it through once more. And to dress."

"Don't you like what you're wearing?"

"I thought something a little...*crisper*. The service is strictly liturgy, nothing secular. There's to be no eulogy."

"No remembrances, no stories to tell? Is that always how Slipstone sees its own to the next world?"

"We're a quiet village, George, and we've each of us always grieved our own way."

"Well, I'd like to say something today. For only a minute or two. This death was different enough for that, don't you think, Grant?"

"I think that's the best reason of all to have it short, and to have it proper."

"I'd like to say something during the service, Grant."

His mouth started to open, but he couldn't decide whether to answer or to return to the book and his slowly descending finger.

"Thank you," I said. "And, Grant?"

"Yes?"

"Only for my curiosity, how did you come in this morning? I've been back and forth to the front door, and I don't think you could have slipped past me."

"Oh, I didn't slip past. I've been here awhile, just selecting these books from the cases downstairs so I can catalog them properly."

"Did you come in that way?"

"Through the cellar? I hardly know how anyone could enter the Chapel down there."

"You grew up in this church. And you've never considered that a dark old place like this might have entrances and passageways that aren't immediately visible?"

"Well, George, it's not something I think much about." His eyes flicked between mine and the desktop, up and down. "Maybe because I *have* spent so many hours in the Chapel is why I don't question it, don't look for mystery where I know there isn't any, like so many of the, the..."

"Tourists? Outsiders?"

"Well, yes, like those who come to look for secrets here..."

"...in our little Gothic sanctuary."

"I don't have time to indulge those fantasies. With seminary, and my work here..." His eyes flicked down as if to watch a small insect walk along a line of text.

"And that cot of yours."

His eyes flicked back up and stayed at mine. "Well, yes, my cot. I've never tried to keep it a secret that I lie there a few minutes now and then, especially when I'm here extra hours. I do try to keep it folded neatly away."

"Why didn't you fold it away Sunday night?"

"George, why are you asking me these questions?" He struggled to keep his eyes at mine. "Besides," his eyes went down and back up, "I believe I did put it away. Did you find it open?"

"Grant," I said calmly, "I would never accuse you of being negligent or untidy."

"I try to keep things in order, George." Eyes back down. "That's hard to do in a place with as many corners as this one."

"That's all I'm saying. This Chapel is nothing but angles, shadows, and noises you can't quite locate. That's the charm; that's what brings our visitors."

"Well, there *is* the Secretary's collection," Grant protested.

"Well, of course. The collection."

I PICKED up Clancy's leash from the iron spike in the railing and started with the dog toward the village proper. Even after nine, and even with the trees not yet fully leafed out, the path was dark and cool. The fallen leaves at the sides of the path were flat and marked with rot. Clancy never paused but led me quickly into the darkest hundred feet of the woods – the air heavy with moisture held in by the trees – and out again, everything lighter and lighter until we emerged onto the village green. We stepped across the little road to the shops.

I hadn't yet eaten, so I tied Clancy's leash to the bicycle rack and stepped into the Franzes' shop, Slipstone Teas. The floor shone with white-and-black linoleum diamonds. Three tables under tidy white cloths were spaced precisely apart within the little space. A glass display presented scones, muffins, and little brown loaves. Steam hissed from two kettles.

There was no one there but me.

I waited a few moments, then called through the door to the kitchen. "Melinda?" Then, "Melinda? Sally?" I heard a single clatter. A spoon onto the floor, a knife in a sink. A Franz came out, wiping her hands on a tea towel. She was bothered.

"Hello, Sally. Is it Sally?"

"It's Gert, George. It's the glasses, remember? Look for the glasses. Mine are gray and round, Sally's are square and gold, Melinda's without."

"Sorry, Gert; I should be better at this by now."

"Here about the service? About the reception? I'll be honest with you, George" – she was drying each fingertip with the tea towel – "I believe your Sara is giving too much of herself to this little event. She's promised to help, but she's not much of a help, is she, always taking charge."

"I'm really very pleased with Sara, the way she's taking all this, a lot stronger than..."

"Oh, she's taking it very well, I'm sure, a chance like this."

"She did tell me you were due at the Chapel at noon to help with the..."

"To help with? To help with?"

"Did I misunderstand? I know that between the two of you..."

"Oh, yes, the two of us will handle things just fine, oh yes indeed."

"Well, good, I am very grateful for all you're doing."

"It is for Jean, after all," she said. The "Jean" dripped with message.

"What I did come for though," I ventured, "is coffee. Just a cup of coffee. And a few of those...those..."

"Those are crumpets. Sally's just brought them out. They're warm and crisp as can be." I crooked my head back toward the kitchen for some sign of another Franz nearby.

"Oh, she's at the pastry dough now. Like a mouse. Quiet,

I mean. Quiet as a flea. Quiet as a secret." She smirked and paused and looked past my shoulder toward the window. "Hadn't you better take a crumpet for Clancy as well? He is so fond of them. He's with you today, I see."

With my coffee I took Clancy back across the street to one of the three village benches, where, after whatever Victor had fed him and after Galen's muffin, he ate all but one of the pale pastries, licking every crumb from the pavers, while I hurriedly managed the one I'd held back. I returned to the tea shop for another, but this time I could summon no one from the back room, no clattering even.

Next door, Elgin's gift shop was locked and dark. Clancy sat just at the glass at the bottom of the door, his nose pushing, his heavy frame shifting on his haunches, impatient to enter the familiar shop. As we stood there, I heard the phone begin to ring through the glass in the door. The sound brought up Clancy's ears and gave a look to his face I hadn't seen before – a sad maturity, a concern, and a sense of something near to intelligence. For those moments of the ringing phone, he abandoned his drool and shudder, and he sat rock still in contemplation, as if the sound through the gift shop door had answered all his questions. I could pull him away only after the ringing stopped.

We walked back past the tea parlor to Galen's shop.

Like Elgin's, it was dark and locked.

And then, like Elgin's, Galen's telephone began to ring, an alarm that carried through the glass of the old shop door. Just the same brrr-ang, brrr-ang of all the Slipstone phones, but hers rang only twice, and then it stopped. What followed was barely a hum, which rose and lowered – and then rose high enough that I heard it become Galen's voice, whether on a machine or not I couldn't tell. I turned the doorknob as quietly as I could, but the bolt was set. I checked my watch; it wasn't yet nine, when she usually opened.

After a few seconds her voice trailed off, and I waited a moment more before knocking on the glass. I tapped gently, but I could see and hear nothing inside. I knocked again, and I looked through the gloom of the shop for Galen to rise behind the counter, where she kept the phone. Nothing moved. After another minute, I walked with Clancy back across the road, and we found our place again at the bench.

Slipstone Village is all white and green and gray, with dots of color in the windows of its three shops – a few books, a few cards, and a half dozen teapots in the tea shop display. Most visitors are older folk, muted, whose own coats and shirts and skirts and pants keep to the village colors – except yesterday, Monday, when the small crowd came to see a place where someone had died in such a way as Jean. The apparel of those visitors had been extravagant against the stones and leaves of the old village. But, contrary to my expectation, none of that crowd was back today, just the one old couple at the Chapel, two regulars, who wanted only to browse the library for the Secretary's treasures, books of birds and trees and Italy before the war.

"Mr. Gilsey."

I jumped, of course, even from the harmless voice of a harmless man, coming up as it did just behind my left ear. So intent was Clancy's gaze at his master's shop across the street that he didn't turn around, even as the fragile Ginger Martin stretched one of his thin long legs and then another over the back of the bench to climb down and sit close beside me. Grease was always streaked somewhere across Ginger's face or hands, and his flannel shirt and old green workpants looked stiff with dirt, but the man never smelled of anything except the fruit he liked to eat. This morning there was something of apples, as he talked close to my face.

"Mr. Gilsey. I see you."

"I know, Ginger. Are you doing all right?"

"No, I see you, Mr. Gilsey. I see you early. With...," he didn't want to say the word, "with *him*."

"With Clancy, with the dog?"

"With him." He threw his head a few times toward the short-haired, tight-skinned beast still slouching toward the shops across the road. Men like Ginger have good reason to fear any dog.

"This morning? On the Path?"

He nodded once slowly, way up and down. "After they take Mr. Brattle," he added as an afterthought.

With his eyes big on me, I didn't know what affected him more, the sight of someone "taking" Elgin Brattle or the image of anyone other than Elgin Brattle escorting Clancy down Center Path.

"Someone took Elgin?" I submitted as calmly as I could. "He left with someone? In a car?"

"He make him leave. But no car."

Ginger was calm again, now that the conversation had left Clancy behind.

"Was this someone you know, Ginger?"

"He got a blue old truck. Mr. Brattle in the back, got rope on him." Suddenly Ginger began to twist himself straight. He stiffened himself against the bench, thrust up his hips, and was able to slide a hand into the pocket of his green workpants. He drew out a small, flattened paper box, squeezed it open, and fingered out a few of the last raisins.

"Ginger, what time did someone take Elgin? Was it dark?"

"Oh, it's dark, Mr. Gilsey."

"If you saw him, Ginger, didn't he see you too?"

"Yes oh yes, Mr. Gilsey. He sees in the dark." He worried the box again for another raisin or two, and then he dropped the empty thing beside our bench.

"Was it Zel Bander?"

"Zel Bander, Zel Bander, maybe Zel Bander."

"How do you know, Ginger? Did you know him?"

"A Tinker man smells that way." Suddenly Ginger was grinning, sharing the secret of the Tinker smell. He still had all his teeth.

"What smell is that, Ginger? What is the Tinker smell?"

"It's the oil," he answered readily.

"The oil?"

"They rub with it. Lincey oil."

"Linseed oil?"

"Lincey, lincey oil. They rub with it."

NO ONE ELSE WALKED PAST; no one tried the shop doors. Galen's light never came on and of course Elgin's didn't. I sat a few minutes more after Ginger left, and then I crossed the street again for the tea shop. Now the door was locked. I left and took the dog to Alder Cottage, the Clacton place, Jean's home.

I hadn't seen the house since late Friday, when I had left Jean, stood awhile by the Hawkson Cenotaph, and first heard the sound of Spinner's violin. This morning, just as then, no one else came within sight. I stood alone on the path and watched Jean's door as if she might crack it open as usual, shyly, just a bit, to see if I was the one outside.

Jean had let the paint fade a year too long on her family's cottage. I knew that if I came close enough to rub against the boards, a dull white mark would stay on my sleeve, evidence no doubt for Sheriff Crisp. But I stayed on the path, watching nothing but the green shutters and the green door of the Slipstone-white cottage. The morning gloom still lingered in the sky and on the ground, not quite damp but ready for rain. The wet smell of the woods came up over the rill to this end of the village. I walked the few yards to the end of the path, pushed my hand for luck down the edge of the worn granite Cenotaph, and, assisted by Clancy, hurriedly left.

14

LATE TUESDAY MORNING

As a map, it was a far thing from the hand-tinted art Zel Bander had left me. Printed cheaply in green and black, handed to me as a new depositor at the Trellis Bank, the map itself was bordered by ads for nearby restaurants, a since-shuttered record store, the hardware store, the palm reader's, and, near a bottom corner, Elgin's gift shop. Now folded out to a few rectangles flattened on the front seat, the map showed county roads so tenuous I couldn't believe they could take my car any distance from Slipstone without trailing off to sets of grassy ditches. On the back seat, Clancy chewed worriedly on a towel spread carefully to absorb his various wetnesses.

I was following no obvious route, only instinct. After coasting down Slipstone Hill, I had turned onto the Trellis road, but in a few miles, halfway to town, I angled off to the right, down a road I hadn't before noticed, opening between last fall's ruined cornstalks on one side and new growth on the other – green just out of the ground, plant life that could still take on any shape in just a week more, maybe soybeans. Big Run Road.

Its faded broken line parting narrow lanes, the road took me straight back over a few hills; then it began to slant in and out between farm ponds and small barns until a bridge pinched the road so tightly I had to brake hard to let a hay truck cross first as it rumbled toward me. Past the bridge, I picked up speed again until a sudden curve brought me too quickly into tree branches hanging so thick with damp leaves their weight flew into the windshield and dragged over the roof of the car as I let off the gas and eased the lever down into low. Clancy managed to keep from sliding forward onto the floor.

Once out of the trees, I sped up. I imagined my wide green sedan from high above. I guided it so far this way, so far that, to make the turns balance each other out toward one direction west, heading, I estimated, toward Needle's Eye River, far back from the place where Slipstone Rill ran in. Then I'd know to go northward, where I hoped to find myself at a place a few forested hills away from Slipstone, close to the village on the map but taking miles of road to reach.

About half the side roads were named in white on faded green atop tall metal shafts. They all ran off at curves and slants, some in cracked pale concrete, some in graying asphalt, others in dirt. Each one I took led me to the next with no dead ends, but finally a road stopped suddenly at a T and required that I decide the way. Instinct took me left, but when the road failed to curve back right as I'd expected, I pulled over at the edge of a farm path. I picked up the map and studied it. Clancy put his head and paws over the seat and examined it with me.

In the green-and-black ink of the map, the county roads were each numbered with four neat digits in no obvious order – 8493, 3367, 9009 – along with some of the names I'd seen: Gypsum Road, Blue Jay Road, Deaf Child Road, all off Big Run to my left. Studying the map with my index finger, I estimated I had driven a quarter of a wide circle, south angling over to west, but it was a guess as to where my big green car now sat on the map's web of insubstantial threads.

My window was down, and I turned the engine off to listen for the rush of water or any other clue, but all I heard was birdsong, and little of that. The sky was so diffuse that the sun could have been any direction, but not far from just overhead, here in the late morning. I started the engine, turned the car around on the narrow road, and sped back past the last intersection. I decided I would find Needle's Eye River past a few more hills, woods alternating with fields both right and left – and I did, just as I topped the highest rise. The river came into view, emerging from a copse of hardwoods far to the left below, snaking to the concrete bridge down the hill from me, then keeping east through acres of open fields into a stretch of dark woods – the forest that I guessed wouldn't end until the rill at the base of Slipstone Hill.

I drove fast down the long descent toward the concrete bridge, my tires changing pitch as I reached its hard surface. The road carried me quickly between the open fields until the woods took me in again, a thin forest of new growth with leafy vines stretching up most of the trees, already in the early spring.

And then for some reason, here in the gap of pavement that split the woods, the morning's murky light gave way, and I was driving under a bright sun so precisely behind that it lit the road without shadows. The dampness of the surface was already steaming into the air. I lowered my window and picked up speed. Beside me, on both sides, the sunlight picked its way around leaves and vines.

After a mile I passed a little cut in the trees.

I stopped, then managed to turn around on the narrow road, careful not to sink my tires into the soft earth at either side. I drove slowly and stopped at the opening.

Haywire Road.

Unlike the other road signs, this was a square concrete post, once painted white with stenciled black letters reading down. With my finger on the map I tried to trace the route I'd followed, but Haywire Road did not appear. And it *shouldn't* have, being only packed earth, with enough gravel to keep it from mudding over in a rain no heavier than last night's. Steering around the ruts as best I could, I followed the way in, as it turned gradually left and then right again with broad curves, a sinuous direction over flat ground that seemed to have no purpose other than to keep the road from being straight. Clancy stirred and sat up on his haunches. He whined and wouldn't stop.

The sunlight teased its way through the upper leaves and then, ahead, a few threads of it fell onto a dark rectangle suspended low on chains from a scaffold at the side of the road. I pulled up just ahead on a small rise, where the mud was more shallow. I managed to leave the car with Clancy inside and walked back to the sign, stepping on old leaves and needles between muddy gravel and the trees. I looked up and pieced the words together from the paint that remained:

CARPENTRIE

&

SHARPNING

The sign was crafted from several wooden boards, once carefully joined but now separating, with a kind of damp gray where the green and tan paint was weathered away. Beneath the words, like some heraldic device in the remnants of paint left behind by the weather, was the image of two crossed instruments, blades of different kinds. A chisel, maybe, and a knife. The two thin chains supporting the sign were brown with rust.

The trees grew less crowded just past the sign; a clearing evidently opened up ahead. I turned back to the car and let out Clancy, noisily eager. With the dog pulling hard on his leather lead, we followed the road to where the trees thinned and opened.

The clearing was an inexact circle, a few hundred feet across. In its center stood a large frame house, nothing unusual in its flat whiteness, the same house to be found anywhere farmland stretched in this county, a county enclosing Trellis, enclosing Slipstone Hill, enclosing the other half-dozen farm towns that inhabited its highest points.

The paint was still white in places, but the brown of the boards had worn through where the sun now shone most directly. The high narrow windows glanced back the sunlight, and I couldn't tell if the whitest part of the glare was a reflection of the clouds or a glimpse of drawn white curtains. At the front stretched a porch with straight, square columns, and nothing along it but two small chairs, set back into the shade. At the left side of the house from my vantage, grasses grew in different greens and heights, except where they had been driven into the dirt by the movement of a hay wagon, the remains of a narrow-bodied tractor, and, nearest to me, a rusted and blue pickup truck.

The grass at the other side of the house had been more carefully tended, where rising from a small and narrow field was a series of carefully spaced but irregularly leaning stones, not unlike those in the Slipstone Chapel yard, though each of these was the same as the others, without ornamentation: short, square, and thin.

As Clancy and I stood at the edge of the clearing, a high metal noise, an unoiled hinge, brought our attention back to the porch and the slow opening of the front screen door.

She came out then, came smoothly out the door, sliding almost. Her hair, straight and brown, fell onto her shoulders. A plain light-blue dress covered her to the knees. Behind the girl a thin arm stretched out to hold open the door, and then a boy came out too. He carried a violin carefully by the neck, and he looked over toward my hidden position for a slow moment, then back to her. She lifted her face only enough to find her chair, one of two just alike. The boy was brown-haired too, in a clean white shirt, buttoned high, and dungarees. He placed the instrument in Spinner's lap, then disappeared for a moment back inside and brought out her bow, all very gently, no slamming of the screen door.

She lifted the violin and began to tune the instrument, the boy straight-backed on the chair beside her, hands folded, his gaze straight out past me. To test the violin, she weaved her way scrupulously over the strings, bowing out a slow but unwavering song, some children's melody maybe, and then she turned the pegs slightly, one by one. Next, she played out the same tune, played it all its short way through, and then she adjusted the four pegs once again. She played her song again, and was ready.

When Spinner began again, a breeze came up and helped carry her song out from the porch, out past the grave markers and up into the woods, through what must be only a mile of trees, if there were such a thing as a straight path to Slipstone Hill. The tune was not quite the one I'd heard late that Friday night, and not quite the same as last night's melody, so quiet and controlled in the dark of my living room. The breeze gained with the song and brought with it something else, a smell not quite like the old wood of the Chapel, but something sweet, like rot. It came around from the back of the porch, toward me at the edge of the wood, and I found myself tilting my head back to catch its vague pungency.

And then something else on the porch. The screen door moving in a slow swing with shadow behind, any sound of its hinges riding just below the voice of the instrument, and then something coming out of the shadow, a figure in light clothes, with neither the boy nor the girl seeming to hear, as Elgin Brattle came up behind to lean one hand on the back slat of each chair. He looked out straight but unseeing, off at my right, swaying gently on his locked-straight legs, emptiness in his face, dreaming, rocking not quite in time with the melody of Spinner's violin.

Until now I'd forgotten the dog, but Clancy's quiet growl brought my attention. He stared hard at the porch, at his master Elgin, and he shifted on his haunches from foreleg to foreleg, his unsteady growl pitching slightly high and then low, harmony of some kind to Spinner's song. He was deciding what to do, and he decided he could not go any closer.

15

TUESDAY AFTERNOON

For the ride back, I spread Clancy's towel beside me on the front seat, and he lay with his head heavy between his stretched front legs, unwilling to sit up and see what might be passing. I drove back just as I'd come, but it was different land now with the sun out, corn and soybean sprouts glinting with the drizzle not yet melted off. We drove back through woods, over the river and up past fields, pausing at intersections that didn't look quite the same as before, everything sunny and almost dry. From time to time I scratched the poor dog's big flat head, but he kept shifting uneasily with what he'd seen. We came to the heavy tree limb that had covered the road. Now, with the weight of the rain steamed off, it had lifted high enough to let us pass under untouched.

Just then a slow tolling began to drift over the air, the biggest of Rachel's bells, heavy but distant. I had known we were late and known that prompt Grant Sweeney and prompt Gert Franz, with or without Sara's cooperation, would have begun the proceedings on time. I drove more quickly now, more sure of my direction, except for a doubtful moment once or twice when a road came in from the side, almost familiar, but then not quite. Finally we were back.

Climbing Slipstone Hill I met no one coming down, but at the top curve I stopped where Victor – it must have been Victor – had situated an unpainted sawhorse in the lane going up. On the sawhorse he had wired the Chapel's wooden Closed sign. I steered wide around it, topped the hill, and pulled to the curb across from the Slipstone shops. There was a car there I recognized, the Franzes' dark sedan, and another, silvery and fast-looking, and familiar from some place recent. Clancy lumbered himself distractedly off my front seat, and, as quickly as he would allow, we paced off the wooded path toward the Chapel, sun now filtering through the leaves, with the green smell of evaporating rainwater.

I tied Clancy's leash as before to the wrought iron fence, not far from a neat and high pile of stony dirt, turned up among the headstones in the time since we'd left for our drive. I imagined Victor, methodical, stooping and lifting, with another shovel in Boz Billings' hands, or Alice Felton's, a community effort to bury the dead. After the ritual inside, they and others would help lower Jean into the earth some twenty paces from the sepulcher, where she would wait for someone to place the next Clacton headstone. I'd seen Jean visit her parents there, not just to speak to the departed but also to contemplate the flat grassy space that would someday be excavated for her own frail form. So much heavy red dirt, so many fist-sized stones – all of it to keep Jean from floating back up to the air.

The thick oak door to the Chapel was shut flat. The reporter Greg Down leaned beside it listening, his white shirt just beginning to sweat through.

"A private event, I'm told," he straightened to tell me. "How about taking me in with you?"

"I'm not sure how welcome I'll be either. We'll stand at the back."

I reached past the reporter to pull open the door. The latch moved down with my thumb's pressure, but the door wouldn't give.

"What about your key?" Greg Down asked.

"You like to ask about keys, I've noticed. But I left the key for this door in my office." He followed my lead as I started down the sunlit side of the Chapel, looking up for any of the green glass windows that might be leaning out on its iron hinge. One was indeed open, as high in the stone wall as I might hardly reach from out here. As Greg Down and I approached it, we heard Grant Sweeney intoning inside, voice as deep as his thin reed of a body could support.

"There is a river," Grant's voice came to us through the open square above our heads, "the streams whereof make glad the city of God, the holy place of the tabernacles of the most High. God is in the midst of her; she shall not be moved."

"Well, where *is* she then?" Greg Down asked in his usual voice, as if he wanted to be heard inside only as far as the eight pews nearest the window.

"Where is...she?"

"The dear departed."

"I don't know exactly," I admitted in a voice gauged to demonstrate a more suitable register than his. "This is the first such service here since I arrived. The first village death."

"But she is there, she's inside?"

"He will not suffer thy foot to be moved," came Grant's recital, surprisingly steady in the unaccustomed timbre.

"And he that keepeth thee will not slumber. Behold, he that keepeth Israel shall neither slumber nor sleep."

"Mr. Down, I really cannot say. I haven't been a party to the...the treatment of her remains."

"All flesh is not the same flesh." Grant's voice was starting to struggle now. Losing power, his voice was taking on passion instead. "But there is one kind of flesh of men, another flesh of beasts, another of fishes, and another of birds. There are also celestial bodies..."

Greg Down's voice broke like a wave over Grant's. "When do they put the script down? When do they remember Jean Clacton? The eulogies?"

"The Lord is thy defence upon thy right hand...," Grant Sweeney told us in his voice, now continuing to hoarsen.

"There will be liturgy here today, Mr. Down, and nothing else, I'd expect."

"...so that the sun shall not smite thee by day, neither the moon by night."

It occurred to me that Slipstone was a place where the sun was forever harmless but where the moon could indeed burn by night. Greg Down gave up talking, and we waited as the service continued.

Ten minutes later, Grant's voice had faded almost to whispering, but he found the capacity for the usual final request, that the Lord lift His countenance upon the parishioners and give them peace, now and evermore.

In a moment I understood that Rachel had ascended, not as far as Jean's departed soul, but to her loft, as she tolled the heaviest of the bells four times, once for each decade of Jean's life.

Through the nearest window, Greg Down and I heard the sound of Grant's shoes as he stepped away from the altar. Then wood creaked as pews were relieved of weight, and we returned to the front door, which now had been unlocked. We let ourselves through to find Victor Blair standing forlornly in the vestibule, no one else in view except the last few mourners toward the front of the Chapel, patiently trailing through the door to the library. Greg Down walked past Victor, but I stopped to catch the sexton's eye.

He wouldn't raise his face to mine. " 'No disturbances' is what Brother Grant said," he finally, reluctantly, told me.

"*Brother* Grant?"

He finally faced me, eyebrows raised in explanation. "He said I couldn't use 'Father' until he was ordained."

"Victor," I tried to be patient, "Grant is not Brother, he's not Father, he's not Mr. Sweeney, he's Grant. He's not God's messenger; he's a part-time librarian. Someday, some very distant day, some faraway church might let him take holy orders. He'll need to grow some first."

"He said you might try to bring in the dog."

"If I ever decide to walk a dog into this Chapel – and, Victor, you know well enough that never will happen – but if it does, if I do, then I *will*, even if that dog is the dog Clancy. It is not a prerogative I would take, but it is my prerogative. Just as it is not Grant Sweeney's prerogative to exclude me from any event taking place on these premises. But I know you understand that, don't you, Victor?"

Tall and perpetually stooped from use of his mop, broom, and shovel, Victor looked toward our feet, our shoes almost toe to toe. He looked up again and spoke quietly, as if he could prevent Greg Down's hearing him at the ten-foot distance at which the reporter stood behind me. "They're in the library," he told me, as if a sudden moment of helpfulness might neutralize whatever consequences I had planned as punishment for his brief revolt. And as if I wouldn't know the only place the mourners might have repaired to.

Greg Down had already begun rapidly up the central aisle toward the altar, and I let him arrive there first, where, tall within her frame, the haloed Virgin folded her hands before her and looked down beyond the lambs at her feet toward a long wooden box, which must have been placed at her feet just before the service. Jean's casket was a beautiful, simple thing, with hand-worked wood that might have come from any of Slipstone's older oaks. The heavy box displayed no ornamentation; the care was all in the smoothing and fitting, with six pewter handles screwed in. The lid was heavily shut. The source of the casket was beyond my knowledge, but I realized my fellow villagers must always be prepared for the passing of one neighbor or another, usually not so young as Jean since the dark days of the illness that brought low Anne, the Secretary's wife, or the unnamed calamity that took their daughter Laura.

From the altar, Greg Down followed me closely toward the door that opened into the Chapel sacristy. We passed Sara's office and entered the library. I might have expected the sound of cloaked conversation to drift out and grow louder as we approached, but there was no evidence of any human presence until we crossed the threshold into the openness of the library itself, where the assembly had now separated into pairs and threes around the Maggini's empty display case, with the library tables moved to the walls. On one of these was arranged the event's offerings of food and drink.

The voices of the Slipstone citizens were almost soundless as I walked in, the reporter close behind. Rachel, now down from the bells, chatted solemnly with Sara, who stood guard attentively at the refreshment table, as if someone might rush the white linen and china, upturning the punchbowl and smashing Gert Franz's dainties. Storekeeper Thorny Webber stood resolute with shirt buttons pulled tight across his middle, Mrs. Webber bringing him little sandwiches to feed his big frame. Two of the Franzes mirrored each other next to Alice Felton, who glanced birdlike at all the groupings in the room as if a shift in someone's posture could alert her to guilt within. Boz Billings crowded the table next to Alice's circling elbow, which threatened to upset the plate from Boz's hand and spill pastry and its fillings onto Victor's polished floor.

A room away, Jean now lay alone in her box at the feet of the Virgin, while her friends in life had removed themselves to speak in hushed phrases in the library. Meanwhile, other necessary characters in any tableau of this village had yet to appear, as if the hand arranging this scene would soon need to lower them carefully into place. Missing were Elgin Brattle, who would be deep in conversation with an inattentive Galen Jones; the homeless Ginger Martin, restive in any indoor situation, who would be approaching the dainties and backing away as if frightened; Victor Blair, who hadn't followed Greg Down and me to the library but had no doubt returned to the gravesite with a spade to smooth any uneven marks from the sides of the well that would soon enclose Jean's casket.

And I saw no sign of Grant Sweeney, who had stolen the day from Jean – Grant Sweeney, ringmaster of the obsequies, self-anointed priest of Slipstone Village, was missing too, was nowhere near the librarian's desk of his day job, stood in no conversational groupings with his communicants. But I knew this slight man could never be far from his scene of ecclesiastical triumph and that through some force of will I could bring him into the room with a hard stare, and so I did, glaring past the display case, and so he came, opening the cellar door, a little dustier than usual, stepping up from below, knob in hand, glancing left to right, and finally locking on my eyes. He knew somehow it was I who had silently summoned him.

He looked away first, then regained composure and marched toward Sara and Rachel. I turned my own gaze and spotted Greg Down, who had quickly overcome the initial, unaccustomed moment of propriety that had given him pause and was now, rumpled, in earnest conversation, pad in hand, with Thorny and Mrs. Webber.

The atmosphere was so thin in the room that I realized I could hear none of the conversations as words – only as the hum of insects in low brush not far away. Even Thorny Webber's usually barrel-chested voice carried across the room only as if it were a distant piece of farm machinery, rumbling but indecipherable. In this scene it looked as if conversations were occurring, soft words without whispers, but my ears picked up only the hum.

Above us all, facing the image of the Virgin in her darker window, old Jonas Hawkson loomed as afternoon sun shone through *his* representation in stained glass, indomitable with his staff before a mighty tree, shadows from the window's lines of lead falling onto our faces below. Lower, and between them on her wall, St. Cecilia in her tapestry anxiously awaited her terrible fate.

And then, from far outside, through the walls or perhaps the closed glass of the lower Chapel windows, another sound came, then again, and repeated, rough and unhappy. We all knew Clancy's voice and here it was, whether with panic or the approach of his master with some morsel from the tea shop. Much like the strokes of a dull saw on thick wood, Clancy's dry barks came faster and louder, each chasing the last with increased insistence.

And then came the sound of the distant front door closing hard, and, as all our voices lay still, fast footsteps walked up the aisle, turned into the sacristy, and brought Galen Jones to the entrance, muddy, and with a message for us, but first for *me*.

"I followed it," she whispered harshly. She had me by the eye, me closest to the door, as if I might understand her by the depth of her stare. Then, again, with a slight but explicit forward tilt of her head, "I *followed* it."

Then she spoke as loudly as it seemed she could, but only soft and hoarse, and she pointed to a spot on the wall below the Hawkson window, dry dirt on her hand, sweater torn, "In that place dug out, for Jean..."

And she stopped, breathed hard, and lowered her hand. I took her gently by the shoulders, and she tilted her head toward the floor. "Out there," she said again.

Then the few of us nearest the door – Thorny Webber, Alice Fulton, and I – moved quickly past her, out from the library and down the dim Chapel aisle, not quite running, shoes clattering all together.

At first there was nothing to see but a dog by the fence, whimpering, pressed hard to the wrought iron. None of us dared touch Clancy once we saw the fact of it, Elgin sitting upright deep in the base of the neat square pit, the shadow of the grave's edge up to his chest, the afternoon light mottled through leaves on his bleached face where his eyes had been.

At the side of his throat I could see a thin and perfect line of red that disappeared into the shadow of his neck.

He seemed military as he sat, his posture measured precisely – or maybe his formal right angle, legs extended straight from his hips, ankles together, was due to Victor's expertise at cutting so exactly the bottom corner of the grave with his shovel. Elgin's arms hung exactly down his sides, and his white hands were stretched out from the neat cuffs of his shirt as if he were about to lift himself. The knees of his pants were torn, and the dirt there was dry.

When the breeze took the shadows of leaves away from Elgin's face, I saw that thin, dark channels ran from his empty eyes, down his cheeks, through a day's stubble. Then more shadows stole the sun from his face, as Thorny Webber, Alice Felton, and Greg Down joined me at the edge of the grave. Then a Franz came over, but only for a second, until she could turn and cry out.

"Oh no."

As the others came close, I did not turn toward their whisperings, as they feared louder voices might wake the dead at this graveside service. I looked for Galen but realized she hadn't followed us out after announcing her discovery.

Somehow the distant dogs across the valley picked up the sounds of our grief and let loose their voices. Still leashed to the fence, Clancy sank to his haunches and cried. The trees had spent all day drying from the rain of the night before, and the birds in the leaves above our heads were joyful in the perfect spring day.

I WONDERED how we all must appear from above, and I looked up toward the tower, where Rachel Wren would doubtless have already returned to prepare for the four o'clock bells, responsible even now to any who might need to know the time. Alice had told Boz to call the sheriff from Sara's office in the Chapel, and the sheriff hadn't yet arrived.

"Don't move him, Alice."

"I know that, Sara."

"He's white, just as white as Jean."

"He's dead, yes, and so of course he's white."

"He's whiter than dead. Don't touch him, Alice."

"Don't worry, Sara. I won't touch him. How could I even reach him from up here?"

Standing beside me, Alice bent low over the edge of the opening and reached in the direction of Elgin's face and his closed and sunken eyelids, from which thin rivulets of brown followed their course down his cheeks.

"But footprints, Alice. What about footprints?"

Alice paused to decide on an answer. "Then maybe you should move *your* feet away from here," she instructed me. "Just back up. Retrace your steps. I'll do the same."

She paused again. "In a minute." And she turned back and kneeled over the grave. Across from us was the hill of earth that Victor had created with his shoveling for Jean's resting place. I left Alice there for her further consideration of the scene.

Past the altar, in the stairway of the tower, I climbed up toward the bell loft. I could sense only the dark slatted walls under the single bulb, the dust smell of old wood, and the clicks of Rachel's shoes above me, as she stepped across her floor. She threw open the door before I knocked.

"Am I next, George? Is that why you're here?" Her small eyes were wide now, her head cocked.

I couldn't answer.

"Because I *could* be next."

"Why you, Rachel?"

"Don't you know?"

"It's you who seems always to know who's *here*, who's

gone *there*, who's locked in the cellar. You from your perch up high. Is that why *you* could be next?"

She consulted her watch and started moving toward the bench at the chime keyboard. She balanced her hands over the batons and almost imperceptibly rocked her small body side to side, readying herself with the rhythm for her four o'clock. When she reached the first lever with the heel of her hand, though, she struck it more slowly than I'd ever seen or heard, dispensing with the Westminster chime, announcing just the hour, exactly as she had tolled the departure of Jean's soul, but a few bells higher.

I walked over and peered through Rachel's window at the tableau below. The villagers were grouped much as in the mourners' room forty-five minutes earlier, where they awaited the arrival of Sheriff Crisp. At some point the third Franz had arrived. From above, the three sisters might have been in identically flowered dresses, but I saw only an unfocused blue, rose, and brown, and once, when Grant Sweeney joined them in their symmetrical huddle, they all hugged him, one by one. The market workers – Thorny Webber, Alice, and Boz, with Mrs. Webber – stood near the grave, but Alice regularly left their circle to attend to another detail in the circumstance of Elgin Brattle, careful to follow her own, earlier, footprints. She seemed not to notice that she shared the graveside with Greg Down but carried on her own examination, never looking toward the reporter, who adjusted his feet as if his own shoeprints would never register. Shifting his feet for better security, he made bold strokes on the narrow notebook, more like a man drawing than writing – a sketch to aid his memory back in the newsroom. As I watched from the height of Rachel's loft, he perched close to the end, squatted, and suddenly tilted forward, just catching himself from falling headlong onto Elgin.

At the window I turned to the right, toward the hill down to Slipstone Rill, near the stepping stones I'd found. Then turning back, I noticed for the first time a pattern in the lawn of the Chapel, a few long, thick lines raised in the grass, an arrangement that might not be noticed from closer below, like the creases in snow where a rodent burrows beneath, but more wide.

And then, immediately beneath me, I saw the top of the green baseball cap and shoulders of Victor Blair, as he leaned onto the Chapel wall below Rachel's window, viewing the villagers near the grave he had labored over, but apart from them.

As the bell just above us reverberated in Rachel's small room, I could hear none of what any of the figures might be saying, and when the fourth tone finally drew silent, I still could hear nothing from below, not even from Thorny's powerful voice. I could see Clancy's mouth snap open and closed, over and over, and that sound did carry up distantly through Rachel's window, now angled open just a little.

"Yes, that *is* why me."

I walked over to my chair. My cup sat on its little table, empty and clean.

"Because of what you know. But what *do* you know? What does it seem to be about, from here on high?"

"It's about putting things back the way they were, of course. You know that, George. Maybe not as well as John did, but you know it."

"The way they were *when*? Before me, before John, before the Secretary?" I hesitated. "Before *Gammel Minken*?"

She didn't answer.

"Gammel Minken," I repeated. "You were children together, you said."

"Yes, that's right," she answered, at the edge of anger.

"And so you *knew* the Secretary."

"As much as a young girl might know a lofty village elder."

"And so the boy Gammel Minken. And Laura Hawkson, all growing up together. Then an illness, you told me."

Her lips tightened, her eyes crept away from my face, and it seemed she would refuse to answer.

But then: "She was my age. Exactly my age. *He* was two years older. We were always together, so few of us here. Just children, and then children...maturing."

"And sharing secrets?"

"Some secrets she didn't have to tell us. And she *didn't* tell us. But I knew, and he knew."

She paused, and I did not interrupt. Then she said, "It was...that I found something. I was *supposed* to find it. She had told me once where she kept her little book, the book she wrote in almost every night. Then, much after it was too late, I went and found it in her room, the same room in what's now *your* cottage. I read it, and then I let Gammel read it too."

She paused again. Then: "She was stronger than that," she said. "We thought she was so strong."

Her eyes came quickly back to mine, and they became angry.

"We wanted to make it right for her somehow," Rachel said, her voice rising. "And Gammel *did*. I stayed, and he went across the rill." Another pause. "And he came back that same night with everything."

"With everything? With...?"

"Or nothing. He didn't want to say, but he was pleased

with himself. He thought it better if he was the only one who knew."

"And now no one really knows," I said. "Is that right?"

I let her be for a few moments. She stood and turned away from me.

"Rachel," I said, "What was it that John Patton knew and that made him leave the way he did? He must have decided, must have taken some time to prepare, to organize his things to carry with him. The office showed almost no sign of him. The Rectory, either, a few cans in the pantry and what's left of that bad beer he made."

"There was never much of John in Slipstone. He came with very little. And what he left.... Well, it was Sara who organized his things, all his things, his clothes, his shoes, after he wasn't coming back. They're all gone now, somewhere of her deciding. She must have told you."

"Sara says very little about any event before I occupied John Patton's office. She has shown me how the phone and lights work, and how Victor does not demonstrate the appropriate deference to her position. But about John Patton's departure, very little, and about his belongings, nothing at all."

"There just *weren't* many belongings," she said. "In his few years in Slipstone he wouldn't have gathered anything of weight or value, not John."

"Sheriff Crisp thinks he gathered the Maggini."

"I don't know what he thinks. He may *say* that, but if Aaron Crisp tells you one thing, he likely believes another." She kept silent for a minute, but then, finally, she spoke – quietly, still at my eyes. "Besides, you know where the Maggini is. Far away, but not *very* far away."

She filled a pan with water for her hot plate and came over to pick up my cup.

"If the violin is with the Tinkers, why has Crisp not gone to pick it up? And to pick up the Tinker who took it? Zel Bander."

"Have you ever spoken to Aaron Crisp about Zel Bander? I think you haven't, and I think I know why."

"The sheriff has no intention of listening to me. When he questions me, I will tell him that I know where Elgin Brattle spent his morning."

At that, Rachel's eyes opened quickly.

I continued. "He will not write that down in his notebook, and then he will ask me some unrelated question that he has asked me before, and he *will* write down that answer. That is the sheriff's interrogation technique with an outsider."

"Aaron Crisp is wiser than you think," Rachel told me severely. "And he knows that if the Tinkers have the Maggini, they intend to keep it."

My tea was ready, and she brought it over. Then she went to sit at her tiny harpsichord.

16

LATE TUESDAY AFTERNOON

I stepped quietly out through the little-used door on the Chapel's west side. Voices came toward me from the front of the building, but I could not make out the words, just the higher register of Alice and a series of measured, slightly lower, responses of Sheriff Crisp, who apparently had just arrived. I could see that the sheriff was now perched over the square-hewn pit, villagers leaning slightly toward him as they stood as near as Alice would have allowed. No one looked over from behind the iron gate as I walked around the corner of the building and, as inconspicuously as I could, untied Clancy's leash and bent to reassure him that we were going away from all this.

And we did. As we began, I saw Victor still resting his lean frame against the front side of the Chapel. He may have glanced at me, may have stared, but his eyes were dark under the bill of his cap. His head did not turn to follow me.

Home at the Rectory, I unleashed Clancy, and he followed me nervously to the kitchen. I gave him a big dish of water to replenish the fluids he had lost through that short, damp skin of his. Then he happily took the cold cuts I offered in my hand. With barking and desperation in his eyes, he did what he could to prevent my leaving, but I was able to close the door behind and make my way quickly back down the path to the Chapel.

I entered through the front door and was quickly through the vestibule.

Dust motes hung to my left in the blue-green light from the western windows. Before me, the illumination was yellow, above the Virgin of the altar and the box below that held Jean. I walked slowly up the aisle to the casket and placed my fingertips at the edge of the lid. It was screwed down tight, of course. Jean was safe here, but alone, no one to carry her to the place so carefully prepared by Victor, and that place no longer ready to receive her. I went upstairs to my office.

Galen hadn't washed off the smudge of dirt on her face. She sat at my desk with the drawer open and didn't look up as I came over and sat in the opposite chair. The high window shed light over her arms. She was holding a pinch of something just above the drawer. Then she opened her fingers to drop it.

"He likes sunflower seeds," she told me. I heard the scurry of the mouse's little feet. "But he's got these other things in here too."

"Those little fan-shaped pieces of wood. He drags them in from somewhere."

The dirt on her cheek was light in color. There was still shock in her face from before, but she tried to smile as she finally looked up. The doll lay before her on the desktop.

I sat on the chair at the corner of the desk. "Have you met my little friend before?" I asked.

"I knew he was here; you must have told me." She

dropped a few more sunflower seeds. "Is Alice still in charge out there?"

"The sheriff won't be able to chase her away. I'm sure he's scolded her for the footprints."

"But he won't object to his own. Is he questioning everyone?"

"Of course. With his little notepad. He hasn't gotten to me yet. I slipped away before he drove up."

"You'll be his special, maybe his *only* suspect."

"Yes. I was the one not back for Jean's service," I said, "and only a dog for an alibi. But the person he'll want to talk to is you, you who discovered...everything. Elgin." And then I realized. "But I was *not* the only one missing from the service. "You..."

She looked up from the drawer and across to my face. "Yes. And it's not just Elgin that I found. I want you to come with me."

"And where would we be going? I should probably go face down Mr. Crisp."

"So should I," she said, "but I want you to know that I found the other thing you'd hidden behind that little metal door in the basement wall."

She reached into the open drawer and pulled out the Tinker map, still rolled loosely within its rubber bands. She released the document and spread it out on the desktop.

"You went back down there. Why?"

"It was a little odd that you'd decided to hide this child's toy in such a way, and I saw that you'd hidden something else in there as well. And, besides, you wouldn't have shown me that place if you hadn't wanted me to...well, at any rate..." She turned her face down toward the map, spread out now between her hands. She secured the corners with items from my desktop – cups, a pencil sharpener, a jar with coins. She circled a finger over the drawing. She found and pointed to the spot at the fallen tree.

"This is where you found the doll, isn't it?"

"How can you know that?"

"Look at it. Have you inspected this map? It's quite plain. You told me the spot was in the woods near the rill, and near a fallen tree, a sort of bridge, and so I went."

"And so you went?"

"George, we both know there are things you don't want to tell me, to tell anyone, I suppose, but you so obviously want to. So I decided to..."

"...to take it upon yourself to remove this...*item*...from the place I'd shown you."

"Well, yes, I returned to the cellar after you gave me the doll."

"And then you examined the drawing and seem to have found this *place*...and then today..."

"I *did* find it, *here*," she insisted, still pointing. "Your boot prints were all over the place. A little smeared in the rain, but yours, I'm guessing. From Sunday."

"So, that's where you've been?"

"With or without a map, there's one logical path into those woods, and so you found the doll. Where you were meant to find it."

"Meant to find it?"

"Somehow you discovered, or were given, this map. And you've kept it in your secret cache and then found this mysterious doll of yours, in a tree, a tree by the rill. Maps are for finding things, you know."

"Treasure maps, maybe, but a doll with no hands isn't a treasure; she's a throwaway."

"Except to some little girl. Who is she?"

I turned away from her and then turned back.

"A Tinker girl, I think."

"A Tinker girl? One of the gypsies in that commune of theirs? Why her?"

I reached down, took the weights away from the drawing and began rolling it up. "Because this is a Tinker map. And I don't believe it was meant to guide me to a doll. But the doll was there. On the way...somewhere."

"Yes. On the way somewhere. Whether or not she was left there deliberately."

She looked suddenly at my face, took the map out of my hand, rerolled the thing within its rubber bands, and picked up the doll. "Then you'd better come with me," she said. "And bring a torch. A flashlight. There's a way I don't think you know about."

Downstairs, we entered the library, where little sandwiches, cakes, and cups from the tea shop remained unclaimed on the refreshment table. Through the wall I heard the first voices, of Grant and others, doubtless the sheriff, coming into the vestibule at the entrance to the Chapel. Galen and I moved quickly past the Maggini case, switched on the cellar light, opened the door, and stepped as quietly as we could down the rough wooden stairs. I followed her past the rows of shelves with the Secretary's collections, under the string of lit, bare bulbs, and to the wall containing my cache, where she stooped at the ash door and pulled it open. As I leaned down beside her we heard footsteps above us in the library, crossing directly overhead, stopping, then circling, probably around the empty display case. Galen quickly pushed in the doll and map and closed the little iron door.

She turned to face me and dusted off her hands. "You don't know your own Chapel very well, do you?" she said, quiet but emphatic.

"I'm sure you're about to prove that, aren't you?"

"It's a matter of curiosity, of a little logic, of just looking around. And, well, of Elgin's showing me. Come over here with your flashlight."

She led a little farther into the dark of the cellar, beyond the last of the overhead bulbs. The large, rough-cut stones of the foundation were less regular here and interspersed with squares of desiccated soil and ancient boards. Galen switched on the flashlight and pointed it to a place where three of the longest boards stood vertical and together against the wall. She then handed me the light and reached for the widest of the boards, gripping some kind of handle just at its base. As she swung it up toward us, I looked and saw two large metal hinges that held the board at its top. Galen brought the end of the board toward us with seeming ease, and she showed me the opening beyond it, as black as I would have imagined such a space would be. Two counter-weights, fist-sized pieces of iron, had descended from thin chains a few feet into the looming dark, lit dimly from the nearest of the ceiling bulbs behind us.

Of course I knew the tunnel must be there, must have known all along. It had to be somewhere, one of the places through which Zel Bander could turn up unexplained. And here it was in the yellow beam from my flashlight, as I let it find the rough cuts of the top and sides of the shaft, its opening wide enough for us both to step together within its edges of hard dry dirt.

I helped Galen let the board descend behind us; then she pushed past me and took the flashlight from my hand.

"Come along," she insisted. "It's all smooth except for the track," and she stopped so suddenly my body pushed against her and we almost fell. She pointed the light at my feet and then behind us toward the door, and indeed a pair of metal rails ran from the opening and in front of us, parallel, a few feet apart, straight into all the distance the light could reach.

Galen moved quickly down the tunnel, brushing with outstretched fingertips the occasional boards above and beside us that held back the heavy earth. The entryway now shut, the light had closed behind us, and all we had was my one flashlight, in her hand, against the utter dark.

She moved quickly through the space, stepping along at the side of the rails, as someone who had surely taken her time earlier to examine her whereabouts but now had no need for curiosity. Without light of my own, I moved closely behind her.

"They must have pushed their carts along this track," she said. The sound of her words bounced up and down the dirt passageway.

"Their carts? With what?" I tried to keep my voice more modulated.

"Supplies. Stones from the quarry, mortar, wood."

"The Chapel, yes," I said. "Piece by piece. Up this shaft. But why dig this tunnel when they could have built their track above ground?"

Now my voice too was echoing in the tunnel, as I realized no one could have heard us, the Chapel cellar now a hundred feet behind and the crowd by Jean's grave, Elgin's current resting place, many tons of packed earth away.

"So rain wouldn't wash it away," she told me. "There was no hurry, you know, if you've read Elgin's history. Jonas Hawkson taking his time for whatever unexplained purpose. And there's another reason too, which you'll see."

"Whatever reason there must be," I told her, "these were people...these *are* people who know their way in the dark."

Along the tunnel we went, and although there was little

light to which my eyes could become accustomed, I quickly worked past the surprise of the situation and began to look around more with curiosity than astonishment. Galen could move upright as we proceeded, but my height required an awkward hunch of my back and a stumbling gait.

"Look here." Galen directed her light toward a pair of sconces near the top of each dirt wall. "And here." She moved the beam farther down to another pair, and I could see how the tunnel was supposed to be lit, with thick candles along the way. The drips of old wax still clung to the black metal holders.

"How could candles stay lit in this airless space?" I asked Galen. "Or how was it that anyone, that *we* could breathe?"

"There have to be air shafts. They must be beside or above us. I haven't found any, or even looked. I haven't spent so much time in here that it's like another home."

She stopped suddenly, and once again I had to stumble toward the side to avoid her. She was aiming her light up and along the passage.

"But how could vents stay open for a hundred years and not grow over where they emerge – weeds and leaves?"

"Do you think no one else travels this tunnel? That no one *maintains* it?"

And so we continued down the square-cut passage, step after step, the angle growing steeper, a constant slope downward cut high and wide, hundreds of steps so far, hundreds of more difficult steps back up if you were pushing a cart of stones. Were there once pulleys of some sort at the head of the rails, the same kind of mechanisms that would have allowed the Chapel's stones to be raised into place?

After five minutes more, Galen's flashlight indicated where not far ahead of us a large square of darkness opened to the left into the dirt wall. The track beside our feet angled away into the aperture, and the tunnel ahead of us narrowed.

"Have you followed that larger branch yet?" I asked, as Galen led us past it.

"It must lead to the quarry, I was guessing, because of the rails," she said, her breath a little shortened now from our walk and the thinness of the air. "I only just followed this direction a few weeks ago, and only the once. It was in the winter, before Elgin and I had our last squabble about his book, when Elgin showed me those boards, that doorway, in the Chapel cellar. He told me about the tunnel and the quarry and so on, and he must have assumed I would never consider burrowing around down here on my own. Then one Sunday, when the shop was closed and the village was quieter even than usual, I decided it was time for a stroll."

"But, Galen, why are you...?"

"Why now? Why am I showing you this?"

"Well, yes, but why did Elgin even tell *you* about it, bring you down here, show you?" As I spoke, I heard my voice echo from some other part of the tunnel in its cool, dry, and thin air. "And, yes, why are we here *now*?"

"That's just it, isn't it, George? Why *did* he show me this?"

As Galen spoke she moved the flashlight beam slowly from our feet, down the black stretch before us and back, angling it unconsciously. We could not see each other's face – at least *I* could not see *hers* – but her breath drifted toward me with each of her words.

"He told me it was a curiosity," she went on, "some vestige of the Chapel's history, something he left out of his little Slipstone book but which I'd appreciate. But there was some other *thing* he wouldn't say, some other purpose in showing me." Galen's voice wasn't echoing like mine; she was speaking more softly, in almost a whisper.

"And that's why we're here now. Because Elgin..."

"Yes. Because I thought you should know before Sheriff Crisp finds you. You should know what there is to know about your own...your Chapel."

"And about what Elgin might have known."

"Or what Elgin *did* know, and why he's..."

"Why he's back there now. Where *we* should go, before the sheriff's posse comes looking."

"No. First just follow me a little. You have to see..." She turned the flashlight beam back down the narrowing tunnel and started on.

Soon the space graded out into a flatness for thirty feet or more and then rose at an abrupt angle, reaching in a short distance a place where Galen's flashlight beam hit something solid and high where the steep path ended.

"It's more damp here," I said. "It's the rill, isn't it? We've just crossed under the rill."

"Yes, back there, but what now? It seems we're stopped dead, doesn't it? But we're not." The beam from her light played in a circle in front of us, as she challenged me to see something in the smooth dirt where the tunnel seemed to end after its short, steep rise. Then I saw that five shallow steps had been cut into the earth, heading upward toward the closure.

"Just show me, Galen, and hurry. What am I looking for, a brass doorknob?"

"Almost," she said. "Not brass, but..."

She handed me the light and climbed the first three steps. Elbows bent and with the flat of her hands she pushed upward against a kind of metal door, which she now angled open to let in some of the shadowy light of the woods.

While I stood below her, she gave a final push, and the thin door swung up and over. The five steps brought us up through the hatchway and out of the tunnel.

We had emerged onto a kind of knoll. I realized how cramped I had been, and I stretched back and forth as I looked to see where we were. The knoll was probably not a natural formation, but it now appeared so, overgrown with mosses and scattered with detritus from the trees. The door that now lay open could have been taken from the entrance to a storm cellar. Galen indicated the area around our feet.

"I think these leaves are supposed to be spread over the entrance."

"Why hide it? It can't have been much of a secret when they used it for bringing construction materials."

"That was a long time ago, George." She bent close to the earth and shone the light through the opening, back into the dimness of the tunnel. "Most people, you and I, we arrive in our little village and, sooner or later, we go back home or to some new place. We don't notice little artificial hills in the forest. But those who came from nowhere else, or who would never consider leaving – maybe they like to keep their secrets. And this isn't the primary entranceway; you saw where the track diverged to the left. That entrance must be back farther into those trees, probably at the quarry, where the Chapel stones were excavated. And other passages must open into this main artery. We passed one earlier, but I don't think you noticed it. They may be disguised somehow but will be easily found."

"Are you so sure we want to find them?" I asked.

"There could be a warren of them under the village."

With one, I knew, that opens into the floor of John

Patton's – my – pantry. And then I said it: "There's one into my house. I've been visited."

Galen had been crouching, digging at lichens with a stick in the dwindling light. Now her head suddenly shot up, her eyes found mine, and she started to speak. But then she didn't.

The rill was twenty feet away; I could hear better than see it now, with the afternoon dimming away. I took the flashlight from Galen and walked around the knoll toward the sound. Under the mat of leaves the earth was still soft from the recent rain. I aimed the light down the stream and then up, where I could see the stepping stones not far away, the only white in the gray water, and so dim they could have been imaginary.

"What else do you have to show me," I asked, handing her back the light.

"Nothing right now. Maybe there's more. But we should go back; the sun's fading quickly – not that it matters in the tunnel, I guess."

She moved ahead of me, carefully onto the first steps of the hatchway at the tunnel's entrance.

"Can you pull that door behind you?" she asked.

"Is it necessary? Has this been a secret visit? It won't be too secret if we can't replace those dead leaves on the other side."

"Just please pull the door."

Return travel is always shorter – is it because now we know the way? – though this time the climb was upward, through the tunnel cut square, but not as square as the corners of a grave that Victor Blair might slice with his spade into the earth of Slipstone cemetery. We walked as quickly as we could, following the pale beam over the same dirt, packed hard with thousands of dry footsteps, past the wider opening where the metal track veered off, and it wasn't long before Galen lifted the light toward the boards into the cellar. She pushed one away as I pushed at one beside it, and we ducked and stooped our way in, letting the boards fall behind us. We walked together to the light of the naked bulbs in the row above, still lit.

"We should have been outside long before now," Galen urged me. I imagined the sheriff circling the gravesite, no doubt hesitating to approach, waiting for the return of the state investigators to come look at another death.

"It's you they'll want," I said, "disappearing like you did just after announcing Elgin's body."

"George, it's you. It's you they're missing. You, who won't even answer *my* questions, you with Elgin's Clancy. We'll go together."

Galen had lost the distraction of showing me the tunnel; her voice shuddered slightly with the chill of remembering Elgin. Where his eyes had been.

Then she asked, "Where *is* the dog, anyway?"

"Oh, Clancy?"

"Yes, that's the one."

"Galen," I said, "would you be willing to take him from my place, from the Rectory, and keep him for just a while? Maybe find him something to eat?"

"He's locked up in the Rectory? That poor, confused beast."

"He's OK, I think, but maybe just for a while, for the afternoon? And he's not locked up, of course. We don't lock..."

"Yes, I know, though I might start locking *my* door. But he'll be inside the house. I'll take care of him."

She started back toward the steps, but I stayed.

"George, aren't you...?"

"I won't go up yet," I told her. "Not yet. I need to learn something." I lifted a hand, a finger, asking for patience. She started to speak, but I retrieved the flashlight from her hand, turned quickly, pulled open one of the boards at the tunnel entrance, and re-entered the dark space.

Deep within a large house, or a building of any size, I'm lost for the outside, with no instinct for which direction I've entered, where the back of the house could be, where the sun might rise or set. Now in the tunnel the simple pattern of streets and paths in the village above were lost to me.

As I retraced the first hundred steps angling down, where Galen had led me earlier, I tried to determine the bearing that might lead under Center Path to my cottage or to the rest of Slipstone Village. Soon my flashlight showed me a dark opening to the right, into a shaft low, narrow, and roughly cut, much like the tunnel that had brought us under the rill and into the woods. It might have been the other passage that Galen had mentioned. As I started in, the flashlight began to dim slightly, but I shook it a few times, and the beam brightened. I thought it might last long enough.

The tunnel floor gradually rose, as I must have been approaching the village, and I walked as quickly as I could, without overtaking the fragile flashlight beam. Before long I saw the passage curve slightly to the right, and I kept moving ahead, but then there was a kind of shuffling sound behind me, quickening, and I was pushed forward hard onto the dirt of the tunnel floor, the flashlight flying from my grip as the flat of my hands tried to diminish the impact of my fall. Even now I don't understand whether I hit my head on the side wall when I dropped, or if *he* hit it when he pushed. It doesn't matter.

I don't know how long I lay there stunned or unconsciousness, but in time I began to understand where this dark place was. In pure blackness it's hard to know if you're finally awake, or if your eyes are open or closed. Was I still with Galen? I wasn't sure, but then I remembered that shuffling sound, and then heard it again, close.

I've said before that I'm a big man, so it shouldn't have been so easy to take me from my feet, but for the suddenness of the attack. The pain now crawled forward along the top of my head, down into my eyes. I tried to shift up onto an elbow, but my stomach weakened and I dropped back down. I must have closed my eyes again – in the dark I couldn't be sure. Maybe I slipped back into the place I'd just wakened from. But just then I could see a tiny flare in some indistinguishable distance, and I could hear the scratch that made the flare, but in what order those events took place I couldn't be sure. Does sound travel faster than light in a tunnel?

"Is there...?"

"Don't be worried. I'm with you, Mr. Gil-sam." His voice was distant and seemed to come from every direction, but it had to originate at the tiny flare – a lit match? "It's fine to see you back. I wasn't sure."

The shuffling receded, and I saw him light a candle in a sconce some thirty feet distant, then another, ten feet closer, and another.

I could start to distinguish up and down, but the rest of the blackness was a mystery, back up the tunnel or under the rill, even side to side. I was up on my elbow again. Two bits of light, and Zel Bander's silhouette, closing.

"Always in the dark," I managed.

"Our talks are better without light. All talk is. When you don't see another's eyes. We work in the light, and we talk in the dark."

"The Tinker People."

"Yes, we Tinkers. We are craft-men. But not so much craft-men as the ones before us, even my father. And *his*." He paused. "That's why you will help us."

"I don't know how to help you. Why you left me the map, the chart, the *story*, you call it. What you want me to find. Those circles in the woods."

"Did you think that book woman would help you, make you understand? So you brought her toward us down these passes of ours?"

"She knows nothing about you." I was finally able to rise as far as my knees, but my head was lurching. "These tunnels – you say of *yours* – these *passes* are no secret if they open so easily into the Chapel.

"Oh, there are secrets, Mr. Gil-sam, and there is understanding that people know but must not share. And there has been much sharing of late, sharing what cannot be taken in your hand but only in sound, only in the music; a stealing is what it is. Sharing without our say, stealing from us, your friend Jean, your friend Mr. Brattle, maybe your friend the book woman. The *taking* though, the taking of something you can take in your hand, was so long ago. My father told me this, about the old man Minkley, not so old then. Minkley. And what Minkley took is what you must bring to me, even after many years."

"Your father told you about the young Gammel Minken? *What* did he tell you?"

"My father told me, and his father too."

"Why can you not tell me plainly what you need from me? What was taken?"

"It's a thing not to talk of straight on. It's a thing words can't do and if they did, there'd be no use of it. Music is the only sound that tells. But *you* know, and I know that you do. John Patton knew, but he made as though he did not."

"What could be his reason for that? Or mine? How can I find what you need when even *you* cannot, when the village, the Chapel, seem entirely open to you?"

Then there was only the sound of his breath, and his odor, the tincture, that sour oil.

And so, as he said nothing, I understood.

"*I* don't know," I said. "*John Patton* didn't know. Because *you* don't know. And your father? Did *he* know?"

He took his breath in sharply, hesitated, and spoke as he released it.

"My father wasn't one to take something back. And he was an afraid man. An afraid man. Too afraid to say just what that man Minkley took from him. From us. He thought maybe *I* might come for it."

"And now you *have*."

"He's gone now. My father. And he used it all up."

"He used all...? All what?" The side of my head now pulsed in the pain and the darkness.

"You're not one for remembering. I touched your hand with this same point that night. That was to remember. This is to remember too."

Suddenly his hand was on my shoulder and found its way down my arm. He captured my wrist and pushed the blade in harder this time, near the other place, and he held me there as I twisted my arm without effect in the strength of his grip. The calluses on his hand were like metal disks.

"I have waited this time since my father went in the ground." His voice was calm as he pushed my wrist harder and kept the blade in my wrist. I realized how cold and dry it was in the tunnel. "I will not wait more."

He rose and backed away, the two candles went dark, one then the other, and I heard Zel Bander's shuffling gait recede as I sank down again onto the packed earth.

. . .

WHAT I REMEMBER NEXT WERE voices. I don't know how I found myself up and standing, peering out through the thick glass of the small window in the Chapel door. I looked across the flagstones and wet grass, past the iron fence, toward the churchyard and the leaning gravestones where the small crowd still huddled, now in the impending darkness, my village neighbors with arms crossed or hands in their pockets. Voices came toward me, but, through the door, their sound was more like a single hum with a low, varying pitch. Farthest from my view were Sheriff Crisp and Thorny Webber, one with his pen and notepad, the other with his usual expansive gestures. And there too was the small blue van of the state crime lab, and, behind the rest, pacing and sketching, were Hella Derry and her assistant Bill.

I eased away from the Chapel door, farther into the vestibule. The back of my wrist stung, and in the light through the little window I looked to see a crease on the back of my hand dried brown and dark. Beside me, I saw that my flashlight lay upon Sara's neatly placed pamphlets. I lifted it and noticed that the lens was cracked and spidered, whether in my fall in the tunnel or by Zel Bander's pointed tool, but the bulb lit faintly when I pushed the switch. Then I turned it back off.

I gradually realized that more painful than my wrist was a thudding from the back of my head, and I reached to find a narrow swelling that stung with my touch. I left my hand there a moment as if it might heal the injury from my encounter in the tunnel, and then I brought my arm back around to see that no blood had seeped out onto my fingertips.

I pushed open the door to the Chapel proper and walked unsteadily up the aisle, leaning on the backs of pews for assistance. As I neared the crossing, where the opening led to the sacristy and small kitchen, I heard the phone ring in Sara's office and no one to answer it. And then someone did, with Sara's muffled voice. "Just a moment, he's here, he's nearby" is what I heard her say.

Still shaken, with my head now more numb than in pain, I passed through without Sara's hearing or calling me, climbed the stairs, and opened the door to my office. Catching my breath. I sat at my desk in the light from the afternoon windows. I pulled open the drawer. No scurrying; my mouse seemed to have left for a while.

Then, when I looked toward the office door only a moment later, the sheriff was already standing there with his pen at his notebook, and it seemed from his glances up and down that he was sketching the floor plan of my office. The small man in his starched uniform saw me watching him, but he continued a moment with his drawing, then snapped shut his little notebook, came and sat in the chair at the corner of my desk, and again flipped open his notebook.

"Go ahead and tell me," he said.

"Tell you...?" My head ached, and I looked down to ensure that my shirt cuff covered the red line on my wrist.

"All this dirt. Where is it from? On your pants, your shirt. On your face."

"There is always work here to be done...," I began.

"Work?" He rested the tip of his pen on his notebook and pointedly turned his gaze left and right across the expanse of the office as if taking it in for his drawing. "Isn't Victor Blair here for the kind of work that soils clothing?"

I paused, and decided. "There is something else more important than the state of my appearance."

"And that *is*, Mr. Gilsum?"

"I drove from the village this morning, a little west of here, across the river, Needle's Eye River."

"And with all the work to be done, as you just mentioned, and the death of Jean Clacton to be resolved, you decided to take a morning drive."

"Sheriff, please let me..."

"Please do."

"I had learned – Victor had told me – that a skilled worker, a carpenter, apparently from a family descended from the original Chapel workmen..."

"The Tinkers."

"Well yes the Tinkers, and that this man could carry out some of the minor restoration work now required within the Chapel proper. He said the man's family lives somewhere beyond the woods west of here."

"And you thought you could find..."

"Victor had said something about the carpenter off Big Run Road and the other side of the forest, and so after the rain..."

"And did Victor Blair provide the name of a particular Tinker, some individual who could do the work you so desperately seem to need?"

"He told me the name Zel Bander, and that's who I went to find..."

"And did you? Find Zel Bander?"

"No, I did not. But I found a little road, more of a path, marked as Haywire Road..."

"And you just happened across this Haywire..."

"Please, Sheriff."

"Go on."

"Haywire was the only road that opened to the right, opened north, and I turned in..."

"Mr. Gilsum, that was an ill-advised mission you decided on."

"When you called me this morning and asked about Elgin, I had no idea where to find him. But Elgin Brattle was at the Tinker house today. He was there. He was alive."

"Please do not tell me any more about the Tinkers. If you were truly there today, and you saw someone you thought you recognized, I can promise you it wasn't your neighbor."

"I also saw Elgin leaving your office yesterday. And he didn't want to see me or me to see him. Sheriff, what do *you* know about all this? Why are you questioning *me*, and not Zel Bander?"

"You need to know something, Mr. Gilsum, and it's this: We don't go to the Tinkers. They have their ways there, and we don't interfere. They take care of their own. Now do we need to go on with this story?" He scraped back the chair as he began to stand, closing the little notebook and sliding it into his uniform's shirt pocket. "Maybe you can continue as we step out of here for a few minutes."

"And step out where? What do you mean?" I hesitated but then stood as well.

"Please, Mr. Gilsum. Just for a moment. I want you to show me what you've got in the cellar."

"The cellar? There are thousands of items in the cellar, as I'm sure you know."

"I've asked you to come with me. Please, can we go?"

Stiff in his tan uniform, the small man raised an arm to usher me through my own office door. At his urging we descended the stairs and walked past Sara, busily ignoring us with some newly found paperwork. The sheriff then moved around me, and I followed him into the library, past the missing glass of the display case, and to the basement door.

"Just down here for a minute, Mr. Gilsum," he instructed, as he opened the door and stepped back to gesture me onto the rough wooden steps. He switched on the light and followed me down, both of us gripping the thin handrail. At the bottom we stood a moment, his hands on his hips as together we peered down the array of shelves and to the back, where the overhead row of light bulbs shone weakly onto the dirt floor. Then suddenly he moved forward.

"Come along here," he said, and I followed him past the rows of the Secretary's relics to the foundation wall near the boards that now, after opening them with Galen, seemed so obviously to lead somewhere. He paused short of them though, and he stooped to rest on his heels at the base of the wall.

He must have felt me looming over his slight build. He twisted his head up and eyed me warily. Then from somewhere he produced a small flashlight and aimed the beam onto the square iron door of the ash cleanout.

"I don't know who might have indicated this opening to you," I said, "and I'm not sure what you expect to find inside, Sheriff. I think you might be disappointed."

But of course he wouldn't be. I stooped beside him and, with a thin rubber glove on this right hand, he brought open the little iron door. As he pulled it away on its hinge, I realized that any dark thing could be behind.

And dark it was, until the sheriff brought his light into the deep square opening.

"I started to extract these," Aaron Crisp said, "but I thought you should be with me." He twisted his gloved hand around something heavy and began to pull.

A brown smear had dried thickly, flaking off the sawblade at its serration. On another tool, a narrow chisel or gouge, the same kind of brown smear extended toward the tan wooden handle. Spinner's doll had been taken; now there were only those tools and nothing more.

I rose, turned from the sheriff, and began to walk away. "You'll need to come with me," he told me calmly, and then insisted, "You'll *need* to come with me, Mr. Gilsum." I walked steadily, past the shelves of the Secretary's memorabilia, past the place where Grant Sweeney slept on his narrow cot, and finally, but no more quickly, up the steps to the library. "Mr. Gilsum," I heard from far behind me.

It had turned even more toward dusk as I left through the front door of the Chapel, and the smells of spring were heavy around me with only the slightest breeze. Ahead, past the wrought iron gate, standing guard at a border of yellow crime tape, was a slight figure, uniformed, pacing. Cigarette smoke rose over the glow of an electric lantern. In the dim light I recognized her as the woman I'd seen at the front desk of the sheriff's office in Trellis.

I continued through the wooded path and found my car by the Slipstone shops. I realized that the silver fast-looking two-door I'd seen there earlier must have been Greg Down's, and now the reporter would be back in the newsroom, filing his story.

The blue crime van was there too, but still it took an instant to recognize her voice.

"Bill is at the gravesite, still at his scrapings and dustings," said Rella Derry, the crime lab detective. "He can be very meticulous. As he must."

She was standing in the dimness under a maple just starting to leaf out, her square form a silhouette. She approached me as my hand was reaching for the door of my car. Her gray hair picked up the light that was threading faintly through the trees from the village shops. She wore her gray suit and white blouse. Rella Derry without color, as before.

"Did you not want to speak with Sheriff Crisp?" she asked.

"We spoke. Rather I spoke and he failed to hear me. It's how we talk together."

"I think he listens but doesn't want to show it. A weakness of personality, but a strength in his profession. In our profession."

"I think he wants to speak with me some more. A few things he found."

"Hidden away, is what I understand, in that cellar of yours."

"Where he was sure to find them."

"Where he was told to find them."

"And who would have done the telling, do you think?"

"The same person who did the hiding, I suppose," Rella Derry said.

"A clumsy attempt," I said. "Too obvious."

"I think Aaron Crisp will know that. Otherwise you'd still be with him."

"I'm not so sure." I opened the passenger door of my car and invited her in. She bent and slowly drew herself onto the seat. I put myself behind the wheel.

"Where are we going?" said Rella Derry.

"I'm not sure. Where *are* we going?"

"Let's just sit. And talk."

And we did. After a while I turned on the engine, and we drove the few short Slipstone streets to Galen's house. Behind the curtains of one room a light was on. I took Rella Derry back to her car, where she could wait for Bill.

17

TUESDAY NIGHT

I let the dimness grow within the walls of my den until I realized I was hungry, turned on some lights, and went to the kitchen. I prepared a stew with the meat and some carrots and potatoes from Thorny Webber's shop and ate it with thick slices of brown bread cut roughly from the loaf. I drank more of the beer that John Patton had made and left behind, a bitter and cloudy drink, but more to my taste than the few thin beers Thorny's store could offer.

Then, with a single dim light on, I played a record, only one, the same Rossini, one of the records least scratched in the rack of John Patton's small collection. I tried John Patton's radio, as I had done many times in the weeks I'd lived here, but Slipstone's magnetic hill sucked up almost every signal that floated by, a few notes, a few words appearing behind static but drifting off. Somehow Sara could capture her one station in her Chapel office, but I'd failed to find it here in my cottage, only the wavering signals with indistinguishable voices and songs moving in and out of reach. Tonight I spent some time with the machine. I found what I thought was an antenna screw in the back panel and wound some thin wire around it. I unspooled the wire diagonally across the den and walked it back and forth, standing on furniture, crisscrossing the room, returning frequently to twist the knob, anything to find a better signal. Whether the voices and stray notes came from nearby Trellis or some far-off transmitter was impossible to determine. Finally I wound the wire back onto its spool and turned off the radio. The static and whining stopped, but then there was something else.

It was the kind of breathing that is not meant to be concealed, and it carried a slight rasp to it, after something strenuous. Accustomed by now to intrusions, I turned my head slowly but didn't understand at first how she could have been sitting there on the thin rug, kneeling really, beside the chair where I'd just perched with the antenna wire.

In her hand was the Maggini.

Or it might have been, or not. How could I have told in the dim light one violin from any other? Or in any light, as close as I could ever be to the old dark dry wood, sound holes, fingerboards, all the same to me without the homework into instruments I should have carried out long ago in this job.

She was so entirely slight in her cotton print dress, where she knelt, feet splayed behind, head bent down with the violin under her arm, the bow tight under there too. Then she looked up so I could read her eyes, but all I could read there was that she had much to tell me. The dress was thin and many times washed, like that of her doll.

"Did you bring that to give me, or just to play again?"

Spinner didn't seem to hear, but she was watching my face closely.

"Is that our Maggini you've been playing, that you've brought?"

The phone rang.

Spinner's eyebrows came together. Was she questioning the nature of the call, the meaning of my words, or even what a Maggini was? Or could she hear any of this? But she *could* hear, I remembered; she had obeyed her father in the dark, in this room, when he demanded she play her instrument.

The phone kept ringing. It finally stopped.

Without much apparent care, Spinner placed the violin and bow on the thin rug and brought out some kind of little notebook from the pocket of a leather bag. She raised it a few inches toward me, and I walked over to sit cross-legged in front of her. Her eyes were gray in the dimness but could have been blue or some other light color. Her expression changed two or three times, but every change was a question as she examined my face. Then she looked down to open the little notebook and find the right page.

I wished for more light to see what she might show me, but I didn't want to change the feeling in the room, where Spinner sat, alert but not nervous, with something to show or tell me, and I doubted that either one of us knew exactly what it was. Then finally, after fingering through pages back and forth with penciled notations in words I couldn't make out, and maybe they weren't words in the way anyone ever writes words on paper, she came to what were not words or lines or symbols but was her doll. Even in this light I could see shades and cross-hatches and careful details, with drawing and erasures and re-drawing, the hands in place before their severing and open toward me in hopelessness. And hopelessness in the face.

It was a notebook like Aaron Crisp's. But not with his ballpoint.

I noticed that Spinner was without smell, without a little girl's smell, without the smell that a Tinker's home must have exuded, without the odor of the tunnel. My living room was the smell of old wood, except where Spinner sat, where there was no smell at all.

SLIPSTONE so far away from town lights, the band of stars was a splash of cream high across the middle of the sky, especially in the winter cold, but also on cool spring nights like this one, looking up through new leaves.

As we walked from my front door to the car, Spinner had the violin wrapped tightly in her bag, a patchwork of leathers sewn carefully together, browns and blacks. She was slight enough that she slipped onto the back seat of the car without bothering to find a way to push the front seat forward. She pulled her sack in behind her. Her thin legs were not long enough to bend down at the knees at the seat edge, and the soles of her shoes just touched the back of the seat in front. One dim light shone through the window of the Rectory as I pulled away from the curb.

Treadle Street was a few turns away, as was every location in Slipstone, and I drove slowly, with headlights off until I knew I needed them, the village's fearless squirrels always darting across their familiar streets. All was quiet in back, Spinner so small she would never creak the springs in the seat no matter how she might twist around. But I think she sat without a movement. I went slowly toward the village center, then turned into and backed out of a diagonal parking space at the tea shop, all dark, and drove back toward my cottage. As I approached at a crawl, I looked toward the front window. The light inside went suddenly dead.

I drove us back toward the village.

I turned left down Treadle Street past the market, where village streetlights gave a nimbus to the haze forming in the early night air. I stopped once to let a mother raccoon and her trailing cubs cross in front, but they decided to turn back and wait. Everything is so close in Slipstone that to drive within the village is an oddity, so Galen should have been surprised to hear a car stop in front of her house and two doors shut – mine and, as I escorted her out, Spinner's.

But she was waiting on her front step in the porch light and showed only mild curiosity at seeing the little girl with her peculiar leather package. She brought us in and sat us on chairs in her small den. Scrambling, claws clicking wildly on the wood floor, Clancy ran in from some other room, happy to see me, circling, dripping.

Galen came over and knelt before Spinner. "This is the one, isn't she? Aren't you?" The little girl met her eyes.

18

WEDNESDAY MORNING

I woke in one of Galen's soft chairs and left her house as quietly as I could, leaving the girl and the dog with Galen in other rooms. The bookshop had no need to open, at least not early that morning, with the road up Slipstone Hill blocked by one of the sheriff's unattended vehicles. I walked to the small lot behind the market where I had moved my car late in the night and drove it back to my cottage. I heard the phone ringing inside. I twisted the knob and pushed, but the door wouldn't open. I stood unsure, then remembered that my only key was beneath a heavy pot with desiccated plant residue in the dry dirt remaining from John Patton's time, or before. You'll never need it, I was told. The key was fouled with peat, and I wiped it clean between my fingers. As I made my way inside, the phone rang a few more times and stopped. In the living room every piece of furniture, every book, rug, and chair looked untouched. I came to the kitchen.

His smell still lingered, and his map had been returned. It now lay unrolled on the wooden counter, each of its corners secured into the surface with a kitchen tool – knives and an ice pick – that must have been punched in with strength and fury. The floor was smeared with the dry, patterned dirt of footprints. I turned toward the pantry, whose door stood fully open. I closed it and returned to the map. There was something on its surface I hadn't seen before, tiny things the color of parchment – a precise drawing of two tiny mittens, stitched at the wrists. The doll's hands had been placed palm down in the woods, in the center of a circle, cross-hatches for trees.

With some effort I unpinned the map, laid the tools on the counter, and left the kitchen.

In the bedroom I pulled down the hinged writing surface of the small desk, marked with years of ink scratches that had bled through the correspondence of those preceding me in the Rectory, among them the Secretary and the Founder. I rolled the Tinker map up loosely and pushed it into one of the dozen pigeonholes. From a drawer I pulled out a single piece of stationery. "Slipstone Chapel" was embossed elegantly at the top, with the village motto along the bottom: *Give to the earth. Take from the trees.*

With a pencil I started a line for Center Path, beginning at the Rectory, which I drew as a quarter-inch square. I continued the line to the Chapel – a cross within a pentagon – and drew a larger, uneven rectangle beside it, sketching in the Hawkson sepulcher, with Jean's gravesite a few memorial stones away. I returned to the line and led the pencil toward the south end of the village, past Alder Cottage, which no Clacton would ever again occupy, and to the Hawkson Cenotaph, where the path ended. I then penciled other lines for the few village streets, the central artery of Gunnell Street along the Slipstone shops, with Treadle Street curving off east past the market and, a half-inch farther, Galen Jones's house, a very small square.

I brought out the next sheet of stationery and taped it onto the edge of the first. This allowed me to broaden my map to the west, down the sloping meadow to Slipstone Rill and beyond to the woods. Tiny rectangles became the stepping stones, and in the woods I curved my penciled line of the rill toward the fallen tree where the doll had been left within its roots. At the bottom of the second sheet, deep into penciled treetops like clouds, I left two clearings, just as in the Tinker map, one with dots around for the sitting stones and the other with tiny x's for the circle of stumps. Finally, pushing hard into the paper, I etched the system of shafts under the earth, as tunneled by the original builders and later by Tinkers, as close as I could imagine it, from the Chapel, under the meadow, under the rill. A branch to here, my cottage, the Rectory. And why only here; did it branch everywhere? Were we all suspended, the village, the Chapel with its thousands of heavy stones, on top of a fragile rabbit's warren?

And, finally, I understood that one branch of the tunnel – it couldn't be much wider than a man's shoulders – must lead somehow to the interior of the Founder's sepulcher. A narrow tunnel through which Jean's maimed body must have been laboriously carried. Or dragged.

I went to the car and brought back and unfolded the map from the Trellis bank that had guided me in the direction of the Tinkers' farmhouse just a day earlier. Depicting the entire county, in a scale a fraction of my hand-drawn map's, it indicated its various advertisers' locations as little green squares and pentagons, most of them huddled in or at the edge of Trellis. Slipstone Village was a cluster of dots atop a modest hillock toward the left of the document, with the Chapel identified as a cross, and the woods to the west stretching beyond a hairline titled *Rill*, just as in the Tinker map. The town of Trellis appeared a few miles to the east at the map's center, exaggerated in size and drawn in some detail as befitted the county seat. A little to the west were the roads I'd driven days before: Big Run Road, Blue Jay Road, Deaf Child Road, and the numbered county designations, with nothing alongside except the fields I'd seen. Needle's Eye River, curled in green ink north to south, was never joined by Slipstone Rill because of hills between, unless perhaps somewhere in the next county, in a map that might be available from a different bank.

I pulled the Tinker drawing from the pigeonhole, unrolled it, and weighted the corners with smooth stones that some predecessor must have collected from the rill. Three maps of different size now lay on the small desktop, overlapping, the Tinker map uppermost. I shifted them to reveal the Chapel in each.

Even in different scales, the maps were much the same. As I examined the three, rearranging as necessary on the small fold-down desktop, I penciled in the word *rill* on mine to match the word on the others. As I had seen when examining the Tinker map in the Chapel cellar, it showed no stepping stones or rough bridge, but a series of little cross-hatches did indicate the tree circle where I'd marked the rotted stumps on my drawing. Unlike the Tinker drawing, the bank map had no suggestion of the quarry, but I added it to mine, though I hadn't yet walked that far into the woods. I was sure I could follow the tunnel there if I chose.

I made a sandwich for breakfast and turned on the radio. Static, static, but eventually something else as I twisted the brown bakelite dial. I watched the indicator thread catch on a particle of some kind and, released, jump toward the higher numbers, then incrementally back and forth to one frequency that tried to hide from the thread until, with an almost imperceptible movement of my thumb and fingers, allowed itself to be heard, faintly, a low register of strings, reception fading and returning as I ate my sandwich and drank my warm tea. Then I pulled on my jacket and canvas pants, lifted my leather bag off its hook, and went into the pantry.

I moved with my flashlight past breads, cereals, and dry fruit, deeper along rows of old cans, rust at the lids, labels loose from the sides, jars packed with uncertain ingredients – uncertain no doubt also to John Patton, who must have let the contents continue simmering in their salt much as I had done. I wondered if Zel Bander knew the contents of my jars and demijohns.

Then I proceeded to the rear of the pantry, and the square of cut boards at my feet there, as I'd found with the disappearance of Zel Bander and Spinner after their night-time visit. The wood of the boards gave slightly as I knelt and put down some of my weight. And there I saw hinges, two of them of the dullest metal, not to be easily noticed in the pantry's dark recess, with a gap across from them, just enough for fingertips. The hatchway lifted, swung open, and rested against the back wall of the pantry. Of course there was a dull metal handle to bring the door back down – and onto a square, black pit.

Within the darkness, my flashlight showed me a wooden ladder, slightly slanted, with flat steps evenly spaced. Carefully I turned myself backward and began to descend, gripping the sides of the ladder, without bothering to close the hatchway above.

Twelve or so steps down, I was standing in the narrowest of the tunnels I'd seen, with sides hewn less smoothly than those of the wider passageways. There was the same, almost pleasant, smell of dryness, and there was no dust in the flashlight's beam. I held the light under my arm and clapped once. Only an echo, and it seemed distant, inviting in an odd way, and I walked quickly along.

Counting my steps, as I proceeded within the earth beneath Center Path, I knew I must eventually near the intersection by the Chapel, where Zel Bander had accosted me the day before. Then the wide opening was suddenly there, before me in the flashlight beam. Entering the larger tunnel with its rails at my feet, I aimed the light to my left, where the rough boards to the Chapel cellar appeared dimly, not so far up the passage.

Now I moved to the right, as Galen had led me yesterday. Here and there along the tunnel, wide beams had been planted to help hold back the walls and give purchase to the sconces. The slope was so gradual as to be hardly sensed, even as it made its way under the hill of the meadow to where it leveled beneath the rill. There, looking up, I saw where heavy boards had been dug in, side by side. How thick was the earth above me? What mechanism, what materials, prevented the stream from falling through? The beams above were tight together and dry, except where several drops collected between two of them and gathered enough weight to fall, one by one, onto a small area of thin mud.

Rising again where the tunnel grew steeper past the rill, I reached the steps cut into the earth, then was quickly at the hatchway and through, detritus around me pushed loose yesterday from the door's opening. I knew my way now. With a crow calling above, I walked into the woods. I easily found the fallen tree. I carefully passed over it and through the opening of roots at the far end, where Spinner had lost – or had placed – her mutilated doll. The water below still ran wide and fast two days after the rain. Above me in the sunlit leaves, smaller birds sang against the angry call of the crow.

The same walk seemed shorter this time, as it will. Ten minutes from the downed tree I passed the sitting stones and arrived at the wide circle of twenty stumps. The trees had been hewn many years before, sawn rather, and no new life had gained hold in the slowly rotting wood, except a variety of mosses, green and gray. Had Rella Derry and Bill found this spot, collecting? Weren't there dogs out? But no crime tape or other evidence of a visit was apparent.

Bending, I examined one stump and then the next, each of them eight steps from the next, all about the same width, in a completely regular circle. The base of every one, toward the center of the circle, still carried a thick smear, now more brown than before. I picked up a fallen stick from behind me and used it to pry up one edge of hardened leaves. The thickness continued into the ground beneath.

I stood at the center of the circle, then turned, trying to imagine if these trees, when tall, would have shaded me from the sun, now just above. But the image wouldn't come, as I had no guess as to whether I'd see leaves or needles. If needles, the trees would necessarily have grown tall, conifers old enough to have trunks this wide. Deciduous trees could have aged into this width without such height. The stumps were far enough apart to have accommodated a wide growth for each tree, planted with such precision. While most of this forest was old-growth, I noticed that none of the trees here now were nearly as ancient as those nearer the rill. Newer oaks, maples, and others had grown vigorously here, but they had not yet widened with the same age. For a moment I closed my eyes and tried to sense some kind of resonance emanating around and past me, a skill I am willing to believe in others but not one I had ever found in myself.

I returned to the stump in what I had come to consider the two o'clock position, as I had first approached the circle on Saturday. I stooped, drew out my pocket knife, and pushed the blade into the wood. The stump gave less to the pressure of the sharp point than I had expected. Though seemingly rotted, the pulp was still tough with fiber, and it was difficult to saw and pry out a four-inch wedge, which I wrapped in a handkerchief and placed in my bag, along with a piece of bark that had remained intact near the roots.

On a notion I re-opened the knife and scraped through the depth of damp oak and maple leaves long since become mulch inches down. I dug away a foot-wide area of rot and desiccation and then finally soil, and then I dug further in, wishing I'd brought something with a wider blade than my pocket knife. The soil was layered more tightly the deeper I went, but I found that I could dig around roots and stones through sediments into looser dirt, a kind of granulate, then damp and hard, finally impenetrable. Lodged there, and with its shape barely intact, a seed cluster, a tiny cone. But all the trees outside the circle were in leaf, nothing with needles, nothing with cones.

19

WEDNESDAY AFTERNOON

To accurately chart the scope of these woods would take some time. The odd shapes of packets and parcels would figure best from the air, a penciled tree in each square of graph paper with cursory shading for cleared spaces and the rill wandering through. But how could the draftsman allow for the crows, crows everywhere around Slipstone, lifting noisily to soar crying over the woods, how many to fit within a square? No, they fly singly, squares apart.

From my office window that afternoon I watched them scour the grass of the churchyard, appearing from behind grave markers, distributing themselves in their own, known pattern, examining the earth for whatever might rise from below and be eaten. I had turned toward my desk when the sudden shouts of the birds began, even more frantic than usual. Back to the window, I saw that a pair of the big birds were diving from oaks at a red fox, pursuing her in the furious confidence of their ownership of the Chapel grounds. The beaten fox, with her head and tail both stretched straight, flew past the edge of my vantage, and I moved to the other window, where I could see the animal reach the rough tangle of vines at the edge of the slope toward the rill, hidden now in the brush but still under siege from the outraged caws of the circling and diving birds. She would slink downhill, I knew, until reaching the stream's flat crossing rocks and then into the woods to sprint to her burrow somewhere. Had she never learned that crows were not easily, or ever, caught by foxes. Was there no better, easier hunting on her side of the rill?

I thought of my map on the hinged-down writing surface of the little desk back in the Rectory, drawn on my two taped pieces of Chapel stationery – how did the mathematics of scale allow for what was in the woods beyond the rill? All I had learned today was that the clouds of leaves I had seen cross-hatched in the tree circle of the Tinker map weren't leaves at all, but thick groups of needles.

The dark boards of my office ceiling had shrunk and slightly separated over the years, and the small but ornate light fixture had descended to have its wiring rub against an edge of wood. How fast was the thing lowering itself? An inch in a year? The safety of the building depended completely on the elaborate fuse box in the cellar, with its row of replacement fuses lined on top. How many of these old wires had become abraded by movement within the walls or chewed to the copper where mice sharpened their teeth? Only Victor would know, if anyone, but likely he would shrug if I asked and remark hesitantly that an electrician cousin had once looked everything over and pronounced it fine. But surely Victor could shore up my ceiling fixture, although I suspected it would not safely accommodate bulbs of higher wattage than the dim ones that now cast barely enough light in the early evening to let me read the titles on the nearest shelves. The Chapel's ancient wiring had been a concern since my arrival, with my most fundamental responsibility that the old, dry wood in the building not catch a spark somewhere behind the walls and leave this part of the hilltop with high but empty stone ramparts.

My desk lamp, left here as everything else by John Patton, was older than I knew fluorescent fixtures could be, but it drew little power as I sat within its range and watched my large hands circling, palms down, on the ink-stained leather of the writing surface. I had not before attended to the nature of these marks, the fading black and blue-black glyphs, as pens had scratched over them, with deliberation or not. But everywhere I was seeing maps – in the way the white clover was taking shape in the grass by the church-yard, and in the contrails above.

I leaned forward to the lines on this old, hard leather. I moved my hands away, and looked to see just where inter-sections might appear, or the wandering line of the rill, or a rough circle of dots, but there was no pattern in the leather that I could eke out.

Sara had alerted me that the frequent storms of summer – but at times of year as early as now – would throw a light-ning flash down onto the electric line that fed the village and cast all there was of Slipstone into a dark afternoon until a workman from Trellis could arrive in his truck. In the corners of rooms throughout the village, candles and oil lamps had a place of easy reach. In the Chapel stairways were the flashlights placed there by John Patton.

There was no threatening weather on this late after-noon, Sara long home and Victor – well, Victor could be quietly sitting in a corner of this dark room for all I knew, his big hand slowly scratching behind Clancy's ears. I peered into every angle, and then I remembered that Clancy was still housed at Galen's. I pushed back my chair and rose to make my way down the narrow stairs, past Sara's unlit alcove, through the library, and to cellar door, where I found that one of us had earlier failed to switch off the lights below those steps. Of course the string of bulbs above the row of shelves was of little use at any time except to prevent stumbling over some misplaced stool or box. Following Grant Sweeney's example from the days I first arrived, I always pulled the Secretary's heavy crates off their dusty perches onto the rough wooden stands that Victor, or perhaps Victor's predecessor, whoever and whenever that might have been, had nailed onto the ends of the shelves, directly under the bulbs. It was damp here underground, and the Secretary's correspondence, much of it in other languages – elegant purchasing arrangements and receipts in French, Italian, or Cyrillic languages I could not read – was in danger of complete annihilation before Grant, in his frustratingly unhurried, mysteriously systematic arranging, could save it from complete dissolution.

Had I ever even counted these boxes? Had Grant? Despite the aura emanating from his hoary legacy, the late Gammel Minken seems not to have quite got around to any kind of system but only scrambled through some of the crates and pulled out what seemed most intriguing to him – and to Elgin Brattle – as they collaborated on the Slipstone history. And now Grant. Grant, who seemed to have inherited Minken's approach to the process of creating history from artifacts selected on the basis of what comes most appealingly to hand from some fifty mildewed cartons and what might display best behind the glass in the library cabinets. It was not, I knew, so different from the creation of most historical records, and very much like writing the story of a species based on the randomness of fossil discovery.

But was there even any chronology among these boxes? Did their fading and peeling labels give any indication of what the Secretary had bundled inside? And over the years under the hands of the caretakers had the materials been haphazardly spilled out and repackaged arbitrarily, with little or no concern for the kinds of approaches that might yield an understanding beyond the myth of the Secretary's years in France, in Italy, in lower Alpine monarchies?

Inside these crates were small wood crucifixes, children's toys of the thinnest metals – a horse and wagon, a colorful top – rusted tools of inexplicable purpose, tiny crumbling pillboxes, on one of which was written *sztrichnin* in a pharmacist's careful hand. It rattled upon my shaking it, and I slid it open to reveal a few tiny white pills. Here also were empty medicine vials of green and brown glass, complete newspapers, folded as purchased, with headlines about the progress of local wars or other matters germane to the Secretary that I could not decode from the unfamiliar words. So many of these crates had been shipped home to Slipstone over his years of travel that I should have already sought funding to hire more assistance than Grant in attempting a rescue of so much.

In my months here, I had searched through the papers of my predecessor in a mostly fruitless endeavor to discover his attempts, if any, to hire workers for the slate roof, to organize the employment records of Sara, Victor, and whoever might have preceded them, to establish proper bookkeeping and other administrative responsibilities, to learn if Rachel's heavy bells were suspended securely enough on old beams not to drop someday onto her fragile harpsichord, her eggshell skull. Did he ever try to trace what little plumbing there was that inhabited the space behind the walls – not difficult because of the noise it made upon the opening of any tap or valve. How completely remiss I also had been as I avoided the central work of Slipstone Chapel – restoring and preserving the stories it had to tell, hidden until now or simply ignored over time by those who should have kept the ghosts of the place – the Hawksons and all the less remembered – somehow alive.

And so tell me, Grant, as you've huddled between these dank aisles down here, removing and replacing these heavy old cartons, and with nights on your cot and in whatever tiny walk-up you inhabit in the village, what would I find in those notebooks you keep so laboriously and with such apparent precision – a precision in no way reflected in an organizing principle for these overstuffed shelves?

The odor of the old boxes trailed Grant in his cassock wherever he walked.

As these thoughts occurred and as I began to leave the aisle I'd last visited, the voice was of course unexpected, like any voice here would be, or any footstep, if footsteps were audible on these packed dirt floors, or any sound at all other than some mouse finding a place among the boxes to hide from the light. And was it his voice or just his breathing that came to me first in the still, heavy air of this old space?

It was a sigh, I suppose. "Um, Mr. Gilsum?" Quiet, as if not to surprise me, but knowing it must.

It was a voice I didn't think I'd heard before, realized later I hadn't, but it was Bill, of course, Bill from the state lab, suddenly under the fifth or sixth light bulb, motioning me toward the aisle from which Rella Derry was slowly emerging, brushing dry dust from the knees of her skirt.

"Yes, hello, Mr. Gilsum," she said, as if encountering me on a village path.

"Yes," she repeated after a pause I did not know quite how to fill. "Not much seems to have changed since the last time I found myself down here."

"Found yourself?" I managed to say.

"Well, yes. When your predecessor, um, vanished. Not so long ago, really."

"I had thought...Jean's death..."

"No, we were brought in when your violin went, um, missing." She was again brushing her hands down the sides of her skirt. "And John Patton too, of course."

"And so it's not just violent death you..."

"No. We're a small group to cover a small territory," she explained. "We have to, um, do it all. Bill and I stay busier than you might believe."

"But today though...down here...?"

"It's quite a collection, isn't it? I mean, um, hard to see how it all...fits. I suppose you have it in some sort of order that you..."

"Not as yet. It has been Grant's..."

"Of course, Grant Sweeney."

"Yes, it is Grant's job to make order out of all these... numberless items from the Secretary's travels. I confess that my own administrative duties upstairs haven't yet allowed me..."

"Of course. You've been here only...a month? Two months?"

"About three, actually, with not as much to show for it as I'd like. For the most part trying to answer correspondence accumulated since John..."

"...since John *vanished*. Or, not to employ such a dramatic word, since he so suddenly...*left*." Here she finally managed to completely straighten her back, and I realized she was taller and little less stout than I had thought.

"I have to ask," I said, "how did you and...how did you and Bill gain entrance today? It's not much of a wonder that the Maggini, or anything, for that matter..."

"Or John Patton?"

"...can...*vanish*...from Slipstone Chapel."

"Our presence today though is considerably less mysterious. Sara, of course."

"Sara? Sara has been home hours by now, with her stitching or quilting, whatever takes her away from here every afternoon."

"Yes, well, Bill and I have been here awhile. The fact is, though, that Sara told us after the theft where you keep the key outside. We've visited a few times since."

"A key outside? There's no key...or is that one of the things that Sara hadn't yet got around to telling me?"

Rella Derry fished in the loose pocket of her trousers and withdrew the massive thing, dangling from some kind of beadwork so evidently crafted by Sara's clever hands. "It's all right. I always put it back in its place."

"Its place? Maybe *you'll* be willing to show me where it's kept. I won't tell Sara you let me in on her secret spot."

"I'm sure she just hadn't got around to telling you. You have your own key?"

"She did allow me that privilege. If I approach her gently enough maybe she'll inform me where the other keys are hidden – to the Hawkson sepulcher perhaps. She kindly provided me with one for my office, although I suppose she has others secreted around. God knows there are enough nooks and fissures in this place that she could hide whatever items she considers vital for our security."

"Possibly not," Rella Derry said. "Most of what is hidden is likely in these boxes."

Then she called Bill to join her from down the aisle where he had just replaced one of the cartons.

"But maybe," she said, "there's nothing hidden at all."

20

WEDNESDAY EVENING

A three-quarter moon hung wreathed in the overcast sky, and dim light framed Alice's hand-drawn posters on the market window as I drove slowly down Treadle Street and stopped at the curb. When I went inside, Boz was wiping down the front counter, and Thorny Webber was preparing to close, covering the meats and salads behind the display.

"George," the shopkeeper said, eyeing me closely, "there you are. Did the sheriff finally locate you?"

"Yes, Mr. Crisp always seems able to find me, wherever I might or might not be."

The day's apron remained loosely draped over Thorny's voluminous belly, stained with smears of deep red from the beet juice with which he flavored his ham salad.

"Is it too late for a sandwich?" I asked.

"Never for you, George. As always?"

He carried himself heavily behind his meat counter and reached for the bread, peeled the wrap from over the ham salad, wiped the broad blade of his spatula across an unsoiled area of his apron, and plunged it into the reddened meat.

Back in the car, I rolled farther down Treadle Street and pulled in across from Galen's house with the small brown bag from the market. I unfolded a corner of the waxed paper and began the sandwich, attending every bite with a sip from my bottle of root beer and considering the pattern of dried rain spots on my windshield. A tapping occurred on my passenger-side window.

I waved Boz in. He smiled thanks and then seated himself but then put away the smile and attempted something more stern on his young face.

"We know that Mr. Crisp never found you. He's been in three or four times. Four times."

"Oh, he found me, but then he didn't."

His expression changed again, trying to smile but settling into something more confused.

"He asked me a question or two," I said, "and that was enough."

"Oh. Oh. Is...is your sandwich...is there enough...your hands; I brought you some napkins. Thorny never..."

"It's fine, Boz, really. I picked some up." I pulled the sheaf of thin deli napkins from the paper bag.

"How about the bike, George? Is the bike doing OK for you?"

"It's just right, Boz. I find I don't use it as much as I should. As you see, I'm driving this thing around the village. Anyway, there's not much to go wrong on a one-speed."

"I greased the chain for you."

"I know. Nice job. It all works very well. Quieter than I'd expected."

"It's a good bike," Boz continued. Then, after a pause,

"Alice just told me I should get the new one. It has more speeds for faster deliveries. That's why..."

"I know. The old bike is great, Boz. Really. Alice was probably right. She generally seems to know the right choices for you."

I waited, and Boz waited too, until he could wait no more.

"I don't think you have to let Mr. Crisp find you. Make you talk to him, I mean." He had turned to me, relief on his face, and then turned back, head down, to examine his folded hands, clasped tight between his knees.

"Why is that, Boz?"

"He doesn't want to help."

"What do you mean, doesn't want to help? Doesn't want to find who..."

"Mr. Crisp...Sheriff Crisp...he knows already." He paused. "You know, don't you, George?"

"What do you mean, Boz? What am I supposed to know?"

Boz struggled with an answer. Then, "You know. J-Jean. And. And. Elgin."

"He doesn't need to know, Boz. It's not his concern, his case anymore. The people from the state..."

"But he wants..."

"He wants me to tell him I know something." I had taken only a few bites from my sandwich when Boz had joined me, and now I resumed eating the first of the two triangles, attempting to keep them both within the waxed paper while I reached for the root beer. But still I watched my companion in his discomfort.

Finally he ventured, "The Tinkers."

"The Tinkers?"

"You know. Zel Bander. And his, his family. His clan."

"His clan, Boz? Just how big is this clan of his? Do you know them all?"

He thought about it. "I know Zel Bander." He turned to look at me, and the light from the nearest streetlamp showed me his troubled face.

"Everyone seems to know Zel Bander. Victor suggested I hire him for carpentry work. Do you know any of the others, of these Tinker People?"

"Maybe there aren't too many. Maybe there's just Zel Bander, and..." He seemed to have finished.

"And who else, Boz? Are there children?"

"The Tinker People come and go," Boz said, with his gaze back down toward the hands clenched between his knees. "Mostly they go. I know they do jobs, they've *done* jobs, in Trellis. They work with old tools. Work that no one else can do. *Lost* work is what Thorny calls it."

"What about Alice? What does she think of the Tinker People?"

"Oh, Alice. You know about Alice. There's not many outside the village she puts much trust in."

With his head down, he seemed to have nothing else. I wrapped an uneaten piece of sandwich in the waxed paper and folded it into the brown bag. I held the root beer bottle by its neck and drank the last of it.

"Boz," I said gently, "what was it? Why did you come find me?"

"I told you. It was Mr. Crisp. He still wants to find you. He says he *needs* to find you."

"Why is it so important for him, Boz? I've told him what I know – and more to the point, what I *don't* know. About Jean. About Elgin. And it's out of his hands anyway."

"I just wanted to tell you." He kept his gaze down as he

paused, and then turned it up toward me. "I just wanted to tell you."

He took the folded brown bag from my hand so he could throw it away for me after he left the car. I leaned my head back against the seat and closed my eyelids against the dim light from the streetlamp through the windshield. Only a minute later I opened my eyes and saw fireflies dancing through the air around the car. In Slipstone they always arrived on time.

I COULD HEAR Galen's footsteps as she approached. She paused to peer through the tiny lens in the door and opened for me, reading glasses poised at the end of her nose and Clancy panting at her feet. Wordlessly she had me follow to a room where she had configured a small chair, desk, and lamp upon a braided rug. Hanging on the back of the little chair was Spinner's leather sack. The girl did not look up from a notepad on which she was carefully drawing with her stub of a yellow pencil.

"How are you two?" I asked Galen.

"You can tell, can't you? We're doing just fine."

"Any long conversations?"

"We've been communicating well enough. She's an artist, you know. She shows me things."

The child wore a faded blue cotton shirt of Galen's, the tail extending past her thin knees. Her long brown hair was tied back with a tan ribbon.

"She seemed a little uneasy about the warmth of the bath water, but she stayed in awhile and came out with wet hair over the shirt. She let me rub it dry."

Clancy had waddled his way over to Spinner's bare feet and now lay there protectively. Spinner reached down and touched the top of his head with two fingers while she continued drawing with the other hand. Then she lifted the fingers from Clancy so she could hold down the notepad while she continued to draw.

"She shows you...what kinds of things?"

"Pictures of stones, for one thing, carefully shaded. A rough wheel of some sort, a grindstone? And then her doll. Over and over, she draws the doll, different angles, different details. She draws carefully and lets me watch when I walk over. She looked up once. She's eaten from time to time today, but only with great care for what I had prepared." Galen paused for the right words.

"I think she's a kind girl," she said. "She's gentle." And then: "How did she learn that? She's doesn't seem fearful, although she looked up suddenly once when the window rattled."

"The window?"

"It rattles all the time, with any breeze at all."

I couldn't be sure if Spinner could hear us in our low voices, and I rose and walked toward Galen's kitchen so she would follow.

"The violin?" I asked quietly. "Have you looked inside...?"

"I offered to take it and place on the table, but she held it to herself and backed away a little, challenging with that little stare of hers. It's not, by the way, your Maggini."

"Do you think...?" I began. "Can you tell what she comprehends, if she can...if she has language?"

"Oh she hears, and she understands. She hasn't spoken, but I don't know if she has much to say, except what she draws. And so I guess what she says most is that she wants her doll."

"The doll," I said. "I'll go for the doll."

"You left it behind? In your house? She wouldn't have..."

"No," I told her. "I think it's over the rill. I have to go back over the rill."

But by the time I had closed Galen's door behind me, the Chapel bells were ringing out in no way I recognized, in no way I had ever heard before, such a clamor from ours or any other steeple.

21

WEDNESDAY NIGHT

Halfway in my hurried walk to the Chapel, the bells suddenly stopped. I hurried along. I used my key at the heavy front door, tried the entrance switch inside the vestibule, and realized at once that power must have been extinguished throughout the building. I knew that somewhere in the corner behind the table with Sara's leaflets was another of the cheap flashlights that John Patton had wisely secreted in corners throughout the building. Crouching, I soon had it in hand. With its old batteries, the bulb glowed a dim yellow, but it cast enough light to help me find my way up the aisle, behind the altar, and to the tower door, where I stooped my way through the miniature opening.

At the first landing I pressed Rachel's bell switch but, hearing no sound above, realized it was useless without power. Then I moved as quickly up the rest of the curving staircase as someone my size could maneuver. I reached Rachel's door, quietly knocked, and then carefully opened it. The oddly shaped room was silent and empty in the dim beam from my light. I could smell Rachel's strong bergamot tea, and whatever had been on her hot plate, but her soup pot and dinnerware must now be in the kitchen sink downstairs. All else was in place, except Rachel. I knew that with some kind of invisibility she strolled the village most evenings, but not tonight, I was sure, after the sort of disordered concert of bell ringing that had substituted for her customary eight o'clock performance. As I looked toward the irregular corners of Rachel's space, the batteries in the flashlight suddenly failed. The darkness was not complete, however. Some kind of ambient light – possibly from the three-quarter moon – stole in from outside through her small window.

I needed to recover my breath, so I squatted with arms outstretched and searched for the visitor's chair, first striking my hip against the corner of the virginal and no doubt repositioning it a few inches, then, as my eyes began to adjust, feeling for the chair and turning to sit. Was Zel Bander's smell in this confined space? I expected it, and moment to moment believed I could perceive it, but finally there was only the bergamot and the broth.

And then the sound of fabric, a kind of scratch against wood, and I turned to the darkest corner of the little attic room, where a small white thing shifted in the dimness, by the curtain that led to Rachel's bed and lavatory. I rose as quickly as I could and went to where she sat, backed into the corner floor, legs in front and ankles tied with some torn material. Leaning her forward, I found that her wrists were bound behind with the same fabric, a strip of which had been twisted across her mouth and tied behind her head.

As gently as I could, I untied the cloth strip from her head and then had to pull another piece of the fabric slowly from between her teeth. It had been multiply folded and was very dry.

"My dress." It was all she was able to say, and, as I looked closely in order to untie her ankles and then, pulling her gently forward by her wrists, I realized with what she had been tied. Sitting in the corner in her thin slip, legs stretched in front, she could not yet rub her wrists but just let her hands sit beside her on the floor. Nearby, along the wall, I saw where more of the torn dress had been thrown.

I lifted one of her tiny hands into the two of mine.

"What time?" she said. And then, when I didn't know how to answer, "What time?"

"I don't know, Rachel. What...?"

She suddenly pulled her hand from between mine and tried to turn my wrist to see the watch there. She lifted my hand, looked inches away, and then was somehow able to push herself forward, away from me, rising with my reluctant help and moving as quickly as she could to the bench at the keyboard of the Chapel chime. She leaned and looked into her clock, nodded a dozen times, lifted her fists and feet onto the levers, and sent nine o'clock into Slipstone Village.

When finished, without looking at me, she said, "George, you can leave me. You have to find them, before..."

"Is that why...the bells...?"

"Please go, George. Go now. Go now!"

Reluctantly I rose and left Rachel's loft, closing her door behind, but not before I found another of John Patton's cheap flashlights, cached at the edge of the narrow stairway. Surprisingly the batteries seemed fresh enough, and I played the beam over the dark vertical boards of the descending walls and the first of the steps as I began to descend, my left hand pushing against the wall in the absence of any handrail.

More rapidly than I should, I made my way down the two series of steps and through the little tower door behind the altar. I paused then and thought I heard water running. I crossed to the vestry and into the little kitchen area. There was no one at the sink, but Rachel's few dishes sat stacked under the faucet, water splashing crazily against them. I turned off both taps and left the room, moving down the darkened hallway toward Sara's office.

Again I paused to sense whether Zel Bander had left his smell behind, but I could not sense his presence. Or that of anyone else.

But then I did hear – I did *think* I heard – the sound of heels on a wooden floor. It was faint and receding, but in the absence of other sounds I knew now I *had* heard something, and, with my flashlight, I began following the sound of the footsteps as they moved within the library. They grew no louder, but there seemed no effort to muffle them.

After the theft of the violin, in their brief visit to discuss the matter on site, a pair of trustees had insisted on a modern lock in the library door, as before the room had been accessible to anyone already in the Chapel building. I knew that Sara conscientiously examined the door every evening on her way out, never trusting Victor, within whose responsibility such safeguards lay.

It was a heavy door, and I could see that it was an inch out of true, so the lock was certainly not engaged. I pulled the door outward, the beam from my flashlight leading me into the room, ranging across the bookcases and the tapestry, then stopping at the cellar door as I saw it slowly, and very quietly, go shut.

Whether it was fear or some other sort of uncertainty that caused my hesitation, I could never say, but I did finally cross the library, where I stopped at the cellar door and bent forward to listen. No sound came through, so I grasped and turned the knob. I flipped up the switch, but of course there was no power for the row of ceiling bulbs in the cellar. I pulled open the door and shone my light down the rough wood stairs, where weeks of footsteps had disturbed the dust accumulating since Victor's last sweeping. Now there was still no sound as I slowly took the first step down and then the rest. On the cellar floor I paused.

During my night alone in this space, before Zel Bander had joined me on Grant's cot, I had listened for whatever sound might move through the aisles, around the Secretary's wooden cases, and along the rough stone walls. But the sound of nothing – shouldn't there have been a ringing in my ears, or dust settling? – was no sound at all. Tonight though, I could hear, or maybe feel, the lingering reverberations from the earlier chaos of the bells.

But then came the slow and unmistakable creak of the heavy tunnel door as it opened upward. And quickly after, the closing, with the counterweights thumping as they swung in syncopation onto the old wood. And then stopped.

Advancing slowly, I shone the light to the left down each aisle of shelves as I moved past, but I expected to see no one, and no one appeared. I continued past the shelves into the narrowed passage, my light ranging back and forth and settling some twenty feet away on the doorway into the tunnel, the underground passage that must have given Tinkers access to the Chapel for all their generations below Slipstone Hill.

I knew I was following Zel Bander, but why was I allowing him more time? Concentrating the beam on the old door I began to step more quickly, continuing past foundation stones and the ash cleanout.

As Galen had demonstrated, I stooped and pulled up one of the boards that opened to the tunnel. Its counterweights, heavy iron fists, lowered before me on their chains, each of them illuminated as I passed the flashlight beam from one to the other.

The dark space was soundless as I entered.

THE WALLS of the tunnel seemed to stand closer together than in my earlier visit with Galen, but of course the width had only to accommodate carts carrying building materials and the men who pushed and pulled them along the rails at my feet. The height of the tunnel was about the same as its width.

It came to me suddenly that this was a place of no life whatsoever. I would have thought some rodent or other vermin might have made its home here, but not even a spider's web caught the light from my beam. The passage was dry of any animal leavings, silent of scratches or scurrying.

I walked as quickly now as I could, past walls of hard earth, long since having given up any of their dust, my flashlight sighting along each, with their sconces placed irregularly. I tilted my beam toward the rails at my feet, and always then ahead.

I continued past reinforcement timbers above and to the sides, unevenly placed. Here was not quite a smell but a *loss* of smell, not rot, just the stale oxygen that came from some source, some series of vents allowing the movement of air without letting rain seep through whatever shafts must exist along these dirt walls.

Then I heard him again. The sound must have been made with deliberation because it came up the tunnel not just once, as the accidental dropping of a tool, but three times exactly spaced – the sound of something against the track, something hard, metal. Was he ensuring I knew the way?

Soon I came to the place where the rails followed the tunnel at my left on their way to the quarry, and I had to decide whether to turn there or to continue straight into the narrower passage ahead that would extend under the rill. Then I saw an insistent flickering some hundred feet ahead, almost a firefly but more rapid, and I followed.

Without another pause, I continued down the gradual slant as with Galen the day before. Soon I saw moisture, the drip from the rill, and wondered how far above me it ran, the vertical distance some tunneler would have had to determine as he worked. Now, shining my light on the sodden boards above and to the sides, I saw that newer beams had been situated beside older, crumbling wood, joined at their ends to similar vertical timbers, and I realized such an effort was a necessary maintenance carried out by anyone with a need to use this passage and to reach its offshoots under the village. As I walked beneath these beams, I could somehow feel the heaviness and movement of the rill above me and imagine its sound.

And then I was at the five steps cut into the earth that led up to the sheet-metal doorway, which was closed and flat above me. From the second step I carefully pushed at the left side as I'd seen Galen manage the day before, and it seemed to swing up and away with less effort than she had required, with almost no effort at all.

Peering side to side, I slowly mounted the steps through the hatchway and brought myself into the dark and wet of the woods.

Chittering all around.

From the utter silence of the tunnel I emerged into a din of night sounds, a high drone punctuated momentarily by something higher – some tinier cricket sounding itself for a few seconds only before disappearing into the steadier and unremitting song of the other insects. There was no bird-song at first, but then crows above me, laughing.

I moved the beam of my light as far into the woods as it could reach, but no movement of any kind appeared ahead. I had followed Zel Bander closely all this while, moving almost as quickly as he, with his deliberate guidance, through the library, down the cellar steps, along and out of the tunnel, then up and here to the damp solitude of the trees. And so where now was I to go?

I moved the flashlight beam closer before me onto last fall's sodden leaves and decided to begin straight into the woods, where the trees seemed most to open for me. The crows soon quieted, and again there were only insects calling, louder as I walked farther into the woods. I soon realized there were no trees or brush to slow me, and so of course this was the path I was to follow.

Before too long, having turned my light momentarily toward the side, I almost stumbled onto the trunk of the upturned tree that spanned the rill and in whose roots I had found Spinner's doll. I suddenly thought the little thing might have been placed on the other side again for me to retrieve. I did not want to cross the makeshift bridge with only my flashlight to guide me, so I followed the stream some way toward the right into the woods but, playing with the light onto the stony course of the water, soon knew that the fallen tree was the only reasonable path across the rill, possibly with the doll and Zel Bander both waiting for me.

"Mr. Gilsum."

I turned to the humble voice behind me, and in the dim light of the moon through so many branches I could just recognize the tall, stooped lank of him.

"I'm sorry, Mr. Gilsum."

"You followed…," I began. "How long have you been…?"

The sexton shrugged, or rather gave a slow twist of his head, and then looked downward toward his hand and the thing he carried.

"It was you followed me, Mr. Gilsum," Victor said. And he hesitantly lifted, dropped, and lifted again the blade in his hand. "It was me who came for you, not someone else. And you coming for me."

"Why are we here, Victor? What are you…?"

"I'm to bring you, Mr. Gilsum."

"To bring me? Bring me where?"

"He's to see you. And you're to put down your light."

I stooped slowly and placed the lit flashlight onto the moist packed leaves. Victor motioned me back, and then he kicked the light toward the stream bed. The beam died but then reappeared dimly from within the ditch carved by the rill.

Then Victor indicated the tree stretching over the stream. At first I refused. I know I must have gaped at this thin figure with his arm slowly circling toward me, but, even in the darkness, his lantern's beam at my knees, there was intent in his face, and I turned and went toward the trunk of the tree. Reaching it, I stopped, then turned slowly back around toward Victor. He had approached nearer, and with a new insistence he pushed the point of his blade toward my ribs.

Still he said, "I'm sorry, Mr. Gilsum. He needs to see you."

My back to the tree, I stumbled slightly but kept upright. Victor did not at all start at the movement, and his hand held steady with its slow circling.

I lifted myself onto the flattened top of the crude bridge,

where I squatted, looking across its carved and notched surface over the black of the stream bed. A dim spot below me, my flashlight remained somehow lit.

He was just behind me. I could feel as much as hear his voice.

"Crossing is easy. You can stand and walk."

As quickly as I could, I lurched back and reached heavily toward him, my arm swinging out at his head.

But Victor easily leaned away, and my weight carried me down hard onto the earth. With the sudden pain of my fall and my breath pushed out of me, there was also the sting of Victor's blade just at my ribs.

"We'll go now," he said quietly. "I'm sorry, Mr. Gilsum. He needs to see you." Suddenly I realized he had placed something over my head and around my neck, some sort of thin rope. I reached behind and my hand closed on a kind of wooden rod from which the rope extended. I was able to turn enough to see Victor three feet behind, shining his beam along the pole, the other end of the rope protruding from it and wrapped tight around the hand that held the light.

"A catcher," Victor told me. "For raccoons and such. We need it at the Chapel."

I stooped and held my arms out for balance and was able to step my way along the flattened tree across the stream, gently pushed when I paused by Victor's rod at the back of my neck. I managed my way to the other side between the roots that had been cut away for passage. After lowering myself gingerly to the earth I could feel a more insistent cinching of the rope from the pole, now that I might try to bolt in any direction. And so he pushed me farther into the trees.

Of course he was guiding me westward, away from the

rill and past the sitting stones toward our right. When we reached the circle of old stumps, I gradually stopped. I tried to turn, but the line around my neck prevented movement except forward.

"Go around," Victor said. "Go on."

I reached to the rope at my throat, but I felt him quickly tighten it before my fingers could find any slack. I spoke only with difficulty.

"Why around?"

"We don't go in there."

"Is there some...?"

"We don't," he interrupted, and he tweaked the rope at his end of the pole. "Go around, please, Mr. Gilsum." I began toward the right as Victor shone his lantern beam ahead of me as a kind of beacon.

I knew that somewhere farther on we would come to the quarry, the source of Slipstone Chapel's high walls. I had not before gone so far into the woods, though I knew that the main tunnel with its tracks must proceed from there.

Soon, with Victor's strong beam guiding me through the increasing dampness amid the trees, I began to stumble over remnants of the sandstone pieces that must have been pulled there from the earth many years before Laura Hawkson had found her way here at the end of everything. I slowed and realized my arms were outstretched to prevent any falling against the line around my neck.

Victor allowed me to gradually stop, and he raised the angle of his light to show me the deep space farther in front. There were no trees ahead, but only darkness stretching above the wide pit. Then came the crows again, loud in syncopation with the insect sounds, which pitched high all around. Somewhere by this pit another mouth of the tunnel began.

"No closer, Mr. Gilsum. You can fall," Victor said. "I fell once."

He allowed me enough slack to slide a few fingers between the rope and the skin of my neck.

"Where...?" I managed.

"We have to go," he answered. "We'll go there. We have to go there."

"Where?" I repeated.

"He said you'd know. We'll go there now. He's waiting."

Slowly we traversed the rim of the quarry pit, my shoes wet with the damp of the forest floor. I stepped as carefully as I could, attempting to maintain the distance from Victor and his end of the catch pole, but when his lantern beam swayed from the area just in front of me, or if my body broke the beam, I would revert to a kind of blind shuffling, unsure what roots or stones or branches were ahead of my feet or face.

It was not only by the shadows of the lantern beam through the trees, but also by the heightened intensity of the insects' pitch, that I knew we had re-entered the thick of the woods past the quarry. I came to realize how the trees opened into pathways that would have been unnoticed except by looking to the sides, where low saplings and small trees would make passing difficult and unnecessary. The farther we walked, Victor and I, the more clear it became that we would stop only upon reaching the house of Zel Bander and his family of Tinkers, however many or few now dwelt there. Though the night was mild, my canvas jacket was too thin for the damp air, and my feet had long since numbed from the soaking of my shoes in the leaves still damp from Monday night's rain.

The roads I had driven the day before had curved in such ways that I knew I had not wound up far on a straight line from Slipstone Village, though how far that line was, I now concluded, I would learn tonight. In hours or minutes we would reach the old house with our long walk straight through the woods, as we now proceeded, with me a few feet from Victor's closed fist onto his end of the roped stick that we shared.

Precise in the distance between us, we moved as steadily as such partners could achieve, each coming to know the expected pace of the other, even as the ground descended toward rivulets. At these, Victor expected me to pause, and he shone his light at flat stones that allowed me, then him, across. As the beam found each step, I could see that the rocks beside it in the water were peaked and thick with green. Our steps, though, had been cleaned clear by someone, without enough time passing for any slippery moss to grow there. After the recent rain, they were just an inch or so out of the water, as it moved quickly past with its brisk, rippling sound.

At one of these I stumbled badly and, as when one falls, time slowed enough that I could twist to the side and bring my arm up to ease my landing in the stream bed. My shoulder stopped me somewhere among rough stones but not big ones. My hip and leg had landed stretched back, my knee on the side of the stepping stone, possibly not injured. Then, as the cold of the shallow water began to make its way through my jacket and clothing, I realized that the thing at my neck had loosened. As I lay stretched across the brook, I looked back to see Victor behind me at the first of the few stone steps, farther away than I had come to expect in the last hour and more, and I knew he had released the catch pole as I fell. There was moonlight through the branches over the stream, and, both motionless, we looked at one another for no more than seconds before I pushed up on my arm and rose as suddenly as I could. I found purchase with one foot and the next as I lifted myself and hurried toward the far bank, the weight of the pole heavy on my throat as it trailed and clattered.

He was quicker than me. And when he stooped for the line at his end of the pole he was able immediately to find and keep the right distance between us so not to further injure my neck.

"We have to take our care, Mr. Gilsum," he explained. "I'm not to hurt you."

He paused thoughtfully as we began our way toward the cleared area between trees.

"Or *try* not to," he decided to add as we took those next steps.

The last ridge was steep enough that Victor found it necessary to climb to my level, at the distance of the instrument that bound us. He motioned me to continue, and I proceeded, not quite on my knees, finding handholds on young trees, while he climbed at my pace, slackening the line around my neck but tightening it again whenever he thought I might be able to twist out of it. We found footholds upward, a few at a time, me, then him, then me. And then the crest of the ridge.

I had seen the clearing before, when Clancy and I had approached through the trees from the end of the rutted road. Tonight's three-quarter moon, and our approach from the side, gave a changed aspect to the Tinker house. The flat slates of the roof, at our level from the ridgetop and maybe fifty yards away, shone back some of the moonlight into the lowest branches of the nearby trees. A stone chimney rose from the slates. Cut into this side of the house a rectangle showed a flickering light within, a kind of yellow.

Between the ridge where we stood and the Tinker house

lay the narrow field with its thin, square gravestones rising from the tended grass, each with its dim shadow from the moonlight. Above them all, fireflies blinked in a fretwork of tiny lights.

Victor allowed me this vantage for a short minute. Then, "Come down now," he said, and we descended the ridge as deliberately as we had climbed, beside one another at the distance of Victor's staff.

As the ground leveled, Victor resumed his position behind me, nudging me with his catch pole toward the left and the porch where I had seen Spinner with her violin, the young boy attending her, and, finally, Elgin Brattle on his last day of life, as he had stepped through the screen door and approached Spinner's chair in a kind of unseeing shuffle.

Nearing the house I saw that a stack of four or five large, flat stones supported the corner. I was able to turn my head slightly to the right, where the side and, farther, the rear corner were footed in the same manner, the house a few hands'-breadths above the hard ground. The earth in the front was packed level, but little vegetation grew except some patches of flattened grass. Unkempt weeds and high bushes grew beyond. As yesterday, the rusted tractor sat beside the old pickup truck, which, though blue yesterday, was now more green in the moonlight.

Nearer, the sound came of a single note, a plucked string. Then another was plucked and a third and fourth, and, as we reached the hard ground below the porch, the sequence again, finding its way through the front door and sounding again as Victor had me climb the two narrow steps. Then, at my weight on the first creaking board of the porch, the notes suddenly stopped, and Victor had me stop too. Someone opened the door inward. The young boy stood there clutching his violin by the neck, unsurprised, and turned back inside toward a small chair at the wall to the left, seating himself, fastening his heels onto the top rung, and beginning again his four notes. Then Victor pushed me far enough inside that he could close the door behind him.

There were circles of light that danced from wicked lamps onto the walls, one illuminating the boy from a small table, another emanating from a lantern on the fireplace mantel to my right. It showed me Zel Bander, as he sat leaning forward. Eyeing me stonily he then settled back, hands folded in his lap, and creaked ahead and back a few times, the sound of his rocking chair playing into the four notes of the boy's plucked violin, string by string. He was far enough away that his sharp smell did not penetrate the must that rose from the old wood of the walls and floor.

"Here you are," Zel Bander said in his low voice, and he rocked slowly a few more times while Victor and I stood before him. Victor shifted the pole at my neck a few times, and Zel Bander motioned to him with a slow, upraised arm. I began to feel the line on my neck loosen; then it tightened again briefly as Victor placed his end on the floor. He came up behind me and pulled the noose over my head and away.

Zel Bander rose carefully from his rocking chair. "I need to show you," he said, coming close, grasping my elbow, and leading me toward a corner of the big room. Briefly I turned toward the boy, and he drew up a bow that had leaned beside him against the wall and began the same four notes, but smoothly, expertly from the strings of his instrument, bowing the same notes but now changing their order into a kind of dance. I could just hear the boards of the floor under Zel Bander's feet as we proceeded slowly toward what I saw in the dimness was a rough-cut door. I had not before seen the man in any light but knew his scent, much like ginger, with some other, not-unpleasant, redolence about him. He was broad, thick in his hips, and he shifted a little side to side as he walked with me, finally releasing my arm to reach down and open the door.

I had thought he was leading me back outside, but then I realized the shape of the main room could not account for the depth of the house as I had seen it from the ridge in the moonlight. He brought me by the arm into someplace dark, and we stopped. I felt, more than saw or heard, as he shut the door behind us, and he left me a moment, moving forward into the darkness. Through the door, from the other room, came the odd dance of the boy's violin. Those four notes had now progressed into something more tonal and, I realized as I waited there in the dark, very beautiful in its deliberate cadence. Then I heard two quick scratches a few feet before me, and Zel Bander was lighting a kerosene lamp on a shelf, the glass chimney in one hand. He adjusted the wick, walked before me across the room, and lit a lamp on another shelf, screwing the flame high.

Zel Bander's workshop was a horseshoe of benches against three walls of the room. Two, at my left and right, were strewn with wooden pieces – a few half-made chairs, what might have been a child's desk, the frame of a small bookcase, and some beginnings of pieces joined at corners, set on their edges. On the center bench, though, in some kind of distinct order, were much smaller things, with a series of square windows above. Zel Bander now struck another match and lit a lamp on a shelf over this workspace. The glass in the little windows began to dance against the light.

"Here," he told me. "Here." And he motioned with his left arm to have me come closer.

As I approached, I felt a gentle cracking under my feet and found myself stepping among curled wood shavings and the shifting accumulation of sawdust. The bench, though, had been cleaned of any detritus of woodworking. Here, from left to right in a kind of lesson in violin-making, were instruments in stages of construction – two maple pieces glued roughly at their edges, another set sawn into shape, a third shaved much thinner with shallow channels. Chisels lay in front, and sharpening stones. Here were dozens of different-sized clamps, a glue pot, a cracked coffee cup with pencils, heavy-looking violin-shaped forms, and, above the scents of worked wood, the smells of Zel Bander: ginger, damp wool, linseed oil. And some other composite, a mixture of scents that I might have identified by themselves but not together. Some kinds of spice.

"Listen now," he told me, and he reached over the bench to sets of hooks in the wall. He took down three unfinished, roughly shaped violin tops, in woods that appeared within the light of the lamp to be slightly different from one another in grain and color. He selected one and secured it into a small clamp, twisting the screw to grip it tightly within the pieces of thick fabric at the jaws of the tool. Then he brought the piece of wood to my ear and rapped it sharply with the blunt end of a small chisel. He released it from the clamp, selected the next violin shape, and repeated the stroke of the chisel against it.

"What is it?" I said, at the third of them. My voice came with a hoarse cough at my first words after hours in the damp woods. "What am I hearing?"

Through the closed door came the sounds of the boy's bowed violin, more slowly now, and then back to the single four plucked notes.

"There's *nothing* to be heard in this bad wood," he said,

suddenly agitated, his voice thinner now but still pitched low. "You know that." And he pushed me hard against the edge of the workbench, causing the tools and glue pot to rattle. "You know that," he said again, louder, close at my eyes, insistent.

"The boy must have better," he told me. "*His* boys will need better."

"And the girl? What does she need?"

"Spinner can play. And she *will* play, when I bring her back from you. And I will bring her back. But she cannot *make*, *we* cannot make any good sound with this bad wood."

"How can we...," I managed. "How can the village be blamed for your trouble?"

"Oh, you know that," he said. "The woman up with the bells told you. She and her friends were young then; they knew my father, and his sister, and some of our others, children and others, when there were others still here. I know this story. I know it from my father. My father now out there with those others beside us under the stones. That girl, that daughter up there on your hill, dropped herself into the pit where the stones were dug, and her friends came over here then, and they stole into this house, and they took what we needed for any new wood."

"But what...?"

"Then the trees shrunk up. They just shrunk up and there was no more of them. I know this story. I know it from my father. We still had wood for years, but that wood is all used, and now we will have back what you took. *I* will have it to make more wood for the boy."

"Your father, in his story, did he explain what...?"

"No!" he shouted, as he held the last of the violin tops by its clamp in one hand. With the other hand he placed down the small chisel onto the workbench and lifted a larger one by its oak handle. Suddenly, with his eyes still deep onto mine, he thrust the blade of the tool into and through the thin wooden piece in the clamp and then threw it all into the sawdust on the floor.

Through the noise and flying sawdust I managed to say, "How do you expect me to help?"

"You *know*," he told me. "You always knew. *He* knew, John Patton knew, but he brought me the other one, the old one, that treasure of yours up there. He stole it. He thought I would want it. I did *not* want it."

Then he finished: "And now you."

He turned quickly and left the room. He shut the door hard, and I heard an outer bolt jam into place.

The boy's violin ceased for a moment, then began again with its four notes plucked, then bowed.

DARKNESS CAME SLOWLY with the dimming of the three lamps, dying only minutes apart as their kerosene burned down and away.

During those hours, voices came through the door, low and indistinguishable, minutes or perhaps an hour apart, less a conversation than thoughts of a moment, all punctuated by the boy's violin, which now and then added a new note to its repertoire. Eventually I noticed the music had stopped, maybe long since.

Before the lamplight faded, I had been able to examine the violin pieces that lay on the workbench and were hung from hooks above it. On the wall were more tops and backs, halves and joined, and on a shelf above the bench, beside the oil lamp, were glass jars with tuning pegs and other small, unfinished items of different woods. Arranged before them on the shelf were short, very dark, lengths of wood, heavy when I lifted them. Ebony, I thought, but where did Zel Bander get such a supply?

Turning back toward the door, I saw on the wall across from me a dozen finished instruments, on hooks with their bows. I approached them slowly, lifted one, and tucked it under my chin, but it had no strings. None were strung, but one. I took that one down, with its bow. I tightened the hair along the bow shaft and drew the thing down across one of the strings. A terrible screech of course, but it brought no effect from outside the workshop door. One of the voices came just afterward, unchanged in its calm, low pitch, and the boy's next note was as pure as mine was harsh.

But soon the darkness was complete, and I found myself standing with my back to the violin workbench, one of the heavier chisels in my hand.

22

THURSDAY MORNING

C ould I have slept like that? I woke standing. There was a dim light, and I saw where the chisel had fallen from my grasp onto the floor upon a small mound of sawdust and shavings. I turned and leaned onto the workbench, pushing my feet back and stretching out my arms. There was some kind of soreness at my neck. I reached to my collar and thought of Victor's catch pole.

Light was filtering through the little square windows above the bench, illuminating the shelf with the jars and pieces of ebony. I noticed now that the surface of the bench was covered end to end with dark leather, much like on the desk in my Chapel office. Gouges and scrapes scarred the surface of the thick leather, but no tool had stabbed completely through it.

Leaning on the work surface with my arms outstretched I looked side to side and saw the same series of small square windows above each of the other benches. I realized this narrow workshop must have extended behind the broader width of the main house.

Then a call came, and I turned my head straight back to

look through the small glass panes before me toward a tree branch just outside. The crow called again, its body in silhouette, head upraised, and then it leapt upward from the leafy branch, which trembled and settled.

I turned back. The splintered violin top still lay with the chisel in the center of the floor, but across from me the workroom door was half open. I approached, looked cautiously out, and moved sideways through the opening. The big room was cool, with filtered light entering through tree branches and the large, dirty window above the front porch to my left. No one was in the room but me. The floor creaked as I moved to my right, creaked with almost every step, as I walked the length of the side and back walls, shelves along each.

Old instruments carry the odor of their years, and here were dozens of them, scenting the big room with their smell: violins, some made for the hands of children, many of other dimensions, a few the size of violas I thought, varnish of different darknesses, scrollwork both rough and refined, bows with sprung strands of horsehair leaning among them, and guitars, thick-bodied, strung or not, some with cracks entirely the length of their soundboards and a few with necks warped inward. These instruments were not on display; each sat where its last musician had happened to place it. I would never have recognized the Maggini among them. None rested on the stone lintel of the fireplace; instead a large painting hung on the wall in its thin frame, perfectly straight. Darkened from wood smoke, the picture still revealed a skilled hand: Slipstone Chapel, distant across the rill, with a tiny figure in a dress standing in the side entrance, her indistinct face gazing toward the artist.

To my left was the boy's small chair. His violin sat on the straw seat and leaned back against the highest of three slats.

Its bow was carefully aligned beside it. I lifted them both and sat on the chair. I held the instrument against my chest and tried bowing a few strings, then plucked at them and tried to find the boy's four notes.

Then the hard sound of a door came, or maybe a window slamming or some other intrusion, and I left the chair, still holding the violin and bow. Through the porch window, nothing. Only the clearing there, and the truck gone.

I replaced the boy's violin, crossed the room, pulled the handle of the front door, and walked out into cool sunlight onto the sagging boards of the front porch.

Beside me, her tiny frame upright on the nearest chair, sat Spinner's doll, thin lace circling the empty wrists. Of course its eyes were gone.

RETURNING from anywhere is always faster.

In daylight I walked back through the Tinker grave markers, up the hill to the woods, along what I thought was last night's path, and then located the truer one. I found and crossed the rivulet where I'd fallen and where I now noticed how Victor's line around my neck still badly stung.

I walked quickly now, my direction toward the sun as it slowly rose behind the woods. The quarry, the circle of dead trees, the sitting stones, and I easily found the fallen tree across the deep bend of the rill, broad and notched, from whose roots I had extracted Spinner's doll, which I now carried in the large pocket of my muddy jacket. This time I walked along the makeshift bridge quickly and easily, little need in the light to balance with my arms. I did not bother to look for the entrance to the tunnel with its sheet-metal door, but left the woods, crossed the closer bend of the rill on the stepping stones, and climbed the meadow to the Chapel.

Sara would not have arrived so early, and, muddy and unshaven, I carefully approached the heavy door. I knew as I reached for the brass handle that I had no key with me, but when I grasped and tried to twist it downward, it did turn, and I brought the door out toward me.

Rachel never rang the time before seven, and, as I walked quickly through the vestibule and up the dim aisle, I heard from above, as all the village did, the day's first bells. I slowed my pace and peered around the door to Sara's office, but she would not arrive until 8:30, as always, and precisely.

I continued past the altar, through the little door to the tower, and up the curved stairs. At her bell switch I realized the power may not have been restored, so instead of trying I went the final steps to Rachel's thin attic door, where I tapped lightly. I expected to hear the soft sound of her shoes across the boards of the floor. Instead she spoke from a distance, "Come in, George." I left the doll sitting on the top step and opened the door.

Rachel was freshened somewhat from the brutality of the night but had retreated to her chair after ringing her seven o'clock.

"Can you make the tea this time?" In her voice she attempted to show strength, but it wavered just in those few short syllables.

I lifted the kettle from the hot plate and passed behind the curtain to her bedroom. I drew water from the lavatory tap and returned to prepare the tea.

As we sat, she knew that I wanted to ask about the night before. And about her friend Laura Hawkson, about Gammel Minken, about anything taken from Zel Bander's father. And she must have wanted to know about *my* night and the dry mud on my clothes. But twice when I leaned forward with my teacup in both hands, she gently shook her head and looked down at her lap. I would wait. I quietly left, taking the doll with me.

Back at my cottage midmorning, I bathed and briefly slept.

Then I was up, tried playing a record but couldn't listen, then made eggs. I took up my clothes from the night in the woods, dried with mud and leaf dirt, and laid them in the closet with other items to be taken to the coin laundry behind the market. In the mirror, while I shaved, I touched the red line Victor's thin noose had abraded into my lower neck. My shirt collar, buttoned high behind my necktie, concealed the line if I held my head straight.

Spinner's doll still sat where I had left it, under a throw pillow on the chair where I read each night. I took it up and placed it carefully in my leather bag. I walked the path back toward the Chapel but turned at one of the small gravel side paths through the trees toward Treadle Street. Passing the market I saw that it remained open, despite the barrier on the road prohibiting passage to the village. Between the hand-drawn grocery announcements taped on the window I viewed Alice and Boz, heads down in conversation at the check-out, with Thorny approaching in his apron and holding out a broom. Alice looked up and saw me. She hurriedly came out, joined me, and kept to my pace with her quick, short strides.

"He won't close; he won't let Boz loose, even with no customers," she told me.

I stopped to let her capture her breath. "I suppose he has to keep up appearances."

"Appearances? Who for? The Franz twins? *They've*

closed the *tea* shop. No one's allowed up the hill, so what can be the point? Can't you do something?"

"I don't think I hold much sway over Thorny. Or Sheriff Crisp."

"It's not Aaron, it's that woman, from the state office. And she won't tell me a thing. I've tried to help."

"I'll see if I can talk to her, but she's just..."

"And Aaron Crisp...well, you know how much authority *he* can exert. By the way, did he ever find you?"

"Just where *is* Rella Derry, do you know?"

"She was *here*. She was *there*. She turns up wherever she wants. And with that younger one. That *Bill*."

Finally managing to leave Alice where Treadle Street began its downward curve, I walked the short distance to Galen's house and rang at the door.

Clancy barked wildly, but no one else came. I rang again, then tried the knob.

The door opened onto an empty living room. All the other rooms were empty too. Spinner's little table had been cleared except for a single blue crayon.

Clancy stayed close and nervous at my heels and brushed past me, knowing his way to Galen's basement door. I opened it and followed the dog down the steps. Two small windows high up within the old masonry cast light onto the dusty floor. Shelving held cans of paint, and a few lawn tools leaned here and there. There was no sound at all except Clancy's anxious breathing, and I almost missed seeing Spinner as she sat in a far corner with her violin bag across her folded knees and a look of questions in her eyes.

I stooped and brought the same expression to my own face. Clancy ran around us in a few circles, finally slowing and coming to lie beside Spinner. She reached out, lay a hand on the dog's head, and arranged herself more closely to him. Tongue out, he looked at me happily.

"Oh god, George, it's you."

Up from my crouch I turned to see Galen, with something in her hand. In the light from the small windows I saw a bar of some kind, heavy and long, straight down from her arm.

"I rang and rang again," I told her. "No one came."

"There was a truck. An old blue pickup. It parked and stayed. It drove away and came back, and parked."

"Could you see...?"

"His hat was down. His face was covered. There might have been two inside. When you rang we came down here. We thought..."

"The truck is gone. And the door was unlocked. Didn't you...?"

"I don't know. I don't know. I thought I did. No one ever locks. I hurried her down here."

Spinner had risen from her place on the floor and now stood beside Galen. She took the bar from the woman's hand, brought it to a bench behind them, and returned. Clancy followed close to her heels.

Upstairs the dog ran to a bed of old towels Galen had arranged for him. He sank his head back between his paws and breathed out noisily. Spinner seemed to know where everything was kept. While Galen and I sat, the girl took out cheese and bread, opened a drawer for a knife, and prepared plates for the three of us, along with slices of apple and glasses of water from the tap. After we ate, she unbuttoned a front pocket on her violin bag, removed her notepad and pen, and picked up the blue crayon. With the violin hanging in its bag from the back of her chair, she worked on page after page with the crayon and pen. She did not want to show me what she'd drawn.

"Last night, the bells, the Chapel bells?" Galen finally asked. Spinner looked up from her drawing.

"Some kind of trouble in the mechanism," I said. "Rachel couldn't explain. It's happened before, she told me."

"Not since I've lived here," Galen said.

I suddenly remembered the doll, took it from my leather sack, and offered it to the girl. After a moment's look at my face and back at the doll, she took it gently from my hand. She looked up at me again and stayed awhile with her face on mine. Then with one finger she carefully wiped the places where the eyes had been.

"Where...?" Galen asked.

"I found it," I told her.

23

THURSDAY NOON

"Oh, there you are," Sara said, looking up from her typing and turning down the volume of her desktop radio, tuned as always to murmuring voices in an unidentifiable dialect.

"Did the sheriff find you? Have you been in Trellis? I wish you'd let me know when..."

"No, just catching up on some things at home," I told her.

She glared at me briefly over her reading glasses. "Yes, well, I wish Victor would also tell me when he's decided to take an unscheduled day."

"He called me at home, Sara. I should have let you know."

"Called you at home?" She paused and picked at the neat stack of paper beside her typewriter. "Yes, well, I'm a little surprised he has your telephone number."

"Sara, what about you? You seem not to be terribly apprehensive about, about the deaths. If you need to..."

"George, this is not a time to run away from what needs to be done. The phone calls, the re-scheduling of weddings and so on. I've been here for, well, perhaps not *worse*...but the theft of the Maggini..."

She attempted to lessen the excitement in her voice over her role in the dramas of Slipstone Chapel.

"I know, and please don't think I'm not grateful."

"Someone has to..."

"I know. And I'm sorry I didn't call."

"That reporter kept phoning. Then he came and wanted to wait in your office. He probably thinks I'm rude, but he can think whatever he wants."

"And he's...?"

"He must have parked beyond the barrier and walked up. I'm surprised you didn't see him outside."

As I opened the heavy front door onto the filtered light outside, Greg Down came out from behind the Founder's sepulcher in his heavy tweed jacket and loose tie. He approached and leaned across from me on the short iron gate.

"No stone yet for Jean Clacton, I guess," he observed as I walked slowly toward him. "And soon another one needed for Elgin Brattle. I should trade my typewriter for a chisel and go into business."

"Yes. Maybe you should. Are you here to tell me the sheriff needs me?"

"Sheriff Crisp can take care of himself. Or, maybe he's not even capable of *that*."

"I thought journalists were supposed to be objective."

"Journalists are allowed to *think*. And what I think is that...wait a minute." He glanced up over my shoulder, and I turned.

"I've been looking for you," Grant Sweeney said breathlessly, as he appeared from around the west corner of the

Chapel. Then he stopped suddenly as he saw the reporter across from me at the iron gate.

"Go ahead, Grant," I reassured him. "Mr. Down will likely know already whatever it is you need to tell me."

He took another breath and let it out.

"I think not," he managed. "It's the library. The Maggini."

"The Maggini?"

"It's back."

Greg Down was scribbling madly in his notepad while we stood at the horizontal case in the library. We heard Sara's heels clicking down the wooden floor as she approached.

"I called to tell the sheriff," she announced. "I had to leave a message." She joined the three of us in our tableau at the front edge of the case.

"Ooh, I shouldn't touch anything," she said, as she lifted her hand from almost penetrating the plane where glass had protected the Maggini before its removal. "Don't touch anything," she added for the rest of us.

The small padlock was missing, but I wasn't going to share such observations in the presence of Greg Down. Its bow beside it, the instrument was lying in an oblique angle across the deep-green felt that covered the base of the cabinet. The little display stand still carried Sara's card apologizing for the violin's absence.

"Wasn't there a little padlock?" Greg Down asked, peering up from his notepad. He looked at the three of us in turn. Sara started to answer but glanced at me and decided not to.

He attempted another question: "How do we...how do you know it's the Maggini?"

Never having seen the instrument myself, I turned to Grant.

"Just look at it," he said rapturously.

"Yes, I'm sure you recognize it," the reporter said. "But what about it? Why don't we lift it out?"

"Oh, gosh," Sara said.

"Well, just look at it," Grant repeated impatiently. "There's the color of course, and the double purfling. If I could remove it, *when* I can remove it, I can show you the St. Andrew's cross on the back. But the elaborate scrollwork is enough, can you see there, above the neck?"

"Well, how does it sound? Have you played it?"

Grant sighed. "No one has played it – it hasn't been strung – since the Secretary brought it from Italy. Well, maybe *he* played it."

"And none of us would know how," Sara added. "Would we?"

"I'll have a photographer here in an hour," Down said.

"I think not," I told him. "Tomorrow maybe. *Maybe.*"

The reporter returned to his notepad for a few more words, closed and put the thing in the side pocket of his tweed jacket, then nodded at us and left the library. We heard his footsteps down the center aisle and then the closing of the Chapel's heavy front door.

In my office I lifted the desk phone, dialed, let the other end ring awhile, and then spoke briefly. I unlocked and opened the drawer to find my mouse's detritus scattered within the area he had claimed, but he was away for the moment. His bed of shredded cardboard, now softened with some kind of fluffy insulation, lay neatly in the front right corner of the space. On the left side of the drawer were the three maps I had brought earlier from my cottage – the Tinker chart, the commercial map from the bank, and the sketch I had drawn based on my wanderings in the woods and the drive I had taken days earlier to Haywire Road and the Tinker place. *Carpentrie. Sharpning.* I closed the drawer.

Then there was a muffled scrambling of some kind, and I slowly pulled the drawer back open.

With his little black eyes, the mouse looked up at me for a quick moment and then dropped a tiny, thin, scalloped piece of wood from his little paws next to some of the other bits, similarly fan-shaped, which he had collected over the last few weeks. Then he scampered back to his gnawed entry hole at the rear of the drawer.

I moved back my chair and peered under the desk to see him descending the corner of the back panel. He leapt the last few inches and scampered away, across the room and under the floor molding on the other side of the office. I silently watched the thin space where the mouse had disappeared, and in a minute he scurried, a dot increasing in size to a larger dot in the dimness of the room. He ran back up the rear of the desk and appeared again with another of the little wooden scallops. He dropped it next to the others just like it.

24

THURSDAY EVENING

In the fading light of the afternoon, as I walked my usual circuit of the village, I passed the downhill road and saw that Greg Down had not moved his car from behind the barrier prohibiting access. A breeze began, and I buttoned my jacket as I walked from the road back onto Center Path.

Rella Derry met me at the Hawkson Cenotaph. *Give to the earth. Take from the trees.*

"Bill went to find out, and we can wait for him here."

We stood in the cool, damp air at the end of the path, past a hundred yards of scattered trees behind Jean's empty house.

"And Bill knows...?"

"As much or more than I do. He spent his first years in Trellis. He left when he could."

"Did he know about the Tinkers?"

"He *knew* the Tinkers."

"He *knew* them?"

"As much as anyone. He would see a few of them in town, in one of their trucks, and he spoke with a few. An older man and woman, he said – sister and brother, husband and wife, cousins? – who said a few words but were unwilling to smile. He saw them only a time or two. But now he thinks they're gone. Those two, anyway. It's been years."

"Where would they have disappeared to? Could they have gone anywhere and do more than survive? Were they able even to speak in sentences?"

"Well, they took their eyes and hands with them, and what those eyes and hands had learned to do with wood. And would no doubt continue to do."

"And so...,"

"And so, no one seems to have located the kinds of instruments they were capable of crafting. Some furniture they *might* have made, but chairs and chests are not as individual as violins or violas. Musicians have looked in all kinds of places, everywhere, states away. Somehow these people were capable of replicating the sound of centuries-old violins in new instruments. *Are* capable, I might say, if those few travelers found some other place to ply their craft and the supplies they needed. There used to be some kind of exotic wood, I've heard it said. And the varnish. No one knows what kinds of substances they combined to create the distinctive color and tone of their handiwork."

"And the Maggini? How would the sound of their instruments compare...?"

As I spoke, I began to notice what I had already perceived somehow before it gained strength: the rising sound of mournful strings from deep away in the woods across the valley of the rill. At the same time the breeze rose too. It carried through the wood and stones of the highest point of the Chapel, and among the bells, stirring what I had come to know as the Chapel Song. It played in the wind back and forth in response to the strings across the rill.

"It's not Zel Bander," came Bill's quiet voice, and I saw that he had come to stand beside us on the path.

RELLA DERRY DROVE, with Bill in front. As we passed Greg Down's car parked at the sawhorse barrier, I turned in the back seat and watched through the rear window as the car grew smaller and darker in the fading light.

She knew the way without any kind of map, and we followed the same roads I had driven with the panting dog a few days earlier – along Big Run and down county routes toward Needle's Eye River, and past Gypsum and Blue Jay Roads, but turning earlier than I had that day and more easily, even in the fading light, finding the narrow cutaway that was Haywire Road. She stopped the car soon after we turned, without following the rutted pathway that led to the Tinker sign and the Tinker house. Except for Bill's brief explanation of what we should expect, no one had spoken on the way there, and no one spoke now, as Rella Derry turned off the engine and lowered her window.

We sat and listened a moment to the sound of the strings through the break in the trees. Then, just as Rella Derry did, Bill and I left the car silently, easing our doors not quite shut. We walked together, Bill stumbling a few times in the ruts left by Zel Bander's truck as he hurried us along toward the house. Keeping to the left of the tracks, Rella pushed aside low branches as she followed Bill's pace, one hand on the strap of her shoulder bag. I walked carefully in the weeded mound between the deep ruts.

In a few hundred feet we passed under the old wooden sign that hung from its thin chains, then slowed a little as we approached the treeless space where the house sat on its foundation of stacked stones, and from where the song of the violin came high and loud.

He sat on the porch, knees together while he played, the instrument tight under his chin in the evening dimness, his bow piercing upward and retreating, fingers seeming not to move along the neck until we came closer and saw the elegance of the boy's left hand as he played the slow thrum and cry of his hypnotic song.

From there we did not bother to move so silently, and, as we approached, the boy reached the end of a phrase and gracefully lowered the bow and the instrument to his lap. He brought his face without expression toward the three of us and shifted his head slightly to follow as we stepped onto the porch and passed through the open door into the big room.

Dark as it was, Rella saw her way to the stone mantel-piece, where she found and opened a box of matches, lifted the glass chimney from the lamp there, twisted up the wick, and lit the thing.

To our right, erect in Zel Bander's rocking chair, sat John Patton.

Of course I knew only that it was a person sitting small and still until Bill came up to him and spoke his name. Rella Derry brought over the lamp, and we saw how tightly the skin was drawn over the bones of this man's skull and of his hands, which would have gripped the wooden arms of the chair had they carried any life in them. He wore a suit that looked tan in the lamplight, with a necktie carefully up to his collar. No odor seemed to emanate from the body to carry above the smell of the old instruments arranged within the room. Rella moved the lamp closer. Above the collar was a thin, deep ring circling the puckered skin of his neck, with shreds of rust dried downward from the cut. I realized I had lifted my hand to the same wound on my own neck.

Bill must have known I was about to ask, because he said, "I'm not sure *how* I know with just the bones and skin, but it has to be him."

He turned to Rella Derry. "Doesn't it? Doesn't *he*?"

Before she answered, there must have been a shuffle or a throat clearing at the door, because each of us turned at once to the boy in the doorway, his violin and bow tucked under an arm.

"Spinner is gone," he said, low and clear.

"I know," said Rella Derry.

BILL BROUGHT one of the straight-back chairs across the room, and he sat with the remains of John Patton, the kerosene lamp between them on the floor, while Rella and I and the boy left the house. He was ten or twelve or more; he didn't tell us when Rella asked, and he may not have known. Older than Spinner. He brought nothing except a bag like hers, leather pieces stitched together. His instrument must have been inside; I hadn't seen him put it there.

When we walked the few steps down from the porch, we all paused, and Rella took a flashlight from her shoulder bag, aiming it through the clearing toward the pathway to our car. Then the boy came up to walk beside her, while I followed over the hard dirt of the yard into the narrow opening under the trees. My eyes had become adjusted to the fading light as it spread within the clearing, but then the dark became almost complete in the pathway under the trees. Walking with the boy, Rella Derry turned on the narrow beam of her flashlight.

Leaving, the way seemed longer than when we had

come just a half hour before, and somehow more curved and difficult in the walking. With the dark, insects had pitched their noises louder, but no birds called. There was a breeze, but then it waned and started again, straight toward us down the alley where we walked. Finally Rella's flashlight beam picked up the chrome grill and headlights of her car.

And then, behind, blocking it in, a truck, possibly blue, but surely Zel Bander's.

Rella and I stopped. The boy took a few steps farther, but then he stopped too, just at the side of our car.

There was no one there. And then there was Victor Blair, in from the trees, with Greg Down ahead of him in the loop of his catch pole. The loop must have been tight, because the reporter kept bringing his big hands up toward his neck, where there was no grip to be found. I remembered the sting of the noose from the night before.

"I know you from days ago," Rella Derry finally said.

"At the sepulcher, yes," Victor answered at the side of the truck in that growl of his voice. "You're from the state."

"There was no key," she said. "That's what you said."

"No. No key to nothing. Not anymore."

Tight in the catch pole, Greg Down had stopped pulling at his neck, but then suddenly he tried to wrench away while Victor spoke, reaching his hands back vainly behind him. The loop tightened with his movement, and Victor seemed to pay him little mind as he held the pole in both hands and eyed Rella Derry and me, shifting his feet only slightly as the reporter struggled, then ceased and tried to cough.

"What is it you want, Victor?" Rella asked. "That's your name, isn't it? What is it you want? What does Zel Bander want?"

He didn't seem to know an answer for a moment, and he

looked at the ground as if he did not have Greg Down noosed three feet away from his stout hands, still strong after struggling me through the woods the night before.

Then Victor lifted his head slightly toward my face but spoke to Rella Derry.

"Ask Mr. Gilsum. He knows. *He* knows."

And I did.

BUT FIRST, it was all too sudden, too easy.

"You know I've been needing to see you," Sheriff Crisp told me, his truncheon swinging by its wrist loop. Tucking her flashlight under her arm, Rella was leaning over the fallen Victor to take the catch pole from his limp hands and ease the loop at Greg Down's neck. Now on his knees, the reporter pulled at the noose enough to pry it over his chin, then his nose, his ears, and the crown of his large head. All the while the boy stood straight, still, and completely quiet.

Then the sheriff was gone a minute, but we heard his car start up at a distance. He advanced enough to shine head-lights toward us on the path, at an angle behind Zel Bander's truck and Rella Derry's car. When he reappeared he had slid his truncheon into a leather strap on his belt and was carrying handcuffs. Victor lay prone and still, head twisted to the side, mouth open. The sheriff straddled him and pulled back on the man's hands.

"Help me with these, will you," he said to Rella Derry.

Still kneeling, Greg Down leaned with his hands flat before him on the path as he struggled with his breath. Then he was finally able to rise. Somehow he had managed to find the narrow notepad in his pocket and now he drew it out, reaching for the pen inside his tweed jacket. He rocked his neck gently to test it, then rose and approached the sheriff.

"And so how did you...?" he began, and coughed. "But how did you find me?"

"I didn't *find* you," the sheriff said. "I followed Miss Derry's car, and here you were."

"Thank you, Aaron," Rella Derry told the sheriff, while eyeing the reporter severely in the gleam of the sheriff's headlights.

Suddenly the boy, as quiet as before, stepped over Victor's legs, quickly approached the truck, and was in the driver's seat before the sheriff could stop him with an outreached arm and a shout. The door slammed shut, the engine turned over, the boy backed expertly between some trees, and the truck bounced loudly around the cruiser and up the path toward the dark road.

"Where do you think...?" he began to ask.

"I don't know, Aaron," Rella said. "But you need to come this way."

The sheriff joined his flashlight beam with hers, and we turned back toward the Tinker house, where Bill sat with John Patton.

25

THURSDAY NIGHT

Out the side window the twilight was dotted with fireflies, as Bill drove Greg Down and me back onto Haywire Road and along the black roads back toward Slipstone. No cars came toward us, and I realized only one truck had passed me when I had driven here two days before, when it was so wet. Were there no other cars in the county? Slipstone, Trellis, always so still.

But the hundreds of fireflies yellowed and blinked out, perfectly spaced from each other, as we drove past them over Needle's Eye River. The water rushed loud under the thump of our tires on the wooden planks of the bridge. Then onto Blue Jay and Big Run roads.

We had left Rella Derry with Aaron Crisp in the big room of the Tinker house, where the sheriff had begun setting up his battery, lights, and camera.

"I don't know what it is we're going to," Bill had said after we crossed the bridge. "What we're going to find."

But I knew, because I had lowered the window on my side of the car.

I knew from the way our bells sounded in a kind of

irregular series as we approached Slipstone Village, knew that Grant Sweeney – or that someone, but it *was* Grant Sweeney – would be stretching out his arms, his face down on the flagstones outside the heavy front door of the Chapel, a darkness seeping slowly from where his forehead had been, his cassock loose at his legs like a bat's wing. And I knew that Rachel Wren would be with her bells, and with Zel Bander, in the high tower.

I knew because Zel Bander would have it no other way.

We drove up the hill and stopped at the reporter's car by the barricade, but Greg Down shook his head and said he would stay with us. I left the car to move the sawhorse, and we proceeded up the hill. Slanted at the side of the road across three of the painted parking lines was the blue truck. Bill, Greg Down, and I then walked together the short way to the Chapel. By now there was only one bell and one sound, again and again as we neared, heavy and loud.

Somehow twilight had not yet deepened, and I saw others gathered there, stepping nervously, foot to foot.

Alice, though, was stooped beside Grant, and Bill went over and knelt to join her. Then I looked up to the tower and could see, within the four tiers of bells, the movement of two silhouettes. The figures looked to be dancing in their struggle, bending toward and away from the biggest of the bells, the old G.

"Zel Bander," I yelled.

The figures still danced. He bent her downward and swung her away from sight.

I yelled, "Zel Bander."

His silhouette turned, but now without Rachel. He leaned one hand against the upright frame of the tower. In the other he carried a hammer, and he struck with it at the rim of the nearest of the bells, ringing out the heaviest of the tones that had carried to us along our drive to Slipstone Hill. It was not as full a sound as the swinging clapper would raise from inside the bell, but, still, its rim of heavy bronze was loud against Zel Bander's hammer.

"You? Now?" came his voice, weighted and dark.

Around me, faces turned up, then to me, and up again. Bill at Grant's body, Buz now materializing from the trees with Thorny Webber, both in their aprons. Two of the Franzes, tiny women with hands at their mouths in fear or expectation, stood with Sara, whose arms were crossed within her long sweater. Greg Down paced behind them all, face upturned, hands thrust in his pants pockets under his tweed jacket.

The three chimes had faded, and I called up to the tower: "I have it. I have what you want."

His silhouette became still. "You do not," he shouted, and he struck again at the rim of the heaviest bell. He turned and bent down, and now Rachel was with him again. She was bent forward over his arms.

"I can show you," I told him. "I've found it, and I can give it to you."

"You do not, you *will* not," he shouted, and he turned Rachel back behind him and dropped her small figure onto the floor under the bells.

"This is my music *now*," he yelled, and he hit savagely again on the bell, and again twice more.

"You have nothing to give me now," he called down. "Anything you have, it's for the two of them." He swung down his hammer again and struck hard at the bell.

Then, when the ringing had almost died on the air, some other sound, seemingly in the same key of G, was taken up somewhere away from the Chapel, in a much higher register, just beyond the flagstones and the low iron railing of the churchyard. Without dying fully, the sound of the bell became the pitch of this other instrument, a violin's string, steady, without pause, and then, inexplicably, joined by another in a lower tone, bowed down and up, again and again, together, synchronous. And then the four notes from the night before, from two instruments now, first out of register and then together, again and again, the same four notes.

Above this strange music I could not have heard the sound from the man in the bell tower, but it must have been a cry of some kind, because we all turned back up to see him lean out, head forward, one arm suspending his body from the frame of the tower beside the low, heavy bell.

And then the arm with the hammer rose with a balletic grace and then arced gently downward and up again in a half circle, and I think the same cry came again from his throat, as the strings from the churchyard became not just those same notes down and up, down and up, but now music, a melody, and the melody was the Chapel Song, the song of Slipstone Rill.

As we listened – all the others and I – the motion of Zel Bander's arm directed the melody of the strings. Then his entire body began to sway slightly, and his arm took on more elaborate arcs as he conducted the music.

Then another sound, the smoothest humming sound, and it *was* humming, a gentle music from the throat of poor Ginger Martin, who stood and slowly swayed, foot to foot, a step or two behind my right side. I tilted my head back toward his face, and Ginger tried smiling while he hummed, but his face had never been able to hold a single expression for very long. He gave up and brought his gaze back up to Zel Bander in the tower. This time he was able to retain a small smile while he swayed and hummed.

And so Zel Bander, a silhouette against the dark blue light behind him through the shadow of the bells, conducted the music in the churchyard, his arm with the hammer moving in a slow figure eight, face upward toward a place away, beyond the rill, toward the circle in the forest where his family's trees could no longer grow, to the quarry, to the house perched on flat stones, where his family's instruments had for so long been carved, glued, and strung.

Then, at the movement of his arm, the breeze began to rise.

It lifted its way from the forest, floating above the rill, then up the slope where we all stood and where Zel Bander, above us, conducted the violins in the churchyard and, for me only, the vibration of Ginger Martin's deep humming.

The breeze grew stronger. It came onto us, then rose to the heights of the Chapel, into the wood and stone interstices, past the window in Rachel's loft, and among the nine bells of the tower, where the weight of Zel Bander's hammer kept his body swaying.

I had heard it before, believed or pretended I had heard it, and it was there again, the wind playing the Chapel like an instrument in resonance with the music from the churchyard. It was the song of the rill, the song forbidden to Jean Clacton or any other in the village, and the song that Spinner and the boy now sent up toward their father from the shadows behind us all.

Then, on one upswing of his arm, Zel Bander let loose his other hand's hold on the tower frame, stepped onto and over the lintel there and took another step, maybe two, fast down the slope of the Chapel roof before his body pitched forward toward its tiles. As he fell, the hammer flew from his hand, dropped onto one, two, three slates of the roof and then soared away, slowly it seemed, floating, finally to land with a hard crack into the flagstones near my feet. I felt a few shards hit my pants leg.

Then, on his chest, the man slid downward on the roof slates. His arms were straight and angled upward, and he made no effort to grasp the gutter at the roof's edge as instead he left that surface and flew outward toward the iron railing of the churchyard.

Boz Billings stood nearest but was able to step back as Zel Bander hurtled toward him. The falling man's eyes were tightly shut, Boz told us later, and in the darkness there may have been a kind of smile on his face until he hit the flagstones at the churchyard gate with arms out, and then lay much as Grant now lay nearby, with darkness pooling at his head.

In the churchyard the music stopped, I suddenly realized, its song ended. The wind, though, continued its way through the fissures within the Chapel heights, less a song now but more like whispers.

Moving slowly backward and continuing to look up, I left the circle of yellow light that came from the bulb above the porch, where Bill still knelt by Grant Sweeney. It was almost fully dark as I approached the churchyard, but, looking back and up in the thin evening light that still remained, I saw within the tower a small shadow moving under the rim of the big bell. Then I heard a car stop quickly in the graveled area nearby, and one door slammed, then two others.

Still looking toward the tower, I reached behind myself, and my hand found the latch of the iron gate. It groaned sharply as I pulled, Victor having neglected the hinge, as he had neglected this area of long grass, now wet on my shoes. As I turned toward the churchyard, there was the dark outline of Galen Jones, near me but inside the iron railing, as she leaned onto it, her face up to the tower and to the vague outline of Rachel, who now rested wearily onto the frame at the bells.

Then Rachel's silhouette seemed suddenly more distinct as, behind her, the wind brought up the three-quarter moon. Below, the moonlight caught the figure of Rella Derry joining Boz, where he knelt at the prone body of Zel Bander. And then, too, with the clink of his leg chains sliding across the flagstones, there was Victor, who stopped beside them, fell hard to his knees, and lifted his hands, now bound before him in Sheriff Crisp's cuffs, to his long face. He bowed and lifted, bowed again, as silent as could be. The sheriff left him there and continued toward the still body of Grant Sweeney.

I passed through the gate and stepped slowly into the deeper churchyard, where the moonlight could just now penetrate, and where the children sat on upright grave-stones. Spinner was nearer to me, the boy darker a few stones behind her, both with their violins and bows held upright on their knees, their backs straight, listening with us all now to the rhythmic wind and the far calling of the crows from deep across the rill and into the trees.

DAYS LATER

We found that only one jar had fallen, unbroken but with its contents scattered in the dust of the floor. Its wide cork stopper lay where the fall had jolted it out. Seven other jars sat in an uneven row on the single shelf. Two of them had been shaken by fifty years of thunderstorms to the edge of the thick oak board and would someday have fallen. Corks were still thrust deeply into the rim of each, the lips of thick glass holding them tight.

The air in here was still with must, though I had left open the low and narrow doorway to the recess hidden behind the panels of the office wall. A row of the tiny wooden scallops – the wings, or the *scales*, as the book in my hand told me to name them – had been arranged by my mouse in a row from the fallen jar to the little door, ready for transporting to his home in my desk drawer. Some of the cones on the floor had been shaken of their scales, the dry things having flown loose with the fall.

Within some jars, tiny, unbroken spruce cones were layered between fragments of a colorless twill. Other jars held only deposits of the little wings, each collection different in color and size from the others, but only in slight degree. A square of the twill was tied with twine from the lip of each jar, inked with a short number. Every number corresponded to an entry, logged with the same ink, in the small journal on the shelf beside the jars, in a nomenclature apparently brought by the first Tinkers when they came to help the Founder realize his vision.

The fingers of the boy's hands were white and thin, with knuckles small and round like the spruce cone he now examined close to his eye. But his hands were strong and capable, as he had easily twisted out the cork from the first jar I handed him.

He rolled the cone within his fingertips in a manner seeming of expertise, but then he looked up at me with the same questioning eyes that Spinner had given me once before.

All I could do was refer to the old arborist guide Galen had brought back from the Trellis library.

"You will find the seed at the tip of the wing where it falls from the cone," I read to him. "To be viable, the seed of a spruce must be firm and of a dark brown or black color, much like the seed of a watermelon, though very much smaller." An etching on the page depicted the palm of a man's hand holding five of the wings.

While I read, the boy stooped and retrieved one of the tiny scallops on the floor. He compared it to those in the intact cone, pulling one out with his nimble fingers.

Spinner sat at my desk in one of the dresses Galen had found for her in Trellis, and as I looked up I saw she had opened the drawer. The little doll sat beside her on my desk chair with a thin dark blindfold tied at the back of her tiny head and covering the space where her eyes had been. Galen sat in a chair at the corner of the desk, watching the girl closely but without interfering. Across the office, under the window, Clancy slept unaware.

The boy took a step into the recess and reached past me for one of the jars that held only the separated wings. He struggled but was able to twist off the cork. He pulled out just one of the little pieces, then carefully replaced the cork into the jar and the jar back into its assigned place on the shelf. Then he compared the wing from the jar with the piece from the floor. Both were much smaller than shown in the book's illustration, and their tips were tiny and round, like mustard seeds. The boy secured each between a forefinger and thumb and held them high away from the window so we could both examine them in the late-morning light, one with its perfect round mustard seed pure black, the other with its little dot a dark brown. The boy dropped the brown one with disapproval back to the floor.

At the desk, I saw that Spinner had now reached into the drawer and was moving her hand back and forth within it.

"The seeds from the female cone can be germinated," I continued from the book, "but only those that will sink in water, and not any that will float or swim."

The boy had turned his gaze from the tiny thing in his hand to his sister at my desk, where movement showed along her arm, as she held it outward, shifting palm up, then down, the mouse scurrying from her shoulder to her hand and back again.

"He doesn't have a name," I told her. "You can name him."

Her response was to look up at the boy and me only for a moment, then at Galen beside her, and down again at the little creature on her arm. She shyly smiled.

And then, delivering the mouse gently back onto its nest, she managed to pull the drawer out fully, shifting it gradually side to side and then completely off its runners. She set the heavy thing onto Galen's knees, then turned it halfway around and placed it upon the leather of the desktop. I came and leaned close. Four tiny brass pins held a yellowed card onto the back of the drawer.

"To my friend J. Hawkson at Slipstone," it read in the same elegant, miniature script as in the log book we had found. It was signed simply, "B."

The boy had crossed the room to join us. He lifted the drawer away from Galen's lap and set it on the floor, the mouse still in its nest but looking apprehensive. The girl stood and joined her brother, who, with a penknife brought from his pocket, was picking at the edge of old leather that covered the writing area of the desk.

He saw me watching. I nodded approval, and he returned to the desktop. He slipped the blade under a corner of the thin brown leather, then slid it around one side and then another until we could see that it had been glued only at its edges. Then, after his knife had completed cutting under the final corner, he peeled the leather off the desktop.

Revealed now was the wood of a hundred years ago, without the dark patina that time had given every other part of the desk.

Slowly the children pushed the palms of their hands over the deep red and fluid gnarl of the wood, now tracing the grain with their fingertips, measuring, never looking at one another, but with hands, hers so much smaller, touching here and there as they explored the newly exposed spruce. The Tinkers' wood.

Then, together, they looked up at me where I stood behind them.

"Yes, of course," I told them. "Take and use it. It's yours again."

It was noon now, and just above us, everywhere around us, came the clamor and thud of Rachel's bells, twelve deep peals, heavy and long.

ABOUT THE AUTHOR

Michael Matros grew up in Asheville, North Carolina. Now he lives in New Hampshire.

53288663R00180

Made in the USA
San Bernardino, CA
13 September 2019